Death's
Final
Sting

Also by Tracy Buchanan

Death's
Final
Sting

Tracy Buchanan

embla
books

First published in Great Britain in 2024 by

Bonnier Books UK Limited
4th Floor, Victoria House, Bloomsbury Square, London, WC1B 4DA
Owned by Bonnier Books
Sveavägen 56, Stockholm, Sweden

A CIP catalogue record for this book is available from the British Library.

ISBN: 9781471416446

This book is typeset using Atomik ePublisher.

Embla Books is an imprint of Bonnier Books UK.
www.bonnierbooks.co.uk

To my agent Caroline, my enduring anchor in an
ever-changing literary landscape

Prologue

I've seen *many* unusual things over the past few years, but the item I'm staring at right now takes the crown. It is grotesque. Beautifully grotesque. It *astounds* me anyone would think I'd want a hair clip made from a live beetle as a gift.

It's cradled in an ornate box, the beetle's shell lavishly adorned with tiny green jewels. The poor creature is tethered to the hair clip by a fine golden chain. Surrounding the beetle are veined fragments of what look like wings, iridescent green and yellow.

The beetle twitches its legs, yearning for freedom.

Poor darling thing.

I catch sight of my reflection in the mirror. 'Poor darling thing,' I tell myself because am I not similar to this beetle, tethered by a golden chain to the industry that discovered me, is devoted to me . . . and now devours me?

Honestly? I don't really know what I am beneath the jewels and the fame. Am I the Oscar-winning actress my fans see? A cash cow my agent and film studio see? The vulnerable daughter and sister that my family see?

I move my fingers down my cheek, to my neck and over my collarbone as I watch myself in the reflection. I definitely feel like I am a thing to be pawed, to be ravished, to be adorned like this insect. The truth is, I don't even feel human anymore, skin peeled away layer by layer. Less Cordelia, more a nameless entity that exists to be admired and stroked.

I read an article yesterday about this condition called scleroderma, where sufferers slowly turn to stone, calcifying. I've been feeling like that lately. Numb. Still. A statue. When I told my mother how I felt, she said I needed a break from everything. It felt like a hallelujah moment. She meant a literal break, of course, like the one I took

1

last year to Koh Samui. A physical removal from New York. But I realised it doesn't need to be as drastic as that. I just need a break from all the distorted images I see of myself. The fact is, my phone has become a house of mirrors with versions of myself constantly thrown back at me, pushing me off course. I don't need to go on holiday. I simply need to put my phone away.

So here I am, about to begin my digital detox. But before I do, one last picture for *him*. I need him to know this isn't his fault. That he is one of the few who truly see the real me. It'll be just two weeks and I'll be back to him again.

I go to take a selfie but realise how ridiculous I look, all pouty-lipped and wide-eyed. I need it to *mean* something. To enamour him so much, his beautiful eyes won't stray.

So I return my gaze to my little friend, this beautiful beetle. I decide to let him see both of us, and perhaps he will even understand what I am telling him. About myself, my life. And I know it will capture his attention, the sight of such a rarity attached to my hair. One picture, then I'll find a way to free the beetle from this prison. Maybe it can be my little companion over the coming two weeks?

I carefully remove the hair clip from the box, feeling the beetle's legs twitch against my fingers. It makes me think of summers in the park behind our house, my brother bringing me bugs as gifts as my mother laughed.

'Shhh,' I whisper to the beetle. 'You'll be free soon, I promise.'

It stills, as though it understands.

No, as though *she* understands. I decide she must be a girl, like me. What shall I name her? Mabel, after my grandmother, another actress, another time. She would have understood what I'm going through.

I lift the hair clip to my fringe and gently slide it in. I have to confess, it looks rather beautiful against my red hair. I press it down. *Click.* The cool metal of the hair clip scratches against my scalp and I feel a pinch, subtle but sharp. I wince slightly. Beetles can't bite, can they? I ought to remove it, but all I need is a quick photo. I hold my phone out, ready to capture this bizarre blend of horror and vanity in a single frame. Mona Lisa smile. Alluring eyes.

Click.
Change position.
Click. Click.
As I turn, the room blurs at the edges, a strange haze clouding my vision. The pain in my scalp increases, like a clawed hand is tightening its grip over my head.
Something's not right.
My own hand darts up, my fingers clawing at the clip, but it clings to me, an unwelcome parasite. My breath shortens, each inhale a labour, each exhale a plea for help that won't come. The room spins, my silk sheets crumpling under clenched fists as a cold dread spreads through my veins.

The beetle. Is the beetle doing this?
A silent scream builds in my throat, my muscles seizing. The world fades to a pinpoint of light, as elusive as the fame that hollowed me out. My eyes, growing heavy, fixate on the ceiling above, where shadows dance in a mocking waltz.

Darkness edges in, curtains closing, slowly slowly until . . .
Nothing.

Chapter 1

Dr Vanessa Marwood was a portrait of concentration as she walked around her Manhattan lab, moving seamlessly from microscope to specimen trays, then back again. She adjusted the microscope, bringing one of the flies she'd reared from larvae into sharp focus. As she'd suspected, it was *Musca domestica*, the common house fly which thrived in New York's urban sprawl. And yet the body the larvae had been feeding on – Jacob Rowland, a chef in his thirties – had been discovered by hikers three hours from the city in a secluded woodland area of the Catskill Mountains.

So how had these city-dwelling larvae found themselves in the rural sprawl of the Catskills? Vanessa's guess was this man had died in the city, the larvae that had hatched from the eggs placed on him hitching a ride as he was moved to the mountains. This tied into the detective's theory that the man had been killed in the apartment he shared with his partner. The killer? Maybe the same tear-drenched man who'd told the gathered press his partner must have died while trekking in the mountains. If that was the case then the story told by the two men's smiling photos on social media was a fake one.

But then weren't most photos a study in selective memory? They captured moments not as they were, but as we wished them to be, allowing us to edit out the undesirable, the mundane and the painful.

Vanessa caught sight of the one photo she had in her lab. It was of her with her brother, Vincent, and their parents, taken at an event at the butterfly farm where her father had worked. Vincent was just two in it, Vanessa five, both full of smiles. She *thinks* those smiles were genuine, both unaware that their family would be torn apart by their mother walking out two years later.

Vanessa focused on her mother's smile. Was the seed of dissatisfaction with family life that drove her to leave already sprouting? Not that Vanessa had ever really understood why she left. And what about her father? Had he sensed his wife's disquiet?

She returned her gaze to Vincent's infectious smile, a glimpse of the toddler he once was. Another story scrubbed away by truth down the line. Or maybe the truth was already there in that chubby toddler face. Vincent said it himself, that there was darkness within him, dragged out by a series of events – from their mother walking out, to the life he experienced on the streets. A darkness that had led him to HMP Frankland in Durham, UK.

Vanessa imagined her brother there now. As she did, she felt that familiar need to see him. She'd spent the first few weeks after her arrival in New York six months ago trying to tamp down that yearning. She'd grow angry, telling herself she needed to stop dwelling on a past version of her brother that wasn't real. But now she accepted the yearning. He would *always* be her little brother, despite what he had done. And maybe part of it was being in a new city, away from familiar haunts and old friends. There was a sense of loneliness she hadn't felt as much in the UK, and that made her crave familiarity, even if that was in the form of her serial killer brother.

She shook her head. Damn, she was getting sentimental. Maybe it was six months in the company of Americans, so quick to express and acknowledge their emotions. The first night she'd met her new colleagues from NovaScope Forensics, she'd felt ambushed by their desire for her story, and to share theirs, too. It was all well-meaning. They wanted – *needed* – to show her they cared. That they were there for her after the horrors she'd been through. Vanessa had hoped the move to New York would offer a clean break, but she'd been naïve. It had been impossible to escape the news of her brother's killings back in the UK – the whole sordid story of the Cobweb Killer as salacious across the pond as it was back home. She must have come across as a typical reserved Brit in those early days, all polite smiles while batting away anything that got close to being a personal question.

Thank God she had her work. A chance to muffle those horrors with microscopes and data and larvae. Being in a city that crackled with a never-sleeping sense of urgency helped, too . . . initially, anyway. But lately, she'd felt something buzzing inside her head, like a queen bee trying to find her way out of her hive. Her American colleagues would no doubt tell her to get therapy, to work it through and get it out. But she didn't need therapy to know what was wrong. It was sitting there before her, right now, in that picture of her family. One dead. One imprisoned. And her mother, back in the UK, not one word for so many years and, worst of all, nothing since Vincent's arrest. That irrational – as she saw it – yearning to pull the broken pieces of that family together seemed to grow louder and louder each day.

As she considered this, her new boss and the co-founder of NovaScope Forensics, Dr Bronagh Thompson, stormed into the lab with an energetic stride, her unruly brown hair falling haphazardly around her face. Her well-worn, stained lab coat smelled of the vapes she sneaked puffs from when she thought nobody was looking. She always seemed so chaotic and messy. If it weren't for her phenomenal reputation in digital forensics, Vanessa wouldn't be so tolerant of her interruptions and disorganisation. Plus, she made *damn* good margaritas.

'Just Tuesday and we've already got a big one,' Bronagh announced with a sigh. She slid a crime scene photo across the surface. It depicted the lifeless body of a woman, face marred with decay and maggots, her faded red hair a shroud around her delicate features.

'It's Cordelia Montgomery,' Bronagh said. 'They found her an hour ago.'

Vanessa raised an eyebrow in surprise. Cordelia Montgomery was an actress in her twenties known for her Oscar-winning performances. 'How awful,' she said. 'She is – *was* – so talented.'

'I know, such a waste. See this?' Bronagh said, tapping her finger on the hair clip the actress was wearing.

Vanessa picked the photo up to get a better look. The hair clip was a masterpiece of design, embellished with shimmering gemstones, delicate engravings . . . and what looked very much like a *real* beetle.

'Wow,' Vanessa said.

'Knew you'd love it.'

For a moment, Vanessa was transported back in time to the opulent Victorian parlours she had read about. She thought of the living beetle jewellery that was so popular in that era, a macabre trend that still remained in some parts of the world, where live insects were worn as accessories.

'The beetle's still alive, too,' Bronagh added.

The familiar excitement that came with working on a fascinating case started building in Vanessa's chest. Would it be intense enough to hold that buzzing bee at bay?

'I'm heading to the crime scene now,' Bronagh said. 'You coming?'

'Do you really need to ask me that? Of *course* I'm coming.'

'Bring your coat, it's started to snow again.'

Vanessa grabbed her kitbag and her coat and strode out of her lab after Bronagh, eager to unravel the enigmatic web of secrets that surrounded this actress's untimely demise.

Chapter 2

The opulent decor of Cordelia Montgomery's apartment contrasted starkly with the odour of decay that dominated the air. Vanessa's nostrils twitched beneath her mask. It was a scent she'd encountered more times than she cared to count, but each whiff still brought with it a wave of sorrow. The body she was about to see had until recently lived, breathed, loved. Such a promising young life cut short. An actress in the prime of youth, now food for insects. Vanessa made sure she took a moment to let that sink in before finally stepping into the vast bedroom.

'Harris,' Bronagh said, approaching a short, muscular man in his fifties with a bald head and an impressive black moustache. 'Lieutenant Haworth got you on this one, then?'

'You know how it is,' he said. 'If you're up, you've got it.'

'Oh come on, don't be bashful now,' Bronagh said. 'You're one of the most seasoned detectives they've got. Williams *had* to have you on this.'

'By seasoned, she means *old*,' the detective said, giving Vanessa a wry smile. 'You gonna introduce us?'

'This is Detective Harris,' Bronagh said to Vanessa. 'Harris, this is our forensic entomologist, Dr Vanessa Marwood.'

'Good to meet you, Doc,' Harris said to her. 'Brace yourselves. She's been in there a while.' He stepped out of the way of the inner cordon and Vanessa walked forward, the plastic layers of her protective coveralls rubbing together.

It was a beautiful bedroom, like the entire apartment, with high ceilings crowned with intricately carved mouldings and pale pink walls. Vanessa's eyes settled on the minor details: a messy stack of magazines and romance novels on the bedside table; a rose-gold board pinned with Polaroids of friends, festival tickets and inspirational quotes. Next to the bed was a framed photo of the actress, devoid of all glamour, laughing with an older woman – her mother, Vanessa assumed. Relics of a happier time, now clashing violently with the grim reality of the actress's lifeless form, which lay on the large queen-size bed before them.

Cordelia Montgomery. Hollywood darling with a face made to adorn magazine covers. But now that face was twisted into a grimace, the flesh distorted by time and decay. Even from a few metres away, Vanessa could see a swarming mass of larvae – or maggots as they were more commonly known – clustered at the corners of the young woman's mouth. They wriggled over one another, microcosms of insatiable hunger in the circle of life and death.

Vanessa's eyes travelled up to the actress's distinctive red hair. She remembered thinking how stunning the colour was when she'd watched one of Cordelia's films the year before; a dark, aesthetic film about the competitive world of art galleries. The actress's portrayal of a working-class Irish artist had won her an Oscar for best supporting actress. Now, those famous locks were matted and discoloured by decomposition fluids and insect activity.

But that wasn't the main reason Vanessa's eyes were drawn to her hair. It was the ornate, jewel-embellished hair clip that was attached to the actress's fringe. About two inches long, it was lustrous and intricate. Adorning it was an object that on first glance looked like a replica of a large beetle glittering with emerald-green jewels. But closer inspection revealed the beetle was very real and very much alive, a gold chain wound intricately around its abdomen attaching it to the clip. Vanessa watched in fascinated horror as its legs twitched minutely, its bejewelled carapace glistening. Even more disturbing were the items that decorated the rest of the clip's centrepiece: what looked like fragments of wing from an endangered species of butterfly, the *Ornithoptera alexandrae*, Queen Alexandra's birdwing. It was a despicable use of such creatures. Illegal, too, if the butterfly had been smuggled live to the US for this item to be created.

'You ever seen anything like it?' the detective asked Vanessa.

She shook her head. 'Not like this. But I've seen videos. Jewellery made from live insects is common in some parts of the world.'

'That's pretty damn gross,' the detective said, shuddering.

'When was she last seen alive, Detective Harris?' Bronagh asked.

'A week ago, on Valentine's Day,' he replied. 'Apparently announced on social media she was escaping from the world for two weeks. A "digital detox", and no visitors. No personal contact. Last person she spoke to was her agent who called her just after 2 p.m. on Valentine's Day, judging by the call information on her phone. Speaking of which, any luck getting hold of the agent, Ramos?' The detective turned to a pregnant police officer standing nearby, with black hair pulled back into a bun and a smatter of freckles over her olive cheeks.

'Still no luck,' Ramos replied, with a heavy Brooklyn accent. 'Her office said she's in a meeting.' She looked at Vanessa. 'Hey. I'm Officer Ramos, by the way. Harris said Bronagh would be bringing a bug lady with her. The kids'll *love* it when I tell 'em.'

'I'm not sure they'd love *these* kinds of bugs,' Harris said, wrinkling his nose as he looked at the squirming larvae.

'On the contrary,' Vanessa replied. 'The more disgusting the better, when it comes to kids.'

Officer Ramos smiled. 'You're damn right there. Got kids yourself, I bet?'

'No, actually,' Vanessa said. 'But I have friends who do.'

'Like this one,' Detective Harris said, gesturing to Bronagh. 'Your three behaving themselves?'

'Just about,' Bronagh replied. 'What about your girls?'

'You gotta be kidding,' the detective replied with a booming laugh.

'That's teens for you,' Bronagh said. 'So, shall I speak to your colleagues here about any devices you found?'

'Knock yourself out.' Detective Harris gestured towards two officers who were gathering up digital equipment from around the room. 'We've already started going through her cell phone, but will hand it over once we've finished.'

'Thanks.' Bronagh turned to Vanessa. 'Time to do what you do best, Vanessa.'

Vanessa nodded and carefully stepped onto the tread plates that were creating a temporary walkway around the room. A man – a forensic pathologist from the New York Medical Examiner's Office, Vanessa presumed – was meticulously taking swabs from the actress's body. When Vanessa's shadow fell over him, he looked up to reveal kind, blue eyes. Vanessa guessed he was in his sixties, judging from the wrinkled skin around his eyes; maybe even older. It was rare to see a senior pathologist at the scene of a crime. But this was a big one.

'Dr Penn,' Detective Harris called over, 'meet Dr Vanessa Marwood. She's a forensic ecologist. She's gonna be checking out the bugs with you.'

'I'm pleased you're here, Dr Marwood,' the pathologist said. 'There are certainly plenty of wrigglers for a forensic *ecologist* like you to collect,' he added with a wry rise of his greying eyebrow as he acknowledged the detective's mistake.

Vanessa crouched down beside him, her dark eyes taking in the deceased actress. 'Any thoughts on cause of death?'

'Some kind of toxin,' the doctor replied. He gestured with his gloved fingers to the actress's mouth region. 'Note the foamy substance around her lips?' Vanessa nodded. 'My first thought is an overdose, but officers have found no drug paraphernalia yet. It *has* been known for staff to remove such items in high-profile cases like this, though,' he added with a sigh. 'However, I did notice this . . .' He pointed to Cordelia's forehead, where a small, discoloured patch of skin was covered with a network of darkened, prominent veins radiating outward.

'Interesting tissue death and vein tracing,' Vanessa observed. 'Close to the clip, too.'

'Quite.' They both watched as the beetle tried to pull away from the golden chains attached to it. 'Are these beetles venomous?'

'Not this species,' Vanessa replied.

'Strange. Maybe the discoloration is a reaction to the beetle's legs rubbing against her skin. What kind of beetle is it?'

'An ironclad beetle, a popular choice for Mexican *makech*.'

Dr Penn frowned. '*Makech*?'

'Brooches made from living beetles.'

'Tough creature, surviving as long as I suspect this poor girl has lain here.'

Vanessa leaned close, taking in the small jewels attached to the beetle's back. 'Yes, ironclad beetles are very hardy, hence why they're chosen for these purposes. But it *will* die if it doesn't get some sustenance soon.' She regarded the doctor over her mask. 'I know you might prefer to remove this during the autopsy, but I'd very much like to examine the clip as soon as I can, especially as I suspect the surrounding wings may belong to an endangered species. Plus I wouldn't like to see this poor creature die.'

Dr Penn considered this before nodding. 'I agree there are benefits to an expert such as yourself taking a look as soon as possible and, of course, ensuring the safety of the specimen. I will observe.'

Vanessa dug a breathable container and a bottle of water out of her kitbag, squirting water onto some cotton wool before placing the cotton wool inside the container. 'One of the officers will need to get some rotting leaves from the pavement outside first. That should sustain the beetle for a bit.'

Dr Penn gestured to one of the forensic officers scouring the room, repeating Vanessa's instructions to them.

'Man, we got a real Dr Dolittle on our hands,' Detective Harris called from across the room.

'I prefer Bug Lady,' Vanessa called back.

'And we prefer the name Joker for Detective Harris over there,' Dr Penn said. 'Likes to keep things light when everything turns heavy. Maybe *too* light, sometimes,' the doctor added, giving the detective a small smile as he did. 'Right, we'd better give you space to do what forensic entomologists do best.'

'Thanks,' Vanessa said.

Dr Penn moved out of the way and Vanessa took his place. Up close, the larval mass was even more vivid as they wriggled in the actress's mouth, eyes, nose and ears, their tiny, elongated bodies giving off a sheen. The sight was unnerving to many, Vanessa could tell that from the way the observing officers around the room looked like they were going to throw up. But for Vanessa, those larvae were crucial evidence, each creature a biological clock that could shine a light on the timeline since death. As she set about collecting samples, placing live larvae in aerated tubes with cat food, Ramos watched in fascination.

'*Cat* food?' she asked.

'Maggots still gotta eat, Ramos,' Harris said. 'Am I right, Bug Lady?'

Vanessa nodded. 'Absolutely, especially as I'm removing their food source by taking them away from the body. In my experience, cat food is the best replacement for flesh.'

Ramos smiled. 'Damn, wait until I tell my cat-loving kids about this.'

Vanessa carefully labelled the samples, then pulled out a canister of recently boiled water, using it to kill some larvae before preserving them in ethanol. Back in the UK, she'd usually have to ask an officer to boil a kettle for her at the scene. But NovaScope had supplied her with a portable travel kettle and canister in one. The perks of working for a private firm.

'Why kill 'em?' Detective Harris asked.

'It freezes them in their development cycle,' Vanessa explained. 'Lets us know what stage they were at on collection.'

'But why hot water?' the detective asked. 'Why not just ethanol?'

'Using the HWK method – that's what we call hot water killing – is actually kinder to the larvae as it takes a while for them to die in ethanol,' Vanessa explained. 'Plus, using this method kills any bacteria, otherwise they'll start to decompose, even in ethanol. It also prevents them from constricting, and therefore shortening, like they would if you put them straight into ethanol. Better all round, really.'

'Fascinating,' Ramos said. 'Man, my kids really *are* gonna love all this. You free for babysitting duties?'

Vanessa smiled. It really was fascinating. Despite the grisly context, she couldn't help but admire the efficient, if morbid, life cycle unfolding before her. The larvae had erased some of the actress's unique markers of humanity, layer by layer, as they fed off her tissue, transforming her once identifiable face into an almost unrecognisable canvas of bloated, discoloured decay.

Sometimes, this stripping away of human features helped with clinical detachment. If someone looked less human, you could convince yourself it was just anonymous organic matter. But this felt different, somehow. Maybe it was that photo of the girl with her mum on the bedside table. The amiable smiles. The signs the deceased wasn't just a face on a screen, but a daughter, too.

Vanessa thought of her own mother then, taking a moment to imagine having the kind of relationship with her that would allow a recent photo of them both to be on her bedside table. The thought – or, more accurately, the *absence* of such a reality – pinched painfully at her. She hadn't even *seen* her mother since she'd walked out when Vanessa was seven.

Vanessa snapped herself out of her pity party and returned to the job at hand. When she'd collected enough samples, she carefully rose from her position, bones creaking in a way she intensely disliked. Damn being forty. Didn't matter how much yoga she tried to do, or how many supplements she took, time was catching up with her.

'Got enough maggot samples?' Detective Harris asked.

Vanessa nodded. 'I'm going to look at the surrounding area now for post-feeding dispersal. Maggots will often move off a body to find somewhere to pupate.'

Harris looked down in horror at his plastic-clad feet as Ramos laughed. 'You're such a pussy, Harris.' She turned to Vanessa. 'You know he cried at the end of *Marley & Me*?'

Harris let out a fake sob and put his fist to his mouth. 'But the dog!'

Vanessa smiled as she got on her hands and knees again and began exploring the thick carpet, finding several pupae cases. Eventually, she ended up near a floor-to-ceiling window that was slightly ajar.

'I presume this was open when the first officer arrived?' she called over to the detective.

'Yeah,' Detective Harris replied. 'Just as well, really, it'd stink even worse otherwise,' he added, wrinkling his nose.

It would also have given the flies and other insects drawn in by the odour easy access to the actress's body, Vanessa thought. She quickly made a note on her iPad, another device she was trying to get used to. How different private forensics in the US was from academic forensics in the UK.

Her back started aching, so she stood up for a moment and stretched, noticing as she did that a crowd had already gathered outside, cameras flashing and onlookers murmuring like a hive of disoriented wasps.

As she watched, a chrome and black motorbike pulled up outside, the crowd dispersing to let it through. The rider came to a stop and swung one long leg over the side, removing his helmet to reveal a sheen of dark hair falling in front of his face, partially obscuring his features. Even from this distance, Vanessa sensed an unsettling intensity about the man as he regarded the apartment block.

'Well, well, well,' Bronagh said as she joined Vanessa, a smile curling on her lips as she looked down at the man. 'This is about to get *very* interesting.'

'Who is that?' Vanessa asked.

'Detective Ru Hoshino. Lieutenant Haworth, the woman who heads up the Detective Squad at the precinct, must've decided to bring him back for this case.'

'Bring him back?' Vanessa remarked. 'Is Detective Hoshino not officially part of the force?'

'Hasn't been for a year,' Bronagh replied in a low voice. 'Nobody quite knows why. There were rumours he had a big bust-up with the precinct captain and was kicked off. With Hoshino, you never know.'

'Do you know him well?' Vanessa asked as they watched the man stroll up to the apartment block entrance.

'More know *of* him. Hoshino's . . . eccentric, to say the least.'

Other officers looked over at the mention of the detective's name, clearly as intrigued by his arrival as Bronagh.

'Hoshino's here?' Detective Harris asked, blue eyes alight with excitement.

Ramos's mouth virtually dropped open. 'No way! The last time I saw him, I didn't have another baby in my belly.'

'Isn't Hoshino a nightmare to work with?' one of the younger officers asked.

'Na,' Detective Harris said. 'He's just . . . misunderstood.'

Vanessa studied everyone's expressions: there was shock, anger, even the odd smile. She'd never witnessed a detective get a reaction quite like this.

Who *was* this Hoshino character?

Chapter 3

Ru Hoshino walked away from his motorbike, snowflakes beginning to dance their way down to Tribeca's cobblestone streets. His attention was unbroken as he looked up at the old-world style apartment building, with its grandiose facade of intricate stonework, expansive arches and tall windows. He hadn't heard of the actress whose life had been snuffed out in this very apartment block – he wasn't a fan of films. But judging by the crowd outside, and the real estate within, she was both famous *and* wealthy. Strange to think this area used to be an industrial zone, peppered with warehouses and factories. But now Tribeca – short for Triangle Below Canal Street – had undergone a remarkable transformation, morphing from its industrial roots into one of Manhattan's most sought-after residential neighbourhoods.

'Detective *Hoshino*?' the officer guarding the entrance to the apartment said, a look of surprise on his face.

Ru nodded. 'Lieutenant Haworth sent me. Where is the deceased?'

The officer opened the door for him as cameras lit up the snow-lashed air. 'Top floor, the penthouse,' the officer said. 'The elevator's down the hallway.'

'I'll take the stairs.' Ru strode towards a large, elegant staircase, ignoring the officer's protests. He walked up the stairs, one hand in the pocket of his baggy trousers, the other on the smooth wood of the banister. Walnut. Expensive. When he got to the top, there was a short hallway before a door at the end: the entrance to the penthouse, Ru presumed. Another officer was guarding it.

Ru flashed his badge. 'Lieutenant Haworth sent me.'

'Sure thing, Detective,' the officer said, opening the door for Ru.

Ru stepped through the door and into a new hallway that exuded contemporary elegance. The space was anchored by a herringbone-patterned hardwood floor, abstract paintings set in gilded frames on the walls. Plush, velvet armchairs in jewel tones were strategically dotted around, with various doors leading off the hallway.

'She's in the bedroom down there,' the young officer said, pointing towards a corridor that led off from the main hallway. Ru walked down it, and was instantly greeted by Officer Ramos. He'd always liked the young – and so it seemed now, very pregnant – officer. That would make three children in the Ramos household soon. Parenthood wasn't an idea that appealed to Ru. But he understood the biological urge to populate the Earth was a strong one.

'Good to have you back, Boss,' Office Ramos said. 'She's inside,' she added with a sad sigh, gesturing to a large bedroom.

Ru didn't need Ramos to tell him where the deceased was. The intensity of the activity within, not to mention the death stench, made its own announcement. Ru pulled on the shoe protectors, gloves and mask Ramos handed him, and paused. It had been over a year since he'd attended a crime scene and he was surprised to feel an unusual tremor of nerves. He examined the sensation momentarily, then swallowed it down and stepped into the bedroom – the officers and forensic investigators inside a blur of white coveralls and navy-blue police uniforms. The morbid centrepiece in this tableau of disarray was a woman lying dead in the middle of her unmade bed.

The room seemed to pause and take in a breath when he entered, but Ru's focus was laser-sharp. This was not a reunion.

'Jesus fucking Christ,' a familiar voice said. 'It really is you, Hoshino.'

Ru dragged his gaze away from the body to see Detective Harris regarding him with a wry smile. His old partner. A great man. A great detective. Also, someone who was relentless in his desire to integrate Ru into normal life. After-work drinks. Weekend barbecues. Even a double date with his wife's sister-in-law. It didn't matter how many times Ru turned these invites down, Harris still persisted.

'I was about to rent out your desk,' Harris said.

'He never used it much anyway,' Ramos called over, as some of the other officers laughed.

Ru didn't respond. He just stayed where he was, processing each detail of the room. A pile of unopened mail was stacked neatly in the corner of a table, except for one envelope that appeared to have been hastily torn open and then discarded. An unpaid bill, perhaps? Blackmail? He picked it up with his gloved hand. No, it was an invite to a fashion show being held by a designer called Maximilian Rossi. Ru tucked that detail away in his mental vault.

Labelled garments were strewn over a nearby chair, and a wilted blood-red rose lay horizontally on the side of the chair, next to a copy of *The Great Gatsby*. A romantic gesture, considering it was Valentine's Day a week ago? He checked inside the book but there was no inscription.

Finally, he turned his attention to the deceased herself. Her eyes were open, the eyeballs deflated from maggot activity, though the maggots themselves were missing. Maybe they had already been collected? Her arms rested at awkward angles, and Ru also noted discoloration around her mouth. An overdose seemed a likely cause, but there was something about this scene that had Ru's instincts screaming.

Ru's gaze finally settled on Cordelia's hair – what he guessed had been a vibrant red now dulled by death and decay. Most interesting of all was the hair clip the lieutenant had told him about, now being carefully removed with an air of practised confidence by a woman he didn't recognise. A forensic entomologist? Ru's thoughts flitted back to a perplexing case from the past where forensic entomology had been instrumental. A series of gruesome killings where the victims were left in secluded areas to decay. The insects had been the silent witnesses, their life cycles providing the timeline that eventually led to the killer's identification and capture.

'Wait,' he commanded. The woman stopped what she was doing and looked up at him. Ru noted her sharply winged eyeliner and the hint of a scar on the skin above her mask. He was sure he hadn't come across her before. He would have remembered. 'I'd like to look at the hair clip before you remove it.'

She nodded and moved out of the way. He leaned down to stare at the clip. Yes, it really was made from a *live* beetle. It was an unsettling juxtaposition – life within death, an uncanny stillness versus nature's ever-present hum. Most important of all, it was a rogue element that, for Ru, screamed louder than anything else in the room. Why here? Why now?

Slowly, he jotted down his thoughts in his recycled paper notebook, giving weight to an observation that might, or might not, be crucial in the grand scheme of things.

'Have you seen anything like this in other cases?' he asked the entomologist.

'No, I haven't.' A British accent. Even *more* interesting. 'I'm Dr Marwood.'

Ru nodded. 'Detective Hoshino.'

'Another detail to note,' the intriguing entomologist said, 'are the wings surrounding the beetle. I think they're real, too. Even more disturbing, they look like they belong to a critically endangered species of butterfly, the Queen Alexandra's birdwing. Whoever created this piece of jewellery may well have broken a few federal laws in the process.'

Ru frowned. He had heard rumours that the Thorsens, a known crime family in the city, were involved in the illegal insect smuggling business thanks to the insect obsession of Nils Thorsen, the son. But they had never been pinned down for it.

He dragged his eyes away from the forensic entomologist and regarded Harris. 'Who was the first officer on the scene?'

'Officer Greenfield,' Harris said, gesturing to a young female officer who glanced nervously at Ru.

Ru walked over to her. 'Tell me what happened.'

'I got a call from the building manager 'cos of the smell,' she said, eyes flitting to the actress and back again. 'I . . . er . . . followed the smell and we ended up here,' she said, gesturing down the hallway. 'The manager had a key. So we came in and . . . that's when we found her.' She shook her head. 'I can't believe it. I watched one of her films at the weekend.'

Ru resisted the urge to tell her such a detail wasn't pertinent to the case.

'One of the officers is taking a statement from the building manager right now,' Harris called over. 'Also getting any security camera footage. We have other officers speaking to residents.'

Ru nodded. 'Good. We need to check if anyone else has a key to the apartment.' He frowned. 'Security seems rather lax, for what I hear is an Oscar-winning actress.'

'I think she liked to keep low-key,' Harris said.

'What about friends, relatives?' Ru asked. 'The lieutenant told me she was taking time out for herself.'

'We're still trying to get hold of the mother,' Harris said. 'The agent, too, who we think was the last person to speak to Ms Montgomery.'

A commotion sounded from the hallway then. Ru turned to see a silver-haired woman in her fifties run down the hallway towards the room, an officer and a young man chasing after her. She froze as she reached the doorway, regarding the deceased with a look of abject horror on her face.

Ru took a moment to note the woman's attire – a smart pair of trousers with a long black cardigan that was inside-out, as if hastily thrown on. Her make-up was smeared, suggesting recent, profuse tears. The deceased's mother?

Behind her, a younger man gasped as he took in the prone body. Brother?

Or Cordelia's lover?

'I tried to stop them,' the officer said, out of breath. 'It's Cordelia's mother and brother. You need to leave, you're contaminating the scene!'

The officer motioned to take them away, but Ru stopped him, silently shaking his head. The room went quiet as the woman took a step towards the lifeless form of her daughter, her face twisted with a grief so raw, it rendered everyone in the room momentarily inert.

Then she let out a howl, collapsing to the ground as Cordelia's brother flinched at the sight of his mother's pain. 'My girl. Oh God, no, my girl.'

Ru observed the scene with interest. He had always found grief interesting to witness, especially grief as raw as this. As a young boy, Ru had been present when his grandmother had died, standing among the adults and quietly observing their varied emotional releases. He remembered being struck by the disparity in how each family member processed their grief, from his mother's wail of loss to his uncle's tranquil stoicism. Even then, he had been more fascinated by their reactions than by the loss of his beloved grandmother; more curious about the human condition in the face of mortality than his own emotions.

Ru crouched beside the grieving mother now. 'I am very sorry for your loss,' he said in an indistinct murmur. 'I believe the last person to speak to your daughter was her agent, seven days ago? Did you speak to her at any point?'

The mother blinked up at him with tear-laden eyes.

'Neither of us did,' the brother said. 'Cordelia was on a digital detox. That extended to communications with family.' Ru observed him. Expensive suit. Neat auburn hair. Good shoes. 'I'm Levi Montgomery, Cordelia's brother.' He put his hand out to shake Ru's hand then paused as he noticed Ru's gloves.

'A digital detox?' Ru asked. Cordelia's mother could barely respond, hand to her mouth, eyes wide and glassy.

'Yes,' Levi replied. 'She told us she was doing two weeks of no contact with the outside world – due to end tomorrow.' He paused, looking away. 'It got pretty hectic for Cordelia after the release of her last film. I think she just needed some quiet time . . . To shut the world out for a while.'

'I understand.' Ru stood up. 'Ramos, will you escort the Montgomerys to another room? We can chat in more detail in a moment.'

'Sure thing, Boss.' Ramos gently helped Cordelia's mother up and led her to the large living room, as Levi followed. When they had left, an officer peered out from an open door at the back of the bedroom.

'We found something you might want to see in here, Detective Hoshino.'

'Show me.'

Ru joined the officer in an impressive walk-in wardrobe. Polished oak shelves lined the walls, stacked with meticulously arranged rows of cashmere sweaters and silk blouses. Leather bags and clutches were displayed like museum artifacts above a spread of designer shoes – stilettos, ankle boots and loafers.

At the back of the room, a young officer was holding up several

Polaroid photos. The first one depicted a naked woman from the neck down, red locks just about discernible over her collarbone. Cordelia? The other photos were similar, but with another body involved. One muscled, hairy leg draped over a long, pale one. A hand palm down on a bare stomach, red hair spilling over it.

'Where did you find these?' he asked the officer as Harris appeared at the door.

The officer pointed towards a tiny open door behind one of the shoe racks. 'They were hidden. Only found them because I leaned on the wall to stand up.'

'This looks like the wallpaper you'd find in a room at the Seraphim Garden Hotel,' Ru said, noting the wallpaper in one of the photos, patterned with finely detailed golden beetles and plump blackberries. 'I recognise it from when we arrested Ebbe Thorsen there.' He peered back out towards the actress in the next room and the hair clip that was currently being bagged up by Dr Marwood. Illegal insects, a trade the Thorsens were rumoured to enjoy. Potential drug overdose. Another trade they were thought to be involved with. And now this Polaroid?

'The Thorsens could've supplied the drugs that led to her death?' Harris suggested. 'These rich millennials are known for their love of exotic narcotics, and the Thorsens sure like to supply them.'

'This is assuming it *is* an overdose that caused her death,' Ru said.

'You think there's more to it?'

'Maybe.'

'Doesn't Nils Thorsen have a thing for redheads? Maybe this is him,' Harris added, tapping the male thigh in one of the Polaroids. 'He's an insect freak, right? Maybe he gave her that weird hair clip as a Valentine's Day gift . . . which could also make him the last person who saw her.'

Ru nodded. As always Harris was not far behind him. 'You stay here,' he said to Harris. 'Keep reading the scene. I'm going to pay the Thorsens a visit. No doubt he'll be at the hotel.'

Harris frowned. 'You sure it's a good idea rushing over there, Boss? After what happened . . .'

He let his voice trail off. Ru ignored the implication in the silence he left behind. All that mattered was doing the best he could for the woman lying dead in the next room. His personal discomfort or the intricacies of his past didn't matter.

'There are too many threads linking the deceased to the Thorsens,' Ru said. 'Hotel. Redhead. Illegal insect.' He looked out at Dr Marwood. 'Dr Marwood, may I have a moment?' She nodded and walked through. 'I'd like you to accompany me on a visit.' He explained what they'd discovered and who he wanted them to see.

The doctor shook her head. 'That's not why I'm here, I'm afraid, Detective Hoshino. My expertise lies in insects, not criminal interrogations.'

'It's precisely your insect expertise I need. If there's a possibility that the Thorsens are involved in this actress's death, then establishing a link to the narcotics trade or the trade of illegal insects may provide proof. As an insect expert, only your eyes could discern the truths I may overlook.'

Vanessa looked like she was about to protest but then another woman appeared: Dr Bronagh Thompson, the digital forensics guru Ru had had the pleasure of working cases with in the past.

'It's fine, Vanessa,' Bronagh said. 'You have my permission. But she stays in the background, right, Detective Hoshino?' she said, turning her hazel-eyed gaze to him. 'An *observer*. I don't want her pulled into any of your cryptic detective games.'

'Of course,' Ru said, bowing his head to her. 'I will be on my best behaviour.'

'Hmmm,' Bronagh said. 'Haven't we heard that one before?'

Ru frowned. He did not understand why he had such a reputation. He gestured to the intriguing entomologist to follow him, impatient to see what would happen when Nils Thorsen, who enjoyed regaling anyone he met with his knowledge of insects, finally met his match in Dr Marwood.

Chapter 4

Vanessa watched the view change as Detective Hoshino drove the unmarked police car through Tribeca's streets and into SoHo, snowflakes drifting sideways in the breeze like moths in flight outside the windows. Beyond the snow, the architectural elegance of Tribeca shifted into the creative soul of SoHo where Broadway served as a living museum of cast-iron artistry. She turned her gaze to the detective, who sat low in his seat, almost crouching, eyes rarely blinking. His gloved hands gripped the steering wheel at an odd angle, as if solving a Rubik's Cube rather than driving a car. He was dressed unlike any other officer she'd met in her time in the city – a white, long-sleeved shirt untidily layered over a baggy pair of trousers, feet clad in expensive trainers, or sneakers, as Americans called them.

Yes, definitely one of the more distinctive detectives she'd encountered.

She thought of her friend Paul Truss. Another detective, from her life in the UK. And more than that, a friend. God, she missed him. He'd promised he'd visit with his wife and kids next year. *He'd better.*

'So, you are British?' the detective asked, cutting through the silence.

'What gave it away, Detective Hoshino? My top hat?'

'No, the crooked teeth,' the detective replied without missing a beat. 'It's Ru, by the way. My name.'

Vanessa smiled. 'Thank you for making me insecure about my teeth, Ru.'

'Now I can see your teeth, they are very good. I haven't encountered you on any cases before.'

'I only arrived six months ago.'

'Ah. How are you finding New York so far?'

She looked out at a man, hunched over in the snow, rocking

back and forth on his heels – an undeniable sign of meth addiction, something she saw a lot around the city. Walking past him was a woman in an expensive fur coat holding a small, beautifully groomed dog in her arms. 'A city of contrasts,' she said.

'An astute observation.'

'Were you born here?'

Ru shook his head. 'Japan. Specifically Kanazawa, a city on the west coast of the country. But I came here with my parents when I was two.' He examined Vanessa's face. 'You have Sri Lankan in you.'

'My mother is half Sri Lankan. How can you tell? People usually assume I'm Spanish or Italian.'

'An old school friend had Sri Lankan heritage. How did your family feel about you leaving the UK?'

'We're here,' Vanessa said, pleased to be able to avoid the question as she noticed the looming presence of the Seraphim Garden Hotel in the distance. She'd passed it a couple of times during taxi rides and had thought it looked rather grand and beautiful with its expansive dark glass facade and intricate gold accents.

Ru pulled up into a space outside and cut the engine, unfurling himself from the seat as Vanessa stepped out of the car.

'*Quite* the place,' she said as they entered the lobby of the hotel, taking in a large water fountain featuring golden dragonfly models balanced on silken lily pads at its centre.

'The Thorsens have a flair for the theatrical.'

'Fan of insects, too, I see,' Vanessa said, eyes catching on insect-themed art and butterfly-etched mirrors.

'That will be Nils Thorsen,' Ru said. 'According to his Instagram account he has travelled the world in search of the most beautiful insects.' Vanessa detected a hint of disapproval in Ru's voice.

'Have you come across the Thorsens much?' Vanessa asked as she followed him past a reception desk towards the lifts.

She noted the way the detective's jaw twitched. 'Yes.'

'Then they're known to the police?'

'Not as known as we'd like. The Thorsens are as adept at camouflaging their crimes as flower mantises.' The doors to the lift opened, and they both stepped in, Ru pressing the button for the top floor. He caught Vanessa's eye in the elevator mirror. 'I hope you're not uncomfortable accompanying me. I know you were reluctant, but your expertise could be invaluable when peeling back layers of a very complicated onion.'

'As long as I'm not crying at the end.'

'No promises with the Thorsens, I'm afraid. But I have a feeling you can handle yourself, Doctor.'

'I certainly can.'

The lift doors pinged, indicating their arrival at the top floor, and Vanessa followed Ru down a long, mirrored hallway towards a cushioned door flanked by two meaty security guards. The larger of the two seemed to recognise the detective. He rolled his eyes and opened the door for Ru without saying a word, a blast of music sounding out as he did.

'Is this a nightclub?' Vanessa shouted over the sound as they walked inside. That was another thing Vanessa was noticing about herself lately, along with the creaking bones. Noise. She hated loud noise. Now she understood why her father used to get so angry when she put her music on loud. He'd have hated this place. The sound of it, anyway. But the look of it? He'd feel right at home. It was like a digital garden in the heart of a concrete jungle with botanical wall art interspersed with neon lights.

'Yes, a nightclub,' Ru shouted back. 'It's open twenty-four hours.'

The DJ, perched in an elevated booth above them, was spinning lo-fi beats, making the entire space vibrate in sync with the glow of the colour-changing mood lighting. Around the room, people sipped cocktails served in bamboo cups, their eyes hidden behind sleek, mirror-tinted shades. It was like an Instagram feed come to life – achingly trendy and meticulously curated.

Beside Vanessa, Ru's eyes scoured the room like a praying mantis before alighting on what looked like an exclusive VIP section behind the DJ area.

'This way,' he said to Vanessa, leading her through the throng of dancing people towards a spiralling stairway. Vanessa put her hand on the rail, noting it was entwined with real vines and ivy. As she looked closer, she saw to her dismay that it was adorned with the dead bodies of various insects – butterflies, dragonflies and beetles. People probably thought they were fake. But Vanessa *knew* otherwise.

'They're real?' Ru asked as he followed her gaze.

She nodded grimly.

'Illegal?' he asked.

'Not from what I can gather.' She took her phone out and snapped a photo. 'I'll take a closer look later, though.'

They got to the top of the stairs and walked towards a large man guarding the entrance to the VIP area. He was less accommodating than the other security man, putting a beefy hand up against Ru's chest. But then a voice hollered out: 'Detective Hoshino! Let him through, Lambi.'

Vanessa's eyes adjusted to the dim lighting of the VIP area as they walked in. The noise thankfully dipped here, allowing the group occupying a booth shaped like a cocoon to talk. Above the cocoon booth was a curved bookshelf featuring a mixture of poetry and puzzle books. In the middle of them all was a blond man with an air of Nordic elegance about him. Behind him stood a wisp of a woman with the same colour hair and a slightly dazed expression. The man turned his green-eyed gaze to Vanessa, cataloguing her like she was an interesting specimen. 'And who is this, Detective? A new prodigy?'

'Dr Vanessa Marwood is a forensic entomologist,' Ru said. 'Vanessa, this is Nils Thorsen and his sister, Anja.'

'Ahhh, a connoisseur of life's minutiae,' Nils said in his lightly accented voice. Scandinavian, Vanessa guessed, which would make sense with the look and surname. Nils gestured to two seats across from him, the people around him slipping out of the booth without saying a word, except the woman whose slim hand remained on Nils's shoulder.

Vanessa and Ru took their seats across from Nils as he leaned back in his booth, spreading his long arms across the back of it as he watched Vanessa with interest. He was in his mid-thirties, with a sharp jawline and platinum-blond hair casually pushed back. He was wearing a tailored charcoal-grey cashmere sweater that subtly accentuated his broad shoulders, paired with slim-fit, dark wash jeans that were no doubt designer. In contrast, the woman behind him looked more dressed for summer in a beige silk slip of a dress.

Nils's eyes settled on the tattoo on Vanessa's forearm.

'*Myrmecorhynchus*,' he murmured. 'Unusual choice.'

Vanessa regarded him with interest. Few people ever recognised that species of ant, much less knew its name. Even more proof he was a connoisseur of insects. The ideal kind of person to run an illegal insect ring.

'Unusual to have a stairway decorated with insect corpses,' Vanessa observed.

'Why have their light diminished with death?' Nils countered. 'This way, they can continue to delight with their beauty.'

'I think they're hideous,' Anja said with a shudder.

'My sister doesn't share my love of insects,' Nils explained. 'I've never understood this aversion to such beautiful creatures. Do you, Dr Marwood?'

'Actually, it's evolutionary,' Vanessa replied. 'As insects can be carriers of disease or venomous, it's an evolved response to avoid these dangers.'

Nils smiled. 'You are a *very* interesting woman, Dr Marwood. How may I assist you?'

Vanessa watched as Ru picked up an emerald-green cocktail napkin from the table and began folding it, fingers busy but precise. 'You're familiar with Cordelia Montgomery, the actress?' he asked as he folded.

Vanessa noticed Nils pause a moment, a crease in his smooth performance. 'Of course, who isn't?' he replied.

Ru's long fingers continued to work over the napkin. 'She's dead,' he said, glancing up.

A ripple of shock crossed Nils's face. Anja, however, barely reacted. But Vanessa noticed her fingers tighten their grip on her brother's shoulder.

'That's . . . horrifying,' Nils said, blinking as though trying to contain himself. 'What happened?'

'Possible drug overdose,' Ru said.

Nils frowned.

'Did Miss Montgomery ever stay here?' Ru asked, dark eyes still focused on whatever it was he was creating with that napkin.

'Never,' Anja said abruptly.

Ru's fingers stopped their rhythmic folding for a moment as he looked up at the woman. 'You seem very sure.'

'My sister has the most *incredible* memory,' Nils explained. 'Much like I hear you have, Detective Hoshino.'

'So you remember every single guest that has stayed here in the five years since the hotel opened?' Ru asked Anja.

'You'd be surprised,' Anja replied.

'That's interesting,' Ru remarked, 'because we may have found evidence that Miss Montgomery was a guest here at the hotel. The wallpaper you use is quite distinctive, if I recall correctly from the last time I was here.'

Anja flinched slightly, turning away. Nils's hands curled into fists, his green eyes going hard. Then he took a deep breath and settled his face back into a calm smile.

'What kind of wallpaper, exactly?' he asked.

'Golden beetles and blackberries,' Ru replied.

'Ah yes,' Nils said. 'I know the room. Or should I say, *suite*? It's one of our best.' His eyes travelled over to Vanessa. 'We've had a cancellation for next week actually, Dr Marwood. As a new British addition to our city, you'd be most welcome to stay. On the house, of course.'

Vanessa frowned. 'How do you know I'm new to the city?'

'Oh,' Nils said, waving his hand around dismissively, 'one gets very perceptive with age.'

Vanessa laughed. 'You're younger than me.'

'Have you ever met Cordelia Montgomery?' Ru asked, cutting through the back and forth.

Nils shrugged. 'A few times, in this club,' he said, gesturing around him.

'How close would you say you were?' Ru asked.

'Not very much. Though I may have experienced a few forgotten evenings last year. Losing my father was . . . difficult.' Again, his hard eyes homed in on Ru.

Ru's fingers suddenly ceased their motion, and he placed his creation on the table. It was a beetle like the one from the hair clip Cordelia had been wearing, the multiple folded layers of the napkin forming a faceted carapace, a painstakingly creased antenna and even legs folded tightly against its body.

Vanessa noticed a slight furrow in Nils's brow as he regarded it.

'Cordelia Montgomery isn't very forgettable,' Ru said.

Nils leaned towards Ru, eyes aflame. 'And my father wasn't very forgettable, but you seemed to *forget* your promise to look after him, didn't you?'

What did Nils mean by 'look after'?

The tension between the two men thickened as they glared at each other.

'How's business?' Ru asked.

'Thriving, as you can see,' Nils replied.

'I mean, the Thorsens' *other* businesses,' Ru said. 'The *less* public businesses. Like narcotics.'

'We have nothing to do with narcotics,' Anja said.

'And Cordelia didn't *do* drugs, if that's what you're implying,' Nils said tightly.

'I thought you didn't know her,' Ru snapped back.

Nils clenched his jaw. 'From what I heard.'

'What else have you *heard* about Cordelia?' Ru asked.

Nils pulled at his jumper, avoiding Ru's gaze. 'I told you, I barely knew her. Darling,' he said, calling over to a server standing by the stairs, 'turn the air con up a notch, will you?'

'Have you heard of ironclad beetles?' Ru asked.

'Of course,' Nils replied. 'Why? One wouldn't usually hear *Zopherinae* being mentioned by a member of the NYPD.' He looked at Vanessa as he said that, clearly hoping she'd be impressed he'd used the scientific name for the species.

'An item of jewellery featuring an ironclad beetle was found at Cordelia Montgomery's apartment,' Ru explained. 'I'd say it's the kind of item an insect enthusiast might give to a lover on Valentine's Day.'

'How lovely,' Nils said. 'I don't know what that has got to do with me. Many people love insects, like Dr Marwood here,' he said, gesturing towards Vanessa.

'Dr Marwood suspects the wings of an endangered species of butterfly also feature on the design,' Ru said.

Nils leaned forward, green eyes lighting up with excitement. 'Which species?'

'*Ornithoptera alexandrae*,' Vanessa replied.

'Ah, the Queen Alexandra's birdwing. Such stunning creatures. Have you seen any yourself, Dr Marwood?' he asked her. 'Up close, I mean, and alive? You really should, it's a sight to behold.'

'I haven't,' Vanessa replied, 'nor would I want to if it was outside its natural habitat.'

Nils leaned back and crossed his legs. 'Well, that's precisely where I saw some, on a trip to Papua New Guinea.'

She narrowed her eyes at him. If, indeed, he was involved with the illegal insect trading business, had he gone there to smuggle insects back to the US?

'Using an endangered species such as these butterflies in a piece of jewellery would make the item illegal,' Ru said. 'The illegal trade in rare and endangered insects is a lucrative business. Lucrative enough to appeal to a man like you.'

Nils flicked imaginary lint off his jumper. 'I don't like what you're implying. Every insect I collect is legitimate.'

'Are you sure?' Vanessa asked, picking up one of the coasters she'd just noticed from the table. Its design featured a blue and yellow butterfly encased within a crystal-clear resin. 'I believe this is a *Bhutanitis lidderdalii* butterfly or, as they're more commonly known, the Bhutan glory. It's listed as rare, so its use in a coaster,' she said with a look of distaste directed at Nils, 'isn't what I would call *legitimate*.'

'It's *real*?' Nils said, taking the coaster from her and examining it. 'I honestly had no idea.'

Ru pulled an evidence bag from his pocket and put his hand out. 'I'd like to take this in and get it tested.'

Nils drew in a long breath and handed the coaster over. Then he stood up to his full six-foot height and stretched. 'As fascinating as this conversation has been, I have several businesses to run and the day is fast running away from me. I will certainly do some digging for you, Detective Hoshino, to see if Cordelia did stay here.' He went to walk away then paused, turning to Vanessa, his icy gaze travelling over her. 'The offer of a night in one of our best suites was genuine, by the way.'

Vanessa crossed her arms. 'I think I'll pass, thanks.'

Nils regarded her with a curious gaze, then he smiled and strode off with his sister.

'God, that man is infuriating,' Vanessa said as she followed Ru to the stairs.

'He is,' Ru confirmed. 'But I also think *he* is infuriated now, too, considering you noticed the illegal item.' He handed the evidence bag to her. 'Can you get this tested?'

'Of course.'

'It *was* very useful having you there,' he said as they jogged down the stairs. 'Your entomological knowledge seemed to throw him off. The problem with Nils Thorsen is he thinks he is too clever for everyone, especially when it comes to invertebrates. But this time, maybe he was outwitted.'

Vanessa considered asking Ru about his history with the family but soon they were back in the thick of the music, so loud Vanessa could barely hear herself think.

They headed downstairs, weaving their way in between the dancers. Just as they were about to exit the club, something caught Vanessa's eye. A woman drifting past, her profile hauntingly familiar: long, greying dark curls; her particular bearing that reached into Vanessa's chest and squeezed around her heart. For a moment, every synapse in her brain fired the same message: Mum.

It can't be.

Turning abruptly, Vanessa wove through the thrumming crowd after the figure, her eyes fixated on the back of the woman. But just as she reached the spot where she'd last seen her, the woman vanished into the crowd, leaving Vanessa standing in an ocean of strangers.

Could it really have been her mother? She'd have been the right age: in her sixties and out of place among all these millennials with her long, bohemian dress, just like the dresses she used to wear. And yet her mother was thousands of miles away in Brighton in the UK. As far as Vanessa knew, anyway. It *was* where she had disappeared off to, after all, when she left the family home all those years ago. It was where the gallery which displayed her sculptures was, too, their regular presence on the gallery website a sign to Vanessa that her mother was at least still alive and making her art. In fact, a photo of one of her mother's new sculptures had been uploaded just the week before when Vanessa had done her monthly check.

So, no, it couldn't have been her mother, all the way here in New York. But then she had gone to art college in this very city, and now Vanessa thought about it, subconsciously, had Vanessa's decision to take this job in the very same city been a way for her to be close to the mother she once knew?

A scream sliced through her thoughts. Vanessa's head snapped around just in time to see a man collapse a foot away from her, convulsing on the floor.

Chapter 5

Ru ran towards the man who lay sprawled on the dancefloor. His curls were damp against his head, his thin body shrouded in an elaborately patterned shirt. Vanessa was already crouching beside him, calling an ambulance as a young, lavender-haired man watched on, wide-eyed.

'Oh my God!' the man cried out. 'What *happened*?'

'How do you know him?' Ru asked.

'He's my friend. We came here together.'

'Your name?'

'Laife Ravenna. Is he going to be OK? After everything with Cordelia . . .' His voice trailed off.

Ru and Vanessa exchanged a look. 'What about Cordelia?' Ru asked as the nightclub's security men ran over, one with a first aid kit.

Laife blinked at Ru through his long fake lashes. 'It's all over my socials. I mean, the darling girl is dead, isn't she? Oh God,' he said, putting his hand to his mouth and shaking his head. 'I still can't believe it if she is.'

'You knew Cordelia Montgomery?' Ru asked.

'Of course, I styled her hair many times. And Maximilian . . .' Laife looked over at his prone friend who was being turned on his side by the security guards, 'he featured her in some of his catwalk shows and adverts.'

'You mean Maximilian Rossi, the fashion designer?' Ru asked, thinking of the torn-up fashion show invite in Cordelia's room.

'Of course. Is it all connected?' Laife asked. 'Oh my God, is Maxxi going to *die*? What if . . . ?'

'What if what?' Ru asked.

Laife quickly shook his head. 'Nothing.'

Ru took an extra step forward, so he was right in the man's face. 'Tell me.'

'We did a little *something-something* earlier. If it's because of that, does that mean *I'll* get ill, too?'

'What did you both take?' Ru asked. Laife hesitated. 'It could save your life.'

'Just some Molly,' Laife replied in a low voice.

Could that be the cause of Cordelia's death? Of this fashion designer's collapse? A bad batch of drugs circulating the city? It had been known to happen. And if it applied to these two cases, were the drugs supplied by the Thorsens? They weren't known for cutting corners. From the intel Ru had read, they supplied to the upper echelons of society. Mistakes were too risky.

'Who's your supplier?' Ru asked.

'No idea,' Laife replied. 'Just some low life on the streets.'

'You don't strike me as the type to buy drugs that way,' Ru said.

Laife shrugged, examining his long nails. 'It happens sometimes,' he said.

Ru sighed in frustration. Behind him, Nils started walking down the stairs, a look of concern on his face. 'What the *hell* is going on?' he said when he got to them.

'Do you know this man?' Ru asked, gesturing to Maximilian.

Nils observed the collapsed form before him, shock flitting across his face. 'It's Maximilian Rossi, the fashion designer.'

Two paramedics ran into the club then, the security guards and Vanessa moving out of the way as Nils called up to the DJ to turn the music off, security directing people out of the club.

'Thoughts on what caused his collapse?' Ru asked as he watched the paramedics tend to the fashion designer.

'Too early to say,' one of the paramedics replied, eyes flicking to the medical equipment briefly before returning to Ru. 'Could be an overdose, or a bad narcotics batch?'

Ru watched Nils for a reaction as the paramedic said that. But he remained impassive, drawing his phone from his pocket and putting it to his ear as the lights in the club turned on.

'Detective Hoshino,' Vanessa said, beckoning Ru over. He strolled over to where she was standing. 'It might be nothing,' she said in a low voice, 'but look at his watch.'

Ru followed her gaze towards Maximilian's watch. It was a sophisticated piece featuring a stunning bright blue butterfly on the watch face.

'I'm pretty sure that's a Lotis blue butterfly,' Vanessa said. 'I thought they were extinct. The last live one was seen in the eighties.'

A frantic shout snapped his attention away.

'He's arresting!' one of the paramedics called out as Maximilian's body started spasming. Ru and Vanessa watched the paramedics work with swift precision, applying chest compressions with rhythmic intensity in an attempt to kick-start the designer's heart. His fingers twitched, the pallor of his skin turning a shade greyer with each passing second. Ru noticed Vanessa put her hand to her mouth.

After twenty long, harrowing minutes, the paramedics ceased their efforts. The fashion designer was dead.

Chapter 6

Vanessa exited the lift, the heels of her red Mary Janes clicking on the polished marble floors of her new workplace. She was still rattled from what had happened an hour ago. Seeing that woman who looked so like her mother, then witnessing a death before her very eyes. She'd seen many insects die, but she'd only seen one human die before this: her father, who had taken his last breaths in hospital after being diagnosed with lung cancer over fifteen years ago. That moment had been blurred with emotion, *her* emotions. The denial and the utter devastation. As her father's body had succumbed to peace, hers had been taken over with the visceral reactions of grief. Later, when she'd calmed down, she'd considered the difference between human and insect death. While an insect's demise might go unnoticed due to its minuscule form, the departure of life from a human body was profoundly visible as the face paled, skin cooled and slackened. But most of all, it was the eyes – especially her father's blue eyes, always so full of life – and how they were reduced to glassy, vacant orbs.

Vanessa suddenly got an image of her mother's rich brown eyes losing life, and then her brother's. Those wild eyes that had pierced her own not that long ago. She paused in her footsteps, putting her hand to her chest. It was likely she wouldn't be present when they died. Maybe she wouldn't even be informed for a while?

What of her? Would *she* be alone when she died?

She squeezed her eyes shut. *Stop it, Vanessa, pull yourself together.*

'Vanessa, are you OK?'

She opened her eyes to see Bronagh walking out from the lift, juggling her laptop bag and a cup of coffee.

'I just witnessed someone die,' Vanessa said.

'My God, who?'

'A fashion designer, at the hotel's club. Maximilian Rossi.'

Bronagh placed the coffee cup on the side and rushed over to Vanessa, pulling her into a hug. Vanessa stiffened against her. 'I'm fine, really.'

Bronagh pulled back, searching Vanessa face. 'How did he die? Drug overdose?'

'Maybe. Or a bad batch of drugs. But something feels off about it; about Cordelia's case, too.'

'Your spider tingles going off?'

'Not just mine,' Vanessa said. 'I think Detective Hoshino feels the same. Rossi was wearing a watch featuring an endangered butterfly.'

Bronagh looked surprised. 'OK, now this is getting weird. The sooner we get a look at the clip Cordelia Montgomery was wearing, the better. It should be arriving soon, I had it couriered over.'

Vanessa nodded. 'Good. I'll get set up.' She began to stride towards her lab but Bronagh stopped her, gently taking her wrist.

'It's a lot, seeing someone die,' she said. 'Even more so for someone who went through what you did last year. We have a therapist on call, remember?'

Vanessa smiled. 'Bronagh, I'm British. I'll just stiffen this upper lip,' she said, gesturing to her red lips, 'and, you know, carry on.'

Bronagh sighed. 'I'm serious.'

'And I'm serious when I say I'm fine, I promise.' As Vanessa said that, she thought about that imaginary bee, buzzing, buzzing, buzzing in her head.

'If you're sure,' Bronagh said. 'Right, better get to it. Cordelia's laptop is arriving soon too.' She picked her coffee back up and headed in the direction of her office as Vanessa walked in the opposite direction towards her lab.

NovaScope Forensics was based on the top two floors of a plush, glass-fronted building in the heart of the Plaza District of Midtown Manhattan. Though the university Vanessa had worked at previously had been based in London, it felt a world away from this place. She still couldn't help but marvel at the sheer sophistication compared to what she'd been used to. Each lab she passed was equipped with high-tech equipment, a host of experts across diverse fields just doors away. When she'd arrived six months ago, not quite over the horror of what had happened in the preceding days, somehow the newness of this place, the sterility and the chemical scents, had been precisely the calming balm she'd needed.

She passed the toxicology unit. Whatever the cause of Cordelia's and Maximilian's deaths, it could be toxicology that would end up solving this case. Already, she could see the lead toxicologist and partner in the firm, Dr Egbo Kone, consulting with a junior technician inside. He was a slim man with a penchant for extravagant shirts and colourful glasses. After an inheritance from her mother, Bronagh had called on Egbo, who she knew had money, to see if he'd be interested in launching their own firm. They had worked together for years in the NYPD's Forensics Investigations Division. Vanessa had met him and his partner, an oncologist, during her welcome cocktails the night she'd finally arrived in New York. They'd both made her feel instantly at ease with their banter and warmth.

At the sight of Vanessa, Egbo broke away from the conversation and stepped outside his lab.

'That must've been tough,' he said, with a look of concern. 'Cordelia Montgomery was a wonderful actress, I enjoyed that period drama she was in.'

'Didn't take you for being into period dramas.'

'Not me, the hubby. So?'

Vanessa sighed. 'It was very sad. Even worse, I've just witnessed a fashion designer die.'

'Which one?'

'Maximilian Rossi.'

Egbo put his hand to his mouth in shock. 'No! I have one of his shirts. Cost a small fortune but it's one of my favourites. Two of this city's youngest and brightest talents, snuffed out in a day,' he said, clicking his fingers together. 'How did he die?'

Vanessa explained what she'd witnessed.

'How awful for you,' he said after. 'We have a wonderful therapist on call here.'

Vanessa smiled. 'Yes, Bronagh mentioned.'

'So what do the police think? A tainted drugs batch?'

'Maybe. Also, Cordelia was wearing a hair clip made from a live beetle.'

'No!'

Vanessa nodded. 'I'll get it sent over to you for testing as soon as I've taken a look.'

'Please tell me it will arrive *minus* the creepy-crawly attached?' Egbo asked with a shudder.

'Egbo, the beetle is smaller than your thumb!'

'Too big for my liking.'

Vanessa shook her head. 'Yes, it will come minus beetle. Right, better get on with it.'

She strode to her lab, pausing at the entrance to punch in the access code. The heavy door clicked open, revealing her sanctuary. It still felt so new, like she was just on some kind of sabbatical across the pond, and she'd be heading back to the UK soon. But this was a permanent move. An 'upheave your life and never turn back' kind of move. And based on the past six months, weighing up the pros and cons, it was a good one. Sure, she missed many things about the UK. Yorkshire puddings and gravy. She even missed the slightly chaotic environment she'd worked in at the university. And the people . . . She missed the people. Her old colleagues, and friends she'd made along the way – forged in shouty conversations at university events and conferences. Good friends like Detective Paul Truss and his wife, Helen. Even the people of her childhood town of Greensands, who had welcomed her back at the worst of times. And sometimes, she missed her old flame, Damon Oberlin. A flame she'd rekindled after returning to Greensands . . . and then puffed out.

She took in a deep breath and walked through her lab to the small office within, letting the chemical smells erase the thoughts. As she did, she passed a line of PCR machines and autoclaves, her gaze sweeping over the carefully organised lab benches. Various microscopes, some of which she hadn't even touched yet, were poised, ready to examine the minutiae of whatever specimen awaited them. Oh, how spoilt she was in this lab!

She quickly changed into her PPE – lab coat, gloves and eye protection. As she did, one of the junior forensic technicians walked into the lab. Jamie was a recent forensics grad with a mop of dishevelled brown hair and wire-rimmed glasses who wore the wide-eyed expression of someone both excited and slightly overwhelmed by the real world of this sometimes gruesome science. He was twenty-five, the same age as Cordelia Montgomery, and the excitement in his eyes showed he was looking forward to delving into such a high-profile case with Vanessa.

'Dr Marwood,' he said, pushing a cart laden with sealed evidence bags, 'the hair clip's arrived. I also created a beetle home for you, at your request.'

Vanessa looked over at the stainless-steel table that dominated the room. On top of it was a small glass terrarium with sticks and leaves layering the bottom, mimicking the beetle's natural environment.

'Excellent work, Jamie,' she said.

'Is it true?' Jamie asked. 'There's been another death?'

'Yes,' Vanessa said with a sigh. 'We'll have another item to examine from that scene, too. A watch. But first let's take a look at this, shall we?'

She carefully lifted the lid off the small plastic evidence box, revealing the ornate hair clip, the beetle's vibrant carapace shimmering under the fluorescent lights. With meticulous care, Vanessa used a pair of tweezers to gently grasp the clip, lifting it with the beetle attached. She then transferred them both to the terrarium, pausing a moment to watch.

The beetle remained still for a moment, perhaps stunned by the sudden change. But then it began to tentatively move, its legs working against the gilded clip. Vanessa felt a surge of protective instinct. 'Let's get this chain removed,' she said.

Jamie nodded, leaning closer to the terrarium to watch the beetle. 'We're going to take good care of you, dude,' he whispered.

Vanessa smiled. 'The key is delicacy,' she murmured, grabbing a small wire cutter from nearby. 'We don't want to harm the beetle or startle it into a defensive posture.'

Carefully, she lowered her hand into the terrarium then quickly snipped at the gold chain as close to the beetle's hard shell as she could. With a final gentle tug, the chain gave way, and the beetle, released from its golden shackle, scurried towards the shelter of a leaf.

'Yes! Freedom!' Jamie declared. 'Can we keep it? You know, like a NovaScope pet?'

'I think I'd rather see it free to roam in a more natural habitat,' Vanessa said. 'But it will have to remain here until Detective Hoshino confirms it's no longer needed as evidence. Now, let's look at this clip.' Vanessa lifted the clip out with her gloved hand and laid it on the table. 'I want to see if these fragments,' she said, gesturing to the green and yellow patches on the clip, 'do indeed belong to the Queen Alexandra's birdwing.'

Vanessa picked up a magnifier and leaned in close, examining the texture and patterns for authenticity as Jamie watched in silence.

'Yes,' she eventually murmured, 'from the microstructure of these wing fragments, it looks real. There's a spare magnifier over there. Have a look.' Jamie took the magnifier and brought it over, looking at the wing fragments. 'Notice the intricate veining, the exact alignment and overlap of scales – this is beyond the skill of any forger. Only nature can produce this level of complexity in such minute detail.'

Jamie nodded. 'Oh yeah, I can see it.'

Vanessa turned the clip around, her gaze tracing the edge of the clasp where the decorative elements gave way to the functional. A glint caught her eye – a minuscule anomaly. She leaned in closer, her breath fogging the glass of her magnifier momentarily. As it cleared, she looked again. Yes. There it was. A tiny, almost imperceptible protrusion integrated cleverly within the design. Not a flaw, but a *needle*.

Specifically, an injector. She felt a tremor of unease.

Had this clip been used to deliberately poison Cordelia Montgomery?

Chapter 7

Ru walked through the Lower Manhattan precinct where he'd once been the lead detective, still reeling from what Vanessa had told him. This was now officially a homicide investigation. One that involved a killer who was not only highly *technically* skilled, having managed to attach an injector to a hair clip, but also took a perverse pride in their work.

'Good to have you back, Hoshino,' one of the detectives said as Ru headed into what they all referred to as the 'squad room', the large, open-plan space where all the precinct's detectives conducted their daily work. The space was a maze of desks, each cluttered with the personal flotsam of its occupant: family photos jostling for space with stacks of case files, mismatched mugs holding a rainbow of pens, and the occasional potted plant struggling for light. In the far corner, a worn-out sofa and a coffee table laden with yesterday's newspapers and a constantly full ashtray served as a makeshift break area.

Was it good to be back? Ru wasn't sure. The precinct, with its rigid bureaucratic structures, had never been his natural habitat. Even when he was a regular a year ago, he preferred to get out as soon as he could to continue the rest of his work at home.

Ru's phone buzzed. He looked down to see it was a message from his mother.

> Ru-kun, hope all is well. I know you're always so busy-busy, but I haven't seen you this month. Will you make time for dinner Saturday evening at the restaurant? I will make your special katsudon. It would be good for you to take a break and eat good food 🍥 🍡 🌸

He quickly replied: Probability of attendance remains uncertain due to case variables. But the allure of your katsudon is noted. Will keep you updated. 😋

Harris strolled over with a cup of coffee in his hand and fell into step beside Ru. 'A fashion designer, huh? You think it's all linked?'

'My guess would be *definitely*.'

'So it's a bad batch of drugs?'

'Unlikely.'

Harris frowned. 'There's been a development?'

'There has. Everyone gathered?'

'Yeah, they're inside with Haworth.'

They both entered a room at the back. Inside, the blinds were drawn tight over the windows to keep the room's secrets from prying eyes. A central table was surrounded by chairs and a large screen had replaced the whiteboard that had once dominated the back wall. Clearly, some money had flowed into the department since he'd been gone. Next to the screen was Lieutenant Haworth. Her journey to the precinct after a return that morning from a holiday to the Dominican Republic had been a traffic-heavy scramble, meaning she'd barely made it to the precinct in time to give this briefing. At least it had afforded her time to make all the important calls, including one to Ru. He hadn't been surprised to see her number flash up; he knew he'd be having a conversation with her soon. He just didn't realise he'd be pulled right into a case.

Of course, he'd said yes straight away, half out of intrigue when he heard the details, half out of respect for the lieutenant. He'd always liked her. She was the epitome of dedication, her years on the force and her experience growing up in the Harlem River Housing Project in the sixties and seventies instilling in her a profound understanding of the fine line between hardship and community. This experience had cemented a deep respect for her, not just within the precinct walls but also across the whole of Manhattan.

She gave Ru a nod now when he walked in and gestured to the desk beside her. He headed right there, hopping onto its surface and sitting down with crossed legs just like he used to.

A dozen or so officers were gathered around the table; some Ru recognised, others he didn't. A few exchanged bemused glances, but Harris and Ramos both just rolled their eyes. They were used to Ru's strange ways.

'Right. Let's evaluate what we've unearthed so far,' Lieutenant Haworth began. 'Harris, if you could run through what you know about the victim?'

Harris nodded as he peered down at his notebook. 'Sure, Boss. Cordelia Montgomery. Twenty-five. Well-known actress. Found dead in her Tribeca apartment this morning. Body may have been there for approximately one week. Fast-forward to over an hour ago. Maximilian Rossi, supposedly an icon in the fashion world, collapses and dies in the nightclub above the Seraphim Garden Hotel at the same time Hoshino was visiting Nils Thorsen with Dr Vanessa Marwood, the forensic entomologist on the case.' He looked up at the room. 'That's Bug Lady,' he said, adding an explainer.

'Wait,' Ramos said, 'isn't that the name on the torn-up fashion show invite we found at Cordelia's apartment?'

'Indeed it is,' Ru said. 'I have just come off the phone from Dr Marwood and it appears we are closer to ascertaining Cordelia's cause of death. She may have been poisoned by the distinctive hair clip that was found on her person.'

The looks on the faces around the room were predictable. Surprise. Disbelief.

'You mean the hair clip made from a live beetle?' Ramos asked, as the officers around the room wrinkled their noses in disgust.

'That very clip,' Ru replied. 'Upon closer examination, Dr Marwood discovered that a small injector had been fitted to it.'

'That is *fucking* crazy,' Harris murmured.

'Life *is* stranger than fiction,' Ramos said as she shifted position in her seat, cradling her large belly. 'We've all seen that to be true in this messed-up job.'

The officers around the room nodded.

'So what, some sicko tampered with the hair clip to kill Cordelia?' the lieutenant asked.

'Possibly,' Ru said. 'Furthermore, at the time of his death, Maximilian Rossi was wearing a watch featuring an endangered species of butterfly.'

'*A live* butterfly?' Harris asked with a look of horror on his face, glancing down at his own watch.

'Not this time,' Ru replied. 'Dr Marwood will be taking a look at it to see if there is a similar device.'

'It's gotta be the Thorsens,' Ramos said.

Looks of displeasure crossed the officers' faces at the mention of the Thorsens. Many had had dealings with the family over the years.

'Definitely has my antennae buzzing,' Harris joked as some of the other officers laughed.

'Let's not get ahead of ourselves,' Haworth remarked.

Ru uncrossed his legs and stood up, pacing slowly up and down the room as the officers' eyes followed him, some twisting in their seats to watch him. 'Adiche,' Ru said, addressing an intelligent-looking woman with bright blue glasses framing her big brown eyes. She was the kind of investigator who didn't just scratch the surface; she mined it. Originally a computer science graduate, a relationship with a fellow student who was training to become an officer had drawn her into the world of policing. Her computer training didn't go to waste; instead, it became her greatest asset. 'You should dig deeper into the rare insect trade,' Ru instructed her. 'Check for any recent busts, known players, exotic imports. See if anything connects with the Thorsen family. And find out if we can subpoena the Thorsens' financials, too. You might want to get in touch with the US Fish and Wildlife Service. If you come up against any problems, let me know. I'll see if I can get the funding for NovaScope to look into it. They have a strong financial forensics team.'

Adiche nodded. 'Sure thing.'

'As for the rest of you,' the lieutenant said, turning back to the room, 'deep dive Cordelia Montgomery and Maximilian Rossi's personal lives. Friends, enemies, frenemies, business associates. We need to build a digital footprint of their last days, too.'

'We should also map out all and any connections the two victims have to each other,' Ru suggested. 'We know Cordelia featured in Maximilian's fashion campaigns. But let's see what else we can find.'

'Did you know they share the same agent?' Adiche asked as she looked up from her iPad. 'Heidi Stone.'

'Interesting,' Ru murmured.

'Ramos, any luck tracking this agent down?' the lieutenant asked the officer.

Ramos nodded. 'Yeah, I'm going to see her at the end of the day. I tried to get in earlier but she said she's on the other side of the city and won't be back until then.'

'I'll come with you,' Ru said.

The door opened then, and Captain Williams strode in. He headed up the whole precinct so of course he was making sure to show his face for a case as big as this. He was a hulking figure with a thick-set neck and broad shoulders. The redness of his cheeks painted the picture of a man accustomed to excess – too many late nights, perhaps a few too many drinks. His uniform, though impeccably neat, seemed to strain slightly at the waist, no doubt bearing the impact of countless dinners with officials and VIPs.

Ru was slightly annoyed to see him looking so relaxed considering the day's developments. His hands were casually tucked into his pockets, and there was a placating smile playing on his lips as he approached the centre of the room. But he hadn't been informed yet about the hair clip injector development. He hadn't seen Ru, either. The lieutenant had told Ru she'd discussed assigning him to the case with the captain. To Ru's surprise, he had agreed. However, the actual sight of Ru would be another matter entirely.

As if tuned into Ru's thoughts, the captain's gaze found the detective, his expression turning sour. 'I've been following up on the developments with the fashion designer,' he snapped, 'and I'm leaning towards a narcotics angle on this one.'

Ru shifted slightly, feeling the room's gaze on him.

'Captain, there has been a development that might change things,' Haworth said. 'Detective Hoshino, can you explain?'

Ru shared Vanessa's findings with the room, the captain's expression increasingly incredulous as he did.

'That seems preposterous,' Williams said.

'A scientist doesn't think so,' Ru replied.

'What scientist?' the captain asked.

'The forensic entomologist from Bronagh Thompson's firm that you agreed for us to bring onto the case,' Haworth replied.

'Bronagh?' the captain asked. 'Doesn't she work in the labs in Queens?'

'She did,' Haworth replied with more patience than Ru felt. 'But she left to set up her own firm, which happens to employ one of the world's leading forensic entomologists in the world, Dr Vanessa Marwood.'

'Entomology? Isn't their area maggots and pollen?' the captain asked.

'Dr Vanessa Marwood also has a detailed knowledge of insects,' Ru said, 'and given the hair clip was made from a *live* insect – and that hair clip is now looking likely to be the murder weapon – she will be playing a very important role in this case. In fact, she will soon be receiving the watch Maximilian Rossi was wearing.'

'Watch?' the captain asked, the officers around them all observing the interplay between Ru and Williams in fascination. 'What watch?'

'At the time of death, the designer was wearing a watch that had rare insect elements,' Ru explained.

'Do you realise how *ridiculous* this all sounds?' the captain asked, visibly irritated. 'Until we get definitive evidence, I do not want a *word* of this getting out to the press. We do not need the city panicking over some deranged jewellery-making, insect-loving serial killer.' Ru opened his mouth to protest but the captain continued. 'For now, we pursue the narcotics angle. These young, rich types are well known for getting caught up in substances. Let's not see bizarre patterns where there are none. It's not our main stage.'

Main stage. Interesting choice of words from the captain considering narcotics was his main stage, big drug hauls and dealer arrests being the area where he'd made his name.

'But to ignore patterns could be a mistake,' Ru said calmly, 'especially in a high-profile case such as this.'

'By all means look into your *theories*,' the captain said dismissively, 'but have the narcotics team on speed dial. And Hoshino, let's keep the theatrics to a minimum, shall we? The last thing we need – the last thing *you* need,' he added pointedly, 'is more drama.' Then he stormed from the room.

'That man is living in a *world* of denial,' Ramos said with an eye roll.

'Since when hasn't he been?' the lieutenant added.

Ru's phone rang. It was NovaScope's number. He put the phone to his ear.

'Detective Hoshino?' It was Bronagh. 'Maximilian Rossi's watch just arrived. I think you need to come take a look for yourself.'

Chapter 8

Maximilian Rossi's watch lay on the lab table in a sealed evidence box. Detective Hoshino had arrived a few moments before, his black hair still messy from his bike helmet. He stood calmly beside Bronagh, his notepad open before him. From her position, Vanessa could spy the writing within and was intrigued to see it was Japanese symbols. Or maybe it wasn't so intriguing. It would make sense; a form of encryption should anyone unsavoury get their hands on the notepad. She'd already seen that this detective was the kind of man who covered all angles. He was probably the perfect detective for a case like this. A case, as she'd just discovered, that was about to get very, very complicated.

Vanessa gestured towards the evidence container. 'Like Cordelia Montgomery's hair clip,' she started, her voice steady, 'the watch that Maximilian Rossi was wearing contains an unusual mechanism. I discovered that on the *back* of the watch,' she said, turning the container slightly so Ru could see the back of the watch face, 'there is a pad that depresses with slight movement. When we tested this under controlled conditions,' she said, gesturing to a glove box unit nearby, 'we noticed a liquid substance was expelled. This is currently being analysed by our toxicology team.'

Bronagh shook her head in disbelief as Ru's pen paused on his notepad, his gaze on the watch.

'The watch was clearly designed,' Vanessa continued, 'to deliver a gradual, unnoticeable release of whatever substance was contained within the watch head.'

'Unbelievable,' Bronagh murmured. But Vanessa noticed Ru remained calm.

'I can also confirm that the butterfly within this watch face,' she said, gesturing to the evidence bag where she'd placed the dead creature, 'is a Lotis blue butterfly, a gloss swallowtail species endemic to California, renowned for its exquisite beauty. The species is endangered, considered possibly extinct, having not been sighted since the eighties – meaning it is illegal to catch, kill or import.' She frowned, remembering how she had felt as she'd gingerly opened the glass front of the watch face and removed the delicate creature. 'This poor thing would have been killed as it hatched and opened its beautiful wings for the first time. Hence why it looks so perfect.'

For the first time, Vanessa noticed a flicker of emotion on the detective's face.

'Why do people *wear* stuff like this?' Bronagh asked. 'So sick.'

'It's less about how they look and more what it speaks to,' Vanessa said. 'Rarity. Prestige. People are trying to buy originality when they buy these things. They're trying to make a statement.'

'The statement being they're sick bastards,' Bronagh said. 'So if tests reveal some kind of poison was in the compartment, we're looking at premeditated murder.'

Ru nodded solemnly.

'Jesus,' Bronagh said. 'Who the hell is doing this . . . and why?'

'Indeed,' Ru agreed. 'Another question: why would they stop at two victims?'

'I thought the same,' Vanessa said with a small shudder.

Ru looked at his watch. 'I must go. I'm due to meet with Cordelia and Maximilian's agent.'

'They share the same agent?' Vanessa asked.

Ru nodded. 'Thank you for your work,' he said, eyes lingering on Vanessa. Then he walked out, hands in his pockets.

'He really is quite the character, isn't he?' Vanessa said when he was out of earshot.

'That's one way to describe him,' Bronagh replied.

'What's the deal with him and the Thorsens? I feel like there's some history there beyond the usual cop versus criminal schtick.'

'Ru was with Ebbe Thorsen, the man who ran the whole Thorsen operation, when he died.'

Vanessa raised an eyebrow. 'What happened?'

'He was shot to pieces by a rival gang when Ru was transporting him to the station after arresting him. Ru even took a bullet himself.'

Vanessa thought back to what Nils had said to Ru: *And my father wasn't very forgettable, but you seemed to forget your promise to look after him, didn't you?*

'Wow,' Vanessa said. 'Is that why Ru left the force for a while?'

'I'm not sure. It happened a few months before Ru left. I get the impression something else happened a year ago to have Ru disappear from the force. No idea what, though.'

'Intriguing.' Vanessa paused, before looking again at the items laid out before her. 'So,' she said, 'looks like we might have one sophisticated killer on the loose.'

'One more victim,' Bronagh said with a sigh, 'and we move into serial killer category. Actually, are you OK working on this, considering the last serial killer case you worked on?'

'A hundred per cent,' Vanessa said. 'Anyway, maybe this is more of a gang thing? Ru seems to think the Thorsens are involved in some way.'

'Or Nils Thorsen is doing this . . . a lone wolf. What was he like?'

Vanessa thought of the calm, informed man she'd met earlier. 'Slick. Clever.'

'Serial murderer potential?'

'Maybe.' Vanessa looked at her watch. Nearly five. 'If it's all right with you, I think I'll head home. It's been a crazy day.'

'Why don't you come back to mine, have dinner?'

'I'm coming out with you guys for your birthday dinner Thursday night, remember?'

Bronagh had invited Vanessa out for dinner for her fifty-fifth birthday. Initially, Vanessa thought the whole NovaScope team would be attending, but she'd since learned it would just be her with Bronagh and her family. She'd wondered if it was because Bronagh felt sorry for her, being alone in the city. Vanessa had said she didn't want to intrude on a family dinner, but Bronagh had insisted, saying she needed some female company on a table 'full of the Y chromosome'. And in truth, Vanessa and Bronagh had already grown close, getting drinks most weeks, as well as a few lunches and dinners at the Thompson house.

'OK, if you're sure?' Bronagh said.

Vanessa nodded. 'I'm sure. I just need to be alone with Nancy tonight,' she said, referring to her pet tarantula.

Bronagh smiled. 'Sure thing. Say hi to Nancy for me.'

Vanessa's apartment was in Upper Manhattan, on the western edge of Morningside Heights, not far from Columbia University and overlooking the sprawling greenery of Morningside Park. Situated on a quiet street lined with historic brownstones, her apartment was located on a higher floor, boasting picturesque views of the park below as well as the Hudson River, which was now partially obscured by the falling snow. She shared the block with an eclectic mix of people, from university staff and professors, to long-time residents who carried stories of the neighbourhood's evolution in their every step. Next door was an elderly couple, once lecturers at the university and now happy to watch the campus from afar. To watch Vanessa from afar, too, often inviting her to dinner parties. She'd only been over once, and although she had loved the lively conversation and the couple's warmth, she had found herself reminded of a lunch she'd had back in Greensands in the midst of her brother's killing spree. She'd had to make up a work excuse and leave early, overwhelmed by memories.

She walked into her apartment now, heading straight over to her cobalt-blue tarantula, Nancy, who was safely ensconced in a state-of-the-art terrarium that took pride of place on a table in the middle of the room. She had recently moulted, her vivid blue exoskeleton looking especially vibrant against the substrate that lined her home. Vanessa took a moment to check the moisture level of the enclosure, making sure her eight-legged companion was as comfortable as possible.

'Today was *something*,' she said to Nancy as she placed her palm against the glass. 'You would *not* be impressed by what's being done to your fellow invertebrates.'

She walked to her kitchen, pouring herself a rum and Cherry

Coke before sinking into the plush velvet of her chaise longue, taking in her surroundings. It was a unique space that could only belong to her: a rich tapestry of nature, entomology and gothabilly aesthetics. Victorian-esque illustrations of insects decorated one wall, while a glass box showcased her vinyl records, a combination of surf rock, fifties country and vintage goth. She switched on her TV, finding a twenty-four-hour news channel. The screen erupted with sensational headlines, colourful graphics and rapidly cutting camera angles. Vanessa found it jarring compared to the BBC's more sedate approach. Unsurprisingly, Cordelia's and Maximilian's deaths were taking centre stage.

'The city continues to mourn,' the male anchor proclaimed sombrely, 'over the deaths of acclaimed actress Cordelia Montgomery and fashion designer, Maximilian Rossi. As yet, the city's police have not commented on the nature of their deaths. Nadine is now joined by two close friends of Cordelia and Maximilian. Nadine?'

The camera switched to a live stream of a young female reporter, standing outside Cordelia's Tribeca apartment. 'Yes, Stephen, let's start with Laife Ravenna, the hairstylist who worked closely with both victims.' The camera panned to the lavender-haired man who had been at the nightclub. 'Laife,' the interviewer said, 'I believe you were with Maximilian when he collapsed?'

Laife nodded, tears leaving a trail in his heavily made-up face. 'It's just so devastating. Maximilian was such a close friend. And I did Cordelia's hair for *multiple* red carpet appearances. We were like family.'

Vanessa shook her head. Were they *really* like family?

The focus then turned to a woman in her early twenties, with her brown hair tied up in a 'messy' bun revealing an assortment of piercings along her right ear. Even more noticeable were her large lips. Vanessa couldn't tell if they were fake or real. One thing that seemed real, though, were the tears that drenched her face and the distraught look in her brown eyes.

'Now we turn to social media influencer, Madeline Layton, also known as MadeYouGlow,' the newsreader said. 'I believe you were very close to Cordelia, and she appeared in one of your TikToks?'

Madeline nodded, blinking back tears. 'I just can't believe she's gone. Cordelia was a complete icon and *so* kind.'

'Yes, she was a *queen*!' Laife interrupted. 'She appeared on *two* of my TikToks,' he quickly added.

Vanessa shook her head in shock. Laife, in particular, was like a scavenger beetle, feeding off the tragedy as if it were a source of nourishment for his own ego. She couldn't watch any more so she switched the TV off and padded over to her turntable, putting on a Wanda Jackson record, the hypnotic melodies filling the air. As the rum softened the edges of the day, she swayed back and forth, wondering what it would be like to have someone here with her. No, there was a reason why she didn't get involved with men. It made things too *complicated*. But then, on nights like these, wouldn't a companion that didn't have eight legs and eyes be quite nice?

As the music deepened, Vanessa's thoughts drifted to her mother. Did she live alone in Brighton? Or maybe she had a whole other family? Despite the years, the thought made her stomach lurch with envy.

A buzz from the doorbell yanked her from her thoughts. She sighed and clicked the video feed on her security system, surprised to see a blurry video of a woman holding what looked like a large bouquet.

'Delivery for Dr Vanessa Marwood?' the woman said in a bored voice.

Vanessa frowned. Who on earth would be sending her flowers? She pressed the buzzer to let the courier in. When she finally appeared outside Vanessa's door, Vanessa could see it wasn't a bouquet of flowers after all. It was a large box of exotic plants – a dark purple oxalis, a Black Velvet Alocasia with its striking black leaves, and a bat flower. Among them were carnivorous blooms like a Venus flytrap and a pitcher plant.

Vanessa smiled. 'Pretty.'

She took the delivery, tipping the woman. Gosh, how they *loved* to tip in the States. She then placed the plants on her kitchen table, removing the card that came with them from a thick, cream envelope.

Dr Marwood,
  A belated welcome to our wonderful city.
  The Thorsens.

A chill ran down Vanessa's spine as she looked from the note to the obviously expensive and carefully curated plant collection. How the hell did the Thorsens – specifically, Nils Thorsen – know where she lived?

Chapter 9

Ru and Ramos walked through the corridors of Heidi Stone's Talent Agency. The walls were adorned with glossy photos of celebrities, their smiles frozen in time. It made Ru think of pinned butterflies. There was a fragility to these celebrities' existence, a dependency on the environment crafted by agents like Heidi.

Ramos gave their names to the receptionist and was asked to wait for Heidi's assistant to greet them.

'Man, she really does represent the best of the best, doesn't she?' Ramos commented, starry-eyed as she stared at the photos on the wall.

'Best of the dead, too,' Ru remarked.

Ramos laughed. 'I've missed you, Hoshino. You're a real comedian beneath that nerdy exterior.'

'Comedian is not a word I've ever heard assigned to me, but I'll take it.' His eyes dropped to her belly, which was pressing for freedom from her zipped-up jacket. 'When is this one due, then?'

'End of next month. You should've seen Ed's face when I told him,' she said, referring to her husband. 'Three in five years.'

'Was it an accident?'

Ramos laughed again. 'Hoshino! You can't ask that.'

'Why not?'

She shook her head. 'No, it *wasn't* an accident. I always wanted three and I wanna pop them out quickly so I can travel in my retirement. Speaking of which, did you enjoy your gap year? What did you get up to?'

Ru thought about the year he'd had off. The time had passed in a blur initially, the days melding into one another. For someone who had been part of the NYPD since the age of twenty-one, the sudden absence of structure and purpose left him adrift in a sea of unstructured time. Days which were once marked by the rhythm of working at the precinct felt like echoes in an empty room. But then, gradually, Ru had found himself adapting to the new tempo. He'd settled into a routine. Mornings were no longer heralded by the urgent calls to duty, but by the quiet contemplation of the day's potential. He dived into books with the same fervour he'd once reserved for case files, each page turn a step away from the identity he had worn for so long and a step towards something resembling peace.

And now he was back, shattering that peace.

'I found a routine outside the badge,' Ru said to Ramos, 'a different kind of investigation. It's curious how the mind adapts,' he pondered. 'Detachment breeds clarity, Ramos. I saw the contours of our work, and indeed of myself, with new eyes.'

Ramos smiled. 'You know you could've just said, "Read. Gamed. Exercised." But thanks for the philosophical insight all the same.'

'Well, I did that too. And I built a garden.'

'Garden?'

Ru nodded. 'For the community. My mother signed me up.'

'And now you're back, and as tempting as it is, I'm not gonna ask why you left. I'm just gonna to say I'm pleased you're here.'

Ru risked a small smile. 'And I am pleased I'm here, too, before you disappear on maternity leave. How long will you be taking off?'

'We only get twelve weeks paid leave,' Ramos said with a sigh, 'and I can't afford to take any unpaid leave or give up vacation time, so Grandma Ramos will be helping out again.'

A young, stressed-looking woman appeared then, eyes on her phone as she walked towards them. 'Heidi's ready for you, if you can follow me,' she quickly said, now tapping away on her phone as she led them down a corridor.

They arrived at Heidi's office, where a large desk sat in the middle of the impressive, high-ceilinged room, surrounded by a wall of shelves artfully filled with awards and personal memorabilia. Heidi Stone herself was an interesting figure, a thin woman in her fifties who looked like she dined on cigarettes and Martinis. She didn't even rise to greet them, just smiled thinly from her position behind the gleaming desk, a pair of expensive gold glasses perched on the end of her powdered nose.

She leaned over, moving several unopened envelopes to the side. As she placed them beneath the light of her lamp, Ru noticed one of the envelopes had a watermark pressed into the paper; a distinctive Japanese character: 美. It was the kanji symbol for beauty, not something typically found on Western correspondence.

'Officers,' she acknowledged, gesturing to the seats across from her. As Ru sat down, he noticed how uncomfortable the chair was. Ramos must have, too, grimacing slightly as she tried to hitch her belly up. It occurred to Ru that maybe Heidi had chosen the chairs on purpose. He had a feeling she was a woman who liked to assert her control in any way she could.

'I presume this is about Cordelia and Maximilian? Oh, that reminds me.' She pressed a button on her phone. 'Pamela, get in here, would you?'

The young assistant who'd guided them in appeared at the door.

'Call Biba Seymour,' Heidi snapped in her no-nonsense voice. 'Maximilian's pilot show will need to be cancelled. See if Serena is available; she might be a good fit for the slot.' Her tone was brisk, all business, not a tremor of emotion. The assistant nodded and walked back out.

'You don't seem too heartbroken by the news,' Ramos remarked.

'That's the family's job,' Heidi replied as her eyes dropped to Ramos's belly. 'My job is business. Trust me, they will be thankful.'

'When was your last conversation with Cordelia?' Ru asked.

'A week ago. Valentine's Day, in fact.'

'Time?' Ramos asked, getting her notepad out.

Heidi shrugged. 'I don't know, early afternoon.' That chimed with Cordelia's call records which suggested they'd talked at 2 p.m.

'How did she seem?' Ru asked.

'Her usual self. Fragile.'

Ru frowned. 'Fragile how?'

Heidi took her glasses off and cleaned them with a tissue. 'As all millennials seem to be. Overthinking. Catastrophising.'

'What was she catastrophising about?' Ramos asked.

'That being on social media was crowding her mind, and she

needed a "digital detox". Heidi rolled her eyes. 'That's why we were on the phone, I was trying to talk her out of it. Her deal with L'Oréal meant she was supposed to be sharing regular content on social media related to them. But she was determined.' She frowned slightly, a brief chink in her dispassionate armour. 'It's been rather . . . shocking, really.'

Ru shifted the topic. 'She was wearing an unusual hair clip made from a *live* beetle when she was found. Do you know anything about it?'

For a fraction of a second, Ru thought he noticed a change in her composure. But then she shrugged dismissively. 'No idea. She gets sent all sorts of things.'

'Are you sure?' Ru asked, showing Heidi the photo of the clip on his phone.

Heidi leaned forward, squinting her blue eyes as she looked at it. 'I'm sure.'

'What about this watch?' Ru asked, flicking to the photo of Maximilian's watch.

'Sorry, no,' Heidi said again, her voice firm. It was intriguing how she didn't even ask what it had to do with their deaths.

'Other than having you as an agent,' Ru said, 'and Cordelia appearing in some of Maximilian's campaigns, do you know of any other connections between the two?'

'Well, they would have been in the same social circles,' she said, 'two successful millennials in the city. But other than that, I know of no other connection.'

'Any enemies?' Ramos said.

'Cordelia had plenty of crazed fans,' Heidi said, 'but what actress doesn't? I looked after her post here; we shredded most of it but I can send over a list of some of the more worrying ones. As for Maximilian.' She paused a moment. 'Not as far as I know.'

'Were you aware if Cordelia was taking any kind of medication?' Ramos asked. Ru could tell she was reluctantly asking this question, prompted by the captain's desire for them to follow the narcotics angle.

'Do you mean drugs?' Heidi asked.

Ramos nodded.

'Not from what we know,' the agent replied. 'But who knows? As for Maximilian, that's a different story. I can confirm he took drugs. *Lots* of them.' She sighed dramatically, leaning back in her chair. 'It'll be ODs, sadly, or a bad batch of drugs, *trust* me. Cordelia might have been clean as far as I know, but everyone starts somewhere. Maybe she was just very, very unlucky.'

'And who supplied Maximilian with his drugs?' Ru pressed.

'How would I know?'

'What about the Thorsens?' Ramos asked. 'Are you familiar with them?'

Heidi hesitated, just a moment too long. 'I know they own the hotel where Maximilian died. Otherwise, no.' Ru wasn't sure he believed her. He examined her face but she held his gaze: strong, emotionless. Then she glanced towards the door where her PA was now standing, pointing at her watch.

'Officers, I hope you can understand,' she said, rising, 'but we are receiving an *overwhelming* number of queries from the press. I really must go, I'm sorry I couldn't help more.'

A few moments later, Ru stood outside the agency's offices with Ramos. The snowfall had calmed down now, but had left a decent layer on the paths. In the distance, the sun began to set over the city, softening the edges of the tall buildings as the snow flurries turned pink under the last rays of daylight.

'Not sure we got much out of that conversation,' Ramos said.

'On the contrary,' Ru replied, 'I think we managed to extract something very useful.'

'What's that?'

'We cannot trust Heidi Stone.'

'Yeah, I hear you,' Ramos said, stamping her feet up and down in the snow. 'She clearly knows the Thorsens more than she's letting on, too. You see the way she paused before answering?'

'I did. Can you do some digging on her?' Ramos nodded, yawning as she did. 'Not now, though. You head home. Your shift ended half an hour ago.'

'Sure. Honestly? I think the Thorsens are behind all this,

specifically Nils. Maybe this is the case that will finally help us nail him.'

Ru suspected she was right. As he thought that, he realised he knew someone who might just be able to shine some light on the younger Thorsens: his old friend, Souta.

Chapter 10

Ru parked his motorcycle at the edge of an unassuming street in Lower Manhattan, and scanned the area. Nothing seemed out of place to an ordinary observer. Just a typical street lined with a mix of old brick buildings and nondescript warehouses. But Ru's keen senses picked up the subtle signs: a watchful gaze from a second-storey window, the too-casual loitering of a man by a shuttered storefront, the faint scent of something chemical carried by the breeze.

He approached a dilapidated building distinguished by the faded manga characters etched above a narrow doorway. Memories of his schooldays flashed in his mind, clashing with the present. He was about to visit an old school friend, once a bright student with a promising future thrown away when he got himself entangled in a web spun by the Yakuza, a known Japanese criminal outfit.

As Ru pushed open the creaky door, the dimly lit hallway greeted him with an air of neglect. He moved silently until he reached a nondescript door with the number nine on it. He didn't need to knock. It swung open abruptly, his former friend, Souta, standing before him with a panicked look on his face. The months since they'd last seen each other had not been kind to him. Souta's once vibrant eyes were now dull, shadowed with the heavy toll of drug use. His sallow skin spoke of a dependence he'd long since stopped fighting. His black hair was unkempt, and his clothes hung loosely on his thin frame, painful for Ru to see, considering Souta had once boasted an athletic build.

'What the fuck, Ru?' Souta quickly glanced over Ru's shoulder then gripped Ru's arm, yanking him inside. The door slammed shut behind them.

The room they were in was a chaotic mix of squalor and opulence. One side was cluttered with remnants of drug use – needles, spoons and small bags littered a low table. The other side displayed incongruous luxury: expensive liquor bottles, a high-end sound system and a plush sofa. Gifts or payments from the Yakuza, no doubt.

Souta released Ru and paced nervously. 'You shouldn't be here.' His gaze flitted to the window, then back to Ru. Ru didn't share his old friend's concerns. The Yakuza wouldn't hurt Souta simply for talking to Ru. Anyway, there were more pressing matters to discuss.

'The Thorsens,' Ru said, getting directly to the point. 'I need to talk to you about them.'

Souta's pacing slowed. 'You know how it ended between Anja and me. I haven't seen her in years.' Souta's history with Nils's twin sister was a tumultuous chapter in his life marked by excess and indulgence, coinciding with Souta's ascent to the peak of his involvement with the Yakuza who shared an uneasy alliance with the Thorsens.

'I heard rumours they were tied to illegal insect trading,' Ru said.

Souta shrugged, lighting a cigarette. 'Probably. Anja and Nils ... they were into some dark stuff back then; still are, probably. When Anja and I were together ... well, let's just say I saw things. They had a knack for the black market, especially on the dark web. Made a killing there.'

'In what kinds of products?' Ru asked.

'The usual. Drugs. Fake designer stuff.'

'What about Cordelia Montgomery? Heard any whispers about Nil Thorsen's involvement with her?'

Souta frowned. 'The dead actress?' He shook his head. 'Never crossed paths with her during my time with Anja. But that would've been before she got all famous and shit. Is this why you're here? The Thorsens are linked to her death?'

'Maybe.'

Souta walked over to Ru, placing his hands on his shoulders, the smoke from his cigarette getting in Ru's eyes. 'Dude, why are you picking at that Thorsen scab again? Didn't you already get yourself in enough trouble after what happened with Ebbe Thorsen? You chop one head off, more grow in its place. Best to just leave them to it.'

'No,' Ru said, gently pushing his old friend away and fanning the air around him to get rid of the lingering smoke. 'I will always keep chopping. Nils, in particular, is getting too powerful, just like his father.'

Souta laughed. 'Nils? His father? You haven't caught up, have you? Ebbe wasn't the power behind that family. His wife Jacqueline was. Or should I say, *is*.'

Jacqueline Thorsen. Ebbe's wife. The twins' mother. As far as Ru knew, she had no real dealings with the 'family business' and was just a photographer. The one time he had met her had been brief: when she'd arrived at the scene of her husband's death. In contrast to the way Cordelia's mother had been at her daughter's crime scene, Jacqueline had been quiet, almost as though she were in shock . . . or quietly calculating what had happened and who was responsible. Judging from the way her eyes had settled on Ru as he'd been treated in the back of an ambulance for a gunshot wound, he had a feeling it was him she blamed.

'Why do you say Jacqueline is in charge?' Ru asked.

'Because it's the truth. Always has been.' He looked at his watch. 'OK, you need to get out of here. I got a visitor coming soon who will *not* like the sight of a cop being here.'

Ru looked his old friend up and down. 'You look thin.'

'And *you* sound like your mother.'

'I'm seeing her on Saturday, at the restaurant. Late, like back in the day. She'd like to see you. Like to feed you up, too,' he added, pinching his old friend's skinny arm as Souta batted him away.

'Maybe,' Souta said with a shrug.

Ru nodded. 'In the meantime, if you hear anything related to the Thorsens, or Cordelia Montgomery, let me know.'

'Maybe,' Souta said again.

'You want me to carry on checking in on your grandma?' Ru asked. 'As I said, you let me know.'

Then he walked back out into the dim hallway, the door closing softly behind him. As he did, his phone signalled a message. It was from Harris.

Cordelia Montgomery's autopsy is happening tomorrow afternoon, 2 p.m. Dr Penn wants you there.

Chapter 11

Vanessa observed the climate-controlled chambers in her lab the next morning. The larvae she'd collected the day before from Cordelia's crime scene were already visibly larger, inching closer to the next phase of their life cycle. There had been several colonisation periods at the scene, with the possibility that different species of fly had slipped through that open window each day to lay their eggs.

She had a sudden flashback to those plants Nils had sent her again. He was like a fly, slipping into her home, feeding on her fears. She'd messaged Bronagh who had done her usual, overreacting and insisting Vanessa stay at hers. Vanessa had managed to talk her down, appeasing her with promises to go for dinner the next day, and convince her it was enough to just let the police know. Vanessa felt silly. It was just a plant delivery . . . right?

She turned her attention back to the larvae, which she'd already examined. She was now waiting for the reared flies to emerge to confirm species identification. They were each at varying sizes, from first instar stage that may have hatched the same day Cordelia's body had been discovered to third instar, which would have been feeding off her for several days until they were ready to pupate and turn into flies. Different factors, like the room temperatures, would have determined the rate at which they would have developed. It had been reasonably mild a week ago before the cold snap that brought the snow. By matching the temperatures in these chambers with what she'd recorded at the crime scene the day before, and weather reports, she could try to recreate that growth. Eventually, when these larvae metamorphosed, she'd know what species they were and get a better understanding of when Cordelia's body may have *first* been colonised. All useful for determining minimum time since death. Since different species matured at varying rates, pinpointing the precise timeline of their development – and thus the time elapsed since the body was colonised – hinged on accurate species identification. However, based on the distinctive morphology of the mouth parts, she hypothesised that these specimens likely belonged to the *Sarcophagidae* family, colloquially referred to as flesh flies, which lay hatched larvae on bodies, rather than eggs. And that meant it was possible Cordelia's body was colonised on the same day she last had contact with the world: Valentine's Day. But she'd need to check temperature data logs from the scene to confirm this.

As Vanessa examined each chamber, she jotted down notes on growth, movement, coloration and feeding. Larvae were simple creatures, with a simple aim: to eat and store energy for their upcoming pupation. Vanessa had seen it as a child when she'd observed the maggots that had spilled out from the rubbish bin in their kitchen. She'd been fascinated as she'd watched the creatures wriggle towards the only food source left behind, a few grains of soggy porridge oats. It wasn't bad, really, as far as ambitions went: to sustain one's genealogy, to continue the chain.

She thought of her own ambitions. She'd be lying if she said she didn't want to be the world's foremost forensic entomologist. She'd already been labelled the best in the UK by *New Scientist*. If she could conquer America, then she'd be getting close to that 'best in the world' goal. Did that seem arrogant? Shallow? She'd learned at a young age how ambition and motivation helped distract from the pain. First, simple ambitions. Good school reports. Win the heart of the richest, cutest boy in her village. Then more complex: leave that boy. Leave that village. Studying hard was less about impressing her dad, or her teachers, and more about being able to get into a university that would take her away from Greensands and the memories of her mother leaving; her brother going missing. By the time she achieved that, she'd learned the distracting nature of having ambitions. It just became a natural part of her world.

What about now? Was she like a maggot, squirming towards those porridge oats with no real thought about the whys and the hows? She certainly wasn't squirming towards continuing the chain. No children. No plans to have any. What about if she gained that 'Best Forensic Entomologist in the World' title?

What then?

'Wow, Vanessa,' she whispered to herself, 'deep thoughts for first thing in the morning.'

She walked over to another chamber, this one containing the beetle rescued from the hair clip. Vanessa watched the beetle as it sat hunched among some debris in the chamber's corner. The jewels remained. Removing them would cause more harm than good.

'You're a survivor,' Vanessa whispered to it.

'Why, thank you,' a voice said from behind her. It was Bronagh, her unruly red hair pulled back into a messy bun, her lab coat looking even more stained than usual. She leaned down and looked at the beetle with Vanessa. 'Poor thing.'

'It'll be fine. Ironclad beetles are tanks. So strong, they can survive being run over.'

'Must make it difficult for entomologists to pin them down?'

'Very. But then they're not meant to be displayed.'

'Or decorated and embellished.'

'Exactly.'

Bronagh paused. 'Have you caught up on any news from home yet?'

'Home? As in the UK?' Bronagh nodded. 'No. Why?'

Bronagh handed her phone to Vanessa. 'I thought you'd want to see this. Joe sent it to me just now,' she said, referring to her husband.

It was a headline from a UK tabloid that read: COBWEB KILLER CAUGHT IN TRAP: PRISON BEATING FOR VINCENT MARWOOD.

Vanessa felt a sudden tightening of her heart as she clicked on it. It was a breaking news item about her brother. 'Shit,' she whispered as she looked at the arrest photo of her brother they often reran.

'Have you heard anything from your brother's prison?' Bronagh asked.

'No, nothing.' Vanessa could hardly hear her own voice as the buzzing in her head grew louder.

'That's good news, I suppose,' Bronagh said. 'If he was *seriously* hurt, the prison would need to inform you.'

Vanessa nodded, massaging her temple as though to massage that buzzing away. 'Yes, you're right. They have my number.'

But the rest of the morning, she couldn't stop picturing her brother, injured. It was ridiculous. He'd done far worse to others. Left *their* relatives with far more horrendous images to contend with.

And yet . . . he was her brother.

At lunch, she decided to call someone who might be able to help her wrap her head around it all: Detective Paul Truss.

'Bugs!' Paul's voice crackled with the same robust cheer she remembered, instantly bridging the miles between New York and the UK.

'All right. How's life treating you on the other side of the pond?' Vanessa asked, a smile in her voice despite the gnawing concern for her brother.

'Oh, you know, the usual. Chasing down garden gnome thieves in the village. The adrenaline is just non-stop over here.'

'I can only imagine.'

They both paused and Vanessa knew what was in that pause. The unspoken memories of the adrenaline and horror-fuelled case they'd worked on together before she left for New York. A case that had ended in her brother being exposed as a serial murderer.

'I bet you miss old Blighty?' Paul asked.

'Oh yes, how I miss the great British . . . rain. Every. Single. Day.'

Paul laughed. 'Isn't some snowpocalypse about to land in the Big Apple?'

Vanessa peered out of the window at the snow, which was back to being in full flow. 'The view from my window suggests that might be true,' she said.

'Working on any cases?'

Vanessa smoothed her palm over the brand-new wood of her desk. 'I'm actually working the Cordelia Montgomery case, the actress?'

'Shit, really? It's all over the news.'

'Ah-huh. But I'm not calling about that.' Her eyes drifted towards her toddler brother in the photo on her desk. 'I'm calling about Vincent.'

'Yeah. I heard what happened.' His voice was strained, no surprise considering Vincent had nearly killed Paul.

'I'll be honest,' she admitted, 'I have this irrational need to check in on him. Is that crazy?' She realised the reason for her call when she asked that: she needed Paul to talk her out of getting in touch with her brother.

She heard Paul sigh. 'He's still your brother,' he said. 'I mean, it's hard for me to understand but family is family. Look, I'm not even sure what's possessing me to say this. But maybe you *should* speak to him, get it out of the way? *Remind* yourself what he is. You haven't talked to him since he was arrested, right?'

'Right.'

'Then maybe this is an itch you need to scratch to be able to get on with things. It's less about him and more about yourself, you know? You might not have been as physically hurt as others, but the mental scars . . .' His voice trailed off.

'Don't start insisting I see a therapist like everyone does over here.'

Paul laughed. 'Not a chance.'

'So you won't hate me if I call him?'

'I could never hate you, you idiot!'

'He did try to kill you.'

'He didn't, though, did he? Someone happened to save me . . . and that someone is more important to me than some petty sense of vengeance. You do what feels right, Vanessa. Right for *you*.'

Vanessa nodded. 'Thanks, Paul. And . . . thank you for being there.'

'Always, Bugs. Always.'

As she hung up, Vanessa let out a slow breath.

It was time to speak to her brother.

After most people had left the NovaScope offices later for lunch, Vanessa sat alone in her office, staring at the waiting room screen on her laptop. In two minutes, Vincent would appear on that screen.

She looked at the countdown. *One minute to go.*

She took in a deep breath, telling herself all it took was one click of her mouse to remove herself from the conversation.

Thirty seconds.

She took a quick sip of her water, smoothing her hair back.

Twenty seconds. Ten seconds.

'Oh God,' she whispered to herself.

Nine . . . eight . . . seven . . . six . . . five . . . four . . . three . . . two . . . one.

The screen wobbled. Vanessa held her breath.

Then suddenly, there he was. Vincent Marwood. Her brother. The Cobweb Killer.

His dark hair had been shaved. Circles the colour of violets shaded his eyes. He was pale, skinny. And yes, there, a gauze across his neck.

He leaned forward, blinking. 'Nessy, is it really you?'

Christ. That voice. It made Vanessa's heart contract.

'Yes,' she said, trying to keep her voice professional. 'I heard you might have been hurt.'

His brown eyes softened. 'You're calling because of that? Nessy, you don't know how much that means. It was just some doofus thought he could rough me up with a knife to the throat. How he got the knife, who knows? You'd be surprised at what people can get their hands on in here.'

Doofus. It used to be their favourite insult to each other.

On the screen, Vincent smiled. 'He really looks like a doofus, too. Just how you'd imagine, with a bowl haircut and everything.'

Her heart ached. If she just closed her eyes, she could be talking to the old Vincent. Her kid brother.

'I'm fine, though, just a scratch,' he said. Then his eyes travelled to her cheeks. 'How's your . . . scratch?'

Vanessa didn't answer.

'I didn't mean it,' he said. 'I wasn't thinking properly. My therapist says I have these psychotic breaks and—'

'There's no excuse for what you did. You know that, right?'

Vincent hung his head, rubbing at his neck. 'I know. All I'm saying is, abandonment does things to a child.' He peered up at Vanessa. 'I've been doing this Open University course, you know, on psychology and neuroscience.' Vanessa raised an eyebrow. He'd always been a clever kid. It was probably good he was distracting himself. 'It's fascinating, really. They explore how early experiences, especially abandonment, affect the neural pathways in our brains. There's this concept of—'

'Brain plasticity,' Vanessa finished for him. He looked slightly disappointed she knew.

'That's right,' Vincent said. 'It's all about how experiences can physically shape the brain. For children, especially, who experience neglect or abandonment like I did . . . Like you did, too,' he added. 'Those experiences can alter the development of certain areas of the brain, like the prefrontal cortex, which is responsible for decision-making and emotional regulation. Oh, and the amygdala, too. That deals with fear and stress responses. It can also lead to difficulties in forming attachments,' he added meaningfully.

Vanessa frowned.

'Basically, Mum walking out on us rewired our brains,' Vincent stated.

'We weren't neglected, Vincent. Dad was there,' Vanessa quickly said. 'He provided us with everything we needed. Love. Care. We're not like the kids that feature in those studies.'

'Oh, come on, Nessy, he wasn't *that* great. Let me guess, I bet he blamed you when I ran off.'

He was right. He had. When he was twelve and Vanessa was fifteen, Vincent ran away, not to be seen again until over twenty-five years later: the year before. As he was so young, the assumption was he'd been abducted, was maybe dead. Instead, he'd been living on the streets of Brighton. As Vanessa was supposed to have been looking after him at the time, her dad always blamed her. It was one of the reasons she'd been so keen to leave her childhood village and go to university in London: to escape the guilt.

'I think you're in denial that Mum did this to us,' Vincent said now, teeth clenching as he tapped the side of his head. His eyes began to water. 'She's not even attempted to contact me, you know. I presume she hasn't contacted you, either.' He paused. 'Maybe she's dead.'

'Don't be silly.'

'I'm serious!' He scratched at his face. 'I think I see her sometimes, just wandering by my cell, like a ghost.'

Vanessa thought of that fleeting glimpse of a woman she'd seen at the nightclub.

'We'd know,' she said. 'Plus, she had a new art piece up on the gallery earlier this month.'

'So you check?'

'Yes. She's not dead, Vincent,' Vanessa repeated.

'She'll die one day, though, won't she? Do you think we'll see her before she does?'

Vanessa couldn't deny it, she'd thought the same.

That bee in her head had started buzzing, her temples throbbing painfully. 'I have to go,' she said.

'But Nessy! We haven't talked about the dead actress.'

Vanessa went very still.

Vincent leaned forward, brown eyes ablaze. 'My God, you really *are* working on it, aren't you? It was on the lunchtime news just now. They said she'd been lying in her room for *days*. The insect evidence must have been a real bonanza for you. I bet you're loving it.'

'No, Vincent,' Vanessa snapped back. 'I am not *loving* it. A woman died.' *Was killed*, she wanted to add, *like all those people you killed.*

He put his hands up in a conciliatory gesture. She noticed his right hand was wrapped in a gauze. 'I purely mean from a forensic entomological standpoint. Reading between the lines they're suggesting an overdose, but something doesn't seem right to me. And one of the other prisoners is a big fan and said she was teetotal. Is it murder? And what about that fashion designer? This is giving off serial killer vibes, Nessy.'

A cold whisper trailed down Vanessa's spine.

'I have to go,' she said again. 'Take care of yourself, Vincent.'

'But Nessy, you—'

She slammed her laptop shut, cutting him off mid-sentence. The conversation had served as a chilling reminder that her brother was a predator fascinated by the macabre. Even worse was the cold insight in his words. The absence of their mother, the abandonment, probably *had* fractured something within him. Maybe her, too.

But what chilled her to the core was his dissection of the case, and her growing fear that he could be right.

Chapter 12

Ru stood behind the glass pane of the morgue's viewing area in the New York City Office of the Chief Medical Examiner, his eyes fixed on Cordelia Montgomery. Her dignity was shrouded, for now, by a white sheet that lay over her decayed body.

'Cordelia Montgomery,' Dr Penn said, drawing Ru away from his thoughts. 'Age twenty-five. Female. Preliminary indications suggest poisoning. We'll proceed with the Y-incision now.'

The scalpel descended, making the first cut. Ru watched with a detached curiosity. To him, corpses were a biological conundrum that could help solve crimes. He tried not to assign any emotion in instances such as this.

'This level of decomposition will obscure some details,' Dr Penn continued, peeling back the layers of skin and tissue with practised ease as his assistant shadowed him. 'However, certain signs are obvious.'

'Obvious how?' Ru's voice crackled through the speaker.

With his gloved hand, Dr Penn drew attention to certain discoloured patches of skin and signs of internal haemorrhaging visible through tiny incisions. 'See these areas of discoloration? They're often associated with neurotoxins, although we can't confirm until toxicology comes back.' Dr Penn continued examining the body, his assistants handing him instruments as if they were part of an orchestrated dance. When he looked inside the chest cavity, he nodded.

'Excessive fluid surrounding the lungs,' he muttered, almost to himself but loud enough for his assistant to hear and make a note. 'My guess is Cordelia Montgomery died of a pulmonary oedema.'

Ru frowned. 'Could poisoning cause this?'

The doctor nodded. 'Acute poisoning could theoretically lead to heart failure, which could subsequently result in pulmonary oedema as a secondary complication. But toxicology results will confirm.'

So poisoning, via a tiny injector in that hair clip, was now the most likely cause.

An hour later, the autopsy was over. As Ru stepped out of the autopsy room and into the reception area, he was taken aback to see Cordelia's mother waiting. She wasn't alone, either, but was with her son and two women. Ru suspected one of the women was the family's rabbi, judging from the small black kippot on her short dark hair. The other woman was younger, steely-eyed, with immaculate make-up. Levi's wife? He had read Cordelia's father had passed away two years before from a heart attack.

'Mrs Montgomery,' Ru began awkwardly. 'I wasn't aware you would be here.'

'It's custom,' Cordelia's mother said. 'And please, call me Felicity.' She peered towards the door Ru had just emerged from. 'Is she . . . does she seem at peace?'

For a split second, Ru's mind flashed back to Cordelia's body laid bare on the stainless-steel table, cut open in a way that clashed violently with the notion of 'peace'. He quickly pushed the thought aside.

'She looks like she is sleeping,' he lied.

Felicity took in a sigh of relief. 'Good.'

'Any indication on cause of death?' Levi asked.

Ru paused. There were so many factors involved in Cordelia's death, with some still pending, such as toxicology. He wanted to be able to present the family with a clear picture and he certainly didn't want to tell them in a mortuary.

'We're still awaiting results from toxicology tests,' he said. 'Once we have a fuller picture, I will share it with you.'

'Of course, we understand,' Felicity said. 'I'm pleased you're running the case, Detective Hoshino. I've done some research on you, and Cordelia couldn't ask for a better investigator.'

Levi frowned. 'But I read you were kicked off the force a year ago, Detective. That doesn't fill me with confidence.'

'Levi,' Felicity said in a low, warning voice, putting her hand on her son's arm.

'That is not what happened,' Ru said. 'I took a sabbatical. But I am back now and can assure you I will work day and night until we know what caused Cordelia's death.'

Levi went to speak again but Felicity squeezed his arm, stopping her son. Then she looked back towards the mortuary doors. 'I just wish *I* could be in there, with her. I don't want her to be alone. I even sat outside this place in my car last night and slept. Seems silly but . . .'

'Not silly at all,' Ru said. 'She is your daughter.'

She nodded. 'Yes, thank you. And with that fashion designer dead, too.' She shook her head, putting a trembling hand to her mouth. 'Cordelia was in one of his campaigns, you know.'

Ru nodded. 'I'm aware.'

'It can't be related, surely?' Felicity asked.

'Mother,' Levi said in a low voice, 'you know the detective won't be able to answer questions like that.'

'Your son is right, I'm afraid,' Ru said. 'But we will update you if any concrete information comes in. I believe the funeral is tomorrow?'

Felicity nodded.

'In Judaism,' the rabbi explained in a deep voice, 'the ceremony must be held as soon as the body is released.'

'Yes,' Felicity added. 'Dr Penn was kind enough to expedite the autops—' She shuddered, unable to finish her sentence. 'Anyway, yes, it's tomorrow.'

'I will be in attendance,' Ru said.

Levi frowned. 'I'm afraid it's invite only, Detective. As I'm sure you can understand, with Cordelia's popularity, we can't risk a stampede.'

'Would it be that appropriate for a detective to attend, anyway?' Levi's wife asked in a clipped tone.

'Very,' Ru replied. 'It can be useful to observe potential suspects in an emotionally charged environment.'

'Suspects,' Levi said tightly. 'So this *is* being regarded as a homicide?'

'I used the word "potential",' Ru replied, observing Cordelia's brother with interest. He couldn't decide if the anger he saw in the man's eyes was only a natural response to the idea of his little sister having been harmed . . . or something more than that.

'Of course, it's fine,' Felicity said. 'We will make sure your name is on the list. You will need to bring identification.'

Ru felt a surge of respect for the woman. She reminded him of his own mother with that comforting blend of compassion and steeliness. It made him even more determined to solve this case. Just then, Ru's phone buzzed.

'Please,' Felicity said, 'don't let us keep you from your investigations.'

He nodded and walked off, quickly composing a message to Bronagh from his phone.

I would like Dr Marwood to attend Cordelia Montgomery's funeral tomorrow. I need someone with insect expertise to keep an eye out for guests wearing any insect-related items. I will forward on the details.

He then slipped his phone into the dark recesses of his pocket and walked outside, the thought of attending tomorrow's funeral hanging over him like an unwelcome spectre.

Chapter 13

Vanessa adjusted the hem of her black lace dress as she exited the taxi into the freezing cold air, wrapping her long black military coat around her frame. She paused a moment, taking in the expansive cemetery before her which was offset by a New York skyline clogged with snow-heavy clouds. She was used to the more intimate burial grounds she'd frequented in the UK. This city cemetery's magnitude was obvious, even in the solemnity of death.

Outside the cemetery gates, a barricade of stern-faced security guards held back a restless crowd. Fans and journalists had gathered since dawn, equipped with lenses and smartphones, their breath forming plumes of mist in the cold air. Muted chatter mingled with the low hum of news vans parked on the street. It all seemed so . . . wrong.

Vanessa approached a security guard who was checking people's names and IDs. As she drew close, a man in a T-shirt adorned with imagery from one of Cordelia's films tried to breach the barrier with a bouquet of roses in hand. Security promptly escorted him away. Even in death, Cordelia drew a crowd – her last appearance as carefully staged as any film premiere. Vanessa felt like an outsider in this well-curated theatre of grief. When Bronagh had told her the day before that Ru wanted her to attend, Vanessa didn't feel it was appropriate. But Ru had been adamant. He needed her observational skills – there was every chance the killer could be at the funeral, and only she would notice illegal insect-themed attire or accessories.

Now, as she watched the mourners, she wondered what she would say if anyone asked how she knew Cordelia. It filled her with unease. It was one thing to comprehend the scientific necessity of her work, but another to convey that understanding in a setting saturated with grief and loss.

She approached the security guard standing in front of the iron gates. 'Dr Vanessa Marwood,' she said in a low voice. He checked his list and nodded, opening the iron gates for her to pass through. As she walked into the cemetery, she took a few moments to observe the mourners in their winter coats, a curious blend of the glamorous and the ordinary that painted the two sides of Cordelia's life. Pre-fame. Post-fame.

On the post-fame side were familiar faces from the entertainment industry – award-winning directors and critically acclaimed actors. It felt strange for Vanessa to see people who graced the covers of magazines or flashed across screens right there before her, in the flesh. Most were low-key, quiet. But there was a certain group that seemed to revel in the dissonance. They were the gaudier, more ostentatious attendees, clearly desperate to stand out in garish patterns and overly dramatic hats. Vanessa noticed their voices were a notch louder than others', their gestures a bit more exaggerated, as if they were performing rather than participating in the collective farewell. Among them was Laife, the hairstylist who had been with Maximilian when he died and had been interviewed on TV the night before last: Tuesday evening. He was wearing an outfit that was *screaming* for attention – a glittering black suit beneath a shimmery multicoloured faux fur coat that seemed more appropriate for a club than a solemn event. It was as if he saw the gathering not as a space for mourning but as a runway for self-expression . . . or perhaps self-promotion. Vanessa tried to find any hint of insect symbolism in his attire, but from a distance noticed nothing.

She then turned her attention to Cordelia's family, whose well-tailored coats and understated jewellery spoke of a comfortable life. But it was the stoic expressions that caught her interest. Particularly striking was Cordelia's mother, her face a canvas of deep sorrow meticulously managed, even as she nervously rubbed at her arm and bit her lip. Levi stood beside her, tall and attentive.

Vanessa noticed Ru, then, a casual black blazer beneath his loose, black wool coat – the only concession to the solemnity of the occasion. When his eyes met Vanessa's, he offered a nod and walked towards her.

'Your fascination with insects extends to your fashion choices, I see,' he commented, gesturing to the moth motif in the lace of her dress.

'Always,' she responded.

They made their way to a simple canopy erected for the ceremony. Beneath it rested a plain wooden casket, which seemed at odds with the glamour of those assembled. But Vanessa was aware this was in keeping with Jewish tradition, highlighting humility even in death. It was unusual to hold a Jewish funeral outdoors, though. Absolutely freezing, too, with many gathered around her trembling in the cold, drawing thick coats around them.

The crowd grew quiet as a rabbi stepped forward – a woman in her forties in a tailored black trouser suit. When she began speaking, her voice was almost musical, her articulation precise. As Vanessa's gaze drifted across the mourners, she noticed another observer in the distance, leaning against an ancient oak.

Nils Thorsen.

Vanessa jogged her elbow into Ru's arm. Ru followed her gaze, his jaw tightening as he took in the tall Scandinavian. Nils was dressed impeccably in a black suit, exuding a magnetic, almost predatory, intensity as he observed the proceedings. As he scanned the crowd, he caught Vanessa's eye. She thought of the plant delivery and hardened her gaze towards him. He frowned and moved his attention to Ru. A frosty exchange of glances ensued before Nils turned and walked away.

The ceremony culminated with the mourners reciting the Kaddish. The ancient Aramaic hymn filled the air and Vanessa was reminded of her own father's muted funeral. It had been held in a small, weathered chapel in Greensands, her home town. No media had gathered; no security guards holding back eager crowds. The attendees had been few but earnest, comprising close family and long-time friends. The vicar had been a soft-spoken man who'd delivered a simple yet heartfelt eulogy, as the rain tapped gently against the chapel's stained-glass windows.

As the congregation dispersed, Vanessa watched them all closely.

'Anything of interest?' Ru asked.

'I'm afraid not.'

'Thank you for coming,' a voice said from behind them. They

turned to see Cordelia's mother. She was wearing a modest black dress, the fabric draped elegantly around her petite form. Her silver hair was pinned up. From afar, she had looked composed, but up close, Vanessa could see the tremor of her hands. She recalled her heart-wrenching grief at the crime scene, and was amazed by how she was holding herself together. Again, she was flanked by her son. 'You must be Dr Marwood. Detective Hoshino asked me to add you to the list.'

'Please, call me Vanessa,' she said. 'Yes, I'm part of the forensics team working on your daughter's case. I'm so sorry for your loss, Mrs Montgomery.'

'Felicity,' she said, taking Vanessa's hand for a moment and squeezing it. 'I'm pleased you're here,' she said, nodding as though to convince herself. 'Forensics plays such a crucial role in—' she paused, taking in a shaky breath, 'in cases like this, if indeed Cordelia's death was no accident. Every tiny detail matters.'

'It certainly does,' Vanessa agreed.

'I'm sorry you've had to endure the cold,' Felicity continued. 'Cordelia had always said she wanted an outdoor burial.' She smiled. 'A final little stamp of her personality. I'm pleased to say Jewish traditions resume *indoors*. In fact, why don't you attend the meal of consolation? I can make space for you both? You must be hungry.'

Levi gave his mother a disapproving look.

Vanessa opened her mouth to protest but Ru nodded. 'That would be useful,' he said.

'Good,' Felicity replied. 'Please, make your way inside, I'll ensure you have space on table ten.'

As she disappeared, Vanessa took in a breath. 'Well, this has turned into a more intimate affair than I imagined.'

Ru observed her with interest. 'Does grief make you uncomfortable, Dr Marwood?'

'No. But being part of a congregation for the funeral of someone I don't know does.'

'And you think all these people really knew Cordelia Montgomery?' Ru asked as some of the most ostentatious mourners walked by. 'You are more useful to Cordelia's family right now than most of these people.'

'I suppose you're right.'

They followed the mourners towards the synagogue down a path shielded by erected sheets. The synagogue was beautiful, its exterior made of intricately carved stone and stained-glass windows that glinted in hues of blue and gold. Inside, mirrors were draped in black cloth, and rows of wooden benches had been pushed up against the walls to make space for several circular tables adorned with white cloths. Mourners congregated in small groups, speaking in hushed tones. In one corner, a few mourners washed their hands in a basin of water: a symbolic gesture, Vanessa presumed, of cleansing after being near the deceased.

They both headed towards the table with a 'No. 10' sign. It was laden with plates of hard-boiled eggs, bowls of lentils, freshly baked bagels, as well as pots of chickpeas, and freshly brewed tea and coffee. A few bottles of wine had been placed discreetly among the other beverages. Vanessa sat with Ru, the only people at their table so far. Levi passed by, pausing as he noticed them. He seemed to struggle with something then set his lips in a grim line and walked over.

'Thank you for attending,' he said through gritted teeth. Clearly, he wasn't overjoyed at their presence. 'My mother has spent many hours planning this. I'm not sure if you're familiar with our traditions, but these food choices aren't random.' He gestured towards the plates of eggs, lentils and bagels. 'The round items represent the cyclical nature of life. The egg, especially, has profound meaning. It hardens the longer it's cooked, a reminder that we must find strength in adversity. And just as the lentils have no eyes or mouth, we are reminded of—' he swallowed, pursing his lips, tears flooding his brown eyes, 'we're reminded of Cordelia's absence.' He shook his head. 'Sorry, I sound like a theology professor. My wife says I go into rabbi mode when I'm in company.'

'You're a professor?' Vanessa asked.

'Oh no,' he said. 'I'm a dentist. I *did* train to be a rabbi, though.' He looked over at his mother. 'I must go,' he said, before he strode off.

'The pretence of formality,' Ru observed as they watched him. 'Grief is a complex beast, and societal expectations only add more layers to it.'

People started filling the tables then. One of them was Madeline, the influencer with the swollen lips who'd also appeared in the TV interview. Another older woman took the seat beside her, her head adorned with an extravagant feather-laden mourning hat. The woman reminded Vanessa of a flamboyant peacock spider, flaunting colours and complicated dances to attract attention. Madeline, on the other hand, sat more quietly, silently wiping her eyes with a cocktail napkin. Her grief seemed more genuine.

As more people took their seats at the table, the woman caught Vanessa's eye. 'Ottilli Holmes,' she said, introducing himself. 'I *love* your hair. Very Dita Von Teese. Isn't it awful about dear Maximilian, too? I simply can't bear this amount of tragedy.'

'Did you know Cordelia and Maximilian well?' Ru asked.

Ottilli turned her attention to Ru. 'Of course. I work at *Vogue*. I'm actually wearing one of Maximilian's designs now,' she said, gesturing to her hat. She leaned forward, lowering her voice. 'They're saying it was a bad batch of drugs. Maybe Maximilian, but Cordelia? No. That girl didn't touch the stuff. Am I right, Madeline?'

Madeline nodded, eyes down.

The conversation shifted as they began to eat, Vanessa noticing how Madeline remained mostly silent. Every so often, she'd take a deep breath, her shoulders shaking as she tried to compose herself. Vanessa couldn't help but feel a pang of sympathy for the young influencer. At a table of theatrics, Madeline's emotions seemed raw and genuine.

Halfway through the meal, Madeline reached into her bag for a compact mirror. To Vanessa's surprise, it featured a Bhutan glory butterfly set in resin on its back, just like the coaster from Nils's nightclub. She was about to ask Madeline where she'd got it when the young influencer excused herself. Vanessa did, too, following her into the bathroom. But by the time she got in, Madeline had already disappeared into one of the cubicles. So Vanessa waited outside, reapplying her lipstick.

A woman in her early fifties walked in, joining her at the mirror as she powdered her nose. She was dressed in a green velvet coat, her glossy blonde hair pulled up into a bun. She regarded Vanessa with sharp, calculating eyes in the reflection.

'How did you know Cordelia?' she asked.

Vanessa took in a breath through her nose. 'We had a shared interest in insects. I'm an entomologist.' She really couldn't bring herself to tell the truth. Though was it a lie, really? Vanessa *was* an entomologist.

The woman's eyes lit up and she turned to face Vanessa properly, looking her up and down. Then she thrust her hand forward, golden bracelets clicking together. 'I'm Heidi Stone, Cordelia's agent.'

Vanessa took Heidi's cool hand. 'Hello, Heidi.'

'*And* you're British.'

'I am indeed.'

'How delightful! Do you have an agent?'

Vanessa tucked her lipstick back into her bag. 'I don't need one in my line of work.'

'So you haven't published a book?'

'I've published papers.'

'Ever been on TV?'

Memories from news items she'd appeared in the year before rushed through her mind. 'Not in an official capacity.'

Vanessa was relieved to see Madeline emerge from her cubicle then – eyes red-rimmed, face ashen. She gave the two women a shaky smile then quickly washed her hands before walking out. Vanessa went to follow her but Heidi stood in her way.

'I think you have *such* untapped potential,' Heidi said.

'Potential that's best kept tapped up tight in the lab,' Vanessa quipped.

Heidi laughed. 'And funny, too! With your looks and expertise, you could bring a lot to even a prime-time television series. People *love* creepy-crawlies, don't they? I mean, we pretend we don't, but we really do. Yes,' she said, her eyes travelling over Vanessa again. 'You'd be a producer's dream.'

The thought alone made Vanessa shudder. 'TV presenting is *definitely* not my thing, and I honestly don't think it will be the viewers' thing either.'

'Oh, you Brits. Always so self-effacing!' Heidi dug around in her bag, handing Vanessa a business card. 'Please, do get in touch. You'll be missing a trick if you don't.' Then she walked out as Vanessa watched, shaking her head in disbelief before quickly leaving the bathroom herself. Madeline was now nowhere to be seen. She sighed and was on her way back to the table when she noticed Ottilli, the feather-hatted woman, talking in a low voice to a man with a hipster beard.

Vanessa ducked into the shadows, pretending to check her phone. 'This is what I was telling you about,' she heard the man say as he pulled a business card from his pocket. 'If you loved Maximilian's designs, then you will *love* these items.'

The man handed the card over. Ottilli held it up, squinting as she examined it. Vanessa used the chance to take a discreet photo with her phone.

'A poem?' she heard Ottilli ask.

'No, an address,' the man said. 'If you're clever or connected enough to figure it out, then you're worthy of entry.'

'Well, now I really *am* intrigued,' Ottilli said, pocketing the card.

Vanessa hurried back to the table. Madeline was no longer there, her bag gone. The people who remained were all talking in low whispers while Ru sat awkwardly staring into the distance.

'Three things,' she whispered to Ru. 'One, Madeline, the girl sitting across from you, has a compact mirror like the coaster from Nils's nightclub, but now she's disappeared. Two, I got this business card from an agent – might be useful.' She handed over Heidi's business card.

Ru looked at it and nodded. 'I've already spoken to her.'

'Ah. Interesting character. And three, I just saw someone handing *this* to the woman in the feather hat. They said it features an address, but it just looks like a poem?'

She showed Ru the photo she'd taken. It was a black business card with a green and gold beetle symbol on it. There were a few lines of poetry in minute text. Vanessa zoomed in even more:

Web of the spider, where secrets ensnare,
Oft in the moonlight, fireflies declare.
Nestled in amber, history's door,

Insects of old, tales of yore.
On gossamer wings, truths do sweep,
Navigating darkness, where cicadas weep.

'Intriguing,' Ru murmured. 'A cipher of some kind. Nils Thorsen is a fan of both poems and puzzles, from what I've heard. Maybe he had a hand in this.' He went quiet, eyes running down the poem. 'Already the word "onion" leaps out to me.'

'You mean "wonion",' Vanessa said, tracing the tip of her fingernail down the first letter of each line in the poem.

'No, whoever did this will mean "onion". Websites on the dark web have dot onion domain extensions, preceded by a random assortment of characters.'

Vanessa quirked an eyebrow. 'Interesting. So it's not a physical address but a web address?'

'Yes.' Ru looked up, dark eyes scouring the room. 'Who handed this over?'

Vanessa looked around the room. 'I can't see him now. I should have got a photo of him. Feather hat lady will be back soon, I'm sure.'

'While we wait, let's decipher this,' Ru said in a quiet voice, leaning closer to Vanessa and bringing with him the scent of vanilla and soap. 'Web of the spider . . . interconnected nature, a reference to the web itself?'

Vanessa pointed at the line about fireflies. 'Fireflies use light patterns to communicate. Each species has a distinct frequency, a unique pattern.'

Ru's eyes darted to the word *oft*. 'A frequency . . . Could this be a numerical hint?'

Vanessa thought for a moment. 'There are over two thousand species of fireflies. But in North America, there are primarily six common species. Six . . . the number of legs on an insect.'

Ru nodded, 'And "Nestled in amber". . . ancient insects maybe? Could this hint at a particular period or era?'

Vanessa's eyes lit up with recognition. 'The most famous amber-entombed insects come from the Cretaceous period, which ended sixty-six million years ago.'

Ru's fingers tapped rapidly on his thigh. 'Six species . . . sixty-six million years . . . Are these our numbers?'

The two exchanged a glance, a shared thrill of being on the cusp of a breakthrough. Of course, some of the detectives she'd worked with in the past approached the crimes she'd worked like they were puzzles, in a way. But with Ru, it felt more academic, almost. More like she was working through a scientific conundrum than a crime. In fact, he felt more like a professor to her than a detective.

'Maybe. There's something else, too. The word "gossamer". It's delicate, almost invisible. But in the insect world, it's essential for movement – for life.'

Ru contemplated this. 'Life . . ." Insects of old, tales of yore". . . It's a play on the dot onion domain. Our numbers might represent layers, like the layers of an onion, or the layers of the web.' Ru pulled his notepad from his pocket and started writing his thoughts down. 'Six layers . . .' he said, hunched over the page. 'Sixty-six . . . It's a pattern. It's not just wonion; it's more intricate. Something like this.'

Beneath the table, he revealed what he'd written to Vanessa

w6x66onionxxxxxx.onion.

'A dark web address?' she whispered.

Ru nodded. He tucked his notepad away and looked around the table. 'The woman with the feather hat,' he said, interrupting the animated conversation. 'Where is she?'

'Oh, she had to go,' one of the people said.

'I want to check this web address out,' Ru said quietly. 'Let's do this at my place. It's a twenty-minute walk away. You can come with me.'

'You're going to use a *personal* computer to do police business?' Vanessa whispered.

'The precinct computers are useless.'

'But still, surely it goes against the rules.'

He tilted his head as he looked at her. 'You don't strike me as the type to follow all the rules, Dr Marwood.'

'Actually, I do when it comes to my work. And so should you.'

'I will repeat the search at the precinct and pretend that was the first time I did it. Does that satisfy you enough to join me?'

'I don't know, I—'

'Fine,' Ru said, standing, 'if you do not wish to help me uncover a dark website selling illegal insects, that is your decision.'

Vanessa sighed. 'Okay, I'll come with you.'

Chapter 14

Ru led Vanessa down the snow-dusted streets of the East Village, noticing the way her dark kohled eyes took in the colourful shopfronts and traditional ramen stores. Ru nodded a greeting to passing neighbours. One, an old friend of his mother's, stopped him. 'Your mother didn't tell me you have a woman,' she said, her eyes twinkling.

'Dr Marwood is my colleague, Chiyo,' Ru explained.

'Doctor, huh?' Chiyo said. 'Your mother will be very pleased you have settled down with a *doctor*.'

Vanessa smiled and Ru didn't bother to correct Chiyo. As they passed a small park, a group of kids just back from school were attempting to build a snowman.

'Hey, Ru!' one of them shouted out. 'Can you help?'

'Not now,' he called back. 'Later.'

'You're a popular guy, Detective Hoshino,' Vanessa observed.

'I've lived in this area for forty years,' Ru replied. 'Less about being popular, more about being part of the furniture.'

They arrived at his apartment block with its facade of muted brick. A small, neatly handwritten sign in both English and Japanese welcomed them. Ru's apartment was on the ground floor and when he let Vanessa in, he tried to see the place through her eyes. The clean lines and a notable lack of clutter. The white walls devoid of any artwork or posters. Then there was the minimalistic furniture: a low wooden table, a few floor cushions and a single couch.

'When did you move in?' Vanessa asked, peering over at the moving boxes still neatly stacked in the hallway's corner.

'Two years ago. I was living in a much smaller flat before.'

Vanessa laughed. 'I've been in my apartment six months and every box has been unpacked. I even painted the walls! I feel a bit OCD now.'

Ru shrugged. 'Not at all. We all have our own individual ways. I have what I need. The rest is just . . . stuff.'

He led Vanessa into the living area, passing a framed black-and-white photo of his mother standing proudly outside her restaurant, and a meticulously arranged shelf holding a series of intricate puzzles alongside several manga books.

'Who's this?' Vanessa asked, gesturing to the photo.

'My mother. Drink?' he asked.

'I fancy tea, if you have any?'

'I have green tea.'

'That'll do, thank you. The restaurant she's pictured at,' Vanessa said, continuing to look at the photo. 'Is it local?'

'Yes, she owns it.'

'I presume she was born in Japan? You said you came to the States when you were two.'

'Yes,' Ru said, strolling to his kitchen and reaching for a delicate, hand-painted teapot – a gift from his mother. 'We both moved here forty years ago, after my father passed away.'

'I'm sorry to hear about your father.'

'I was so young. It barely registers.'

With a practised hand, Ru warmed the pot before adding loose sencha leaves, letting the aroma fill the air.

'That must have been hard for your mum, though,' Vanessa said, walking to the kitchen and standing by the island. 'Moving to a new country alone, I mean, especially with a young child.'

'Yes, she regularly reminds me how tough it was,' Ru replied with a small smile, 'and I regularly remind *her* she's the strongest person I know, so it was probably easy. But yes, she started with nothing, worked two jobs, and used her culinary skills to talk herself into an apprenticeship at the very restaurant she now owns.'

Ru poured hot water into the pot, as Vanessa watched, allowing the leaves to steep just right. Then he poured them both a cup. Vanessa raised hers. 'To your mother.'

Ru raised his glass, too. 'To all strong mothers.' Ru was intrigued to notice Vanessa's face cloud over. 'Is your mother in the UK?'

'Yes,' she said, taking a sip of tea. 'My father died a few years back.'

Ru didn't offer his condolences. He knew they would only be empty; a mere social grace. In fact, he sensed she didn't enjoy talking about that part of her life. So he put his tea down and grabbed a black swivel chair, wheeling it over to his computer area in the corner of the living room. Then he gestured for Vanessa to sit on it as he sank down into his own gaming chair.

'Impressive,' Vanessa said as she took in the sleek, large-screen monitor before her, now displaying an array of windows with data streams and code as Ru tapped on the keyboard.

'I spend most of my spare time here,' he said. 'So, let's look at this poem. I'm going to use the Tor browser – the browser favoured for dark web searches.' The familiar browser with a purple and green onion logo appeared on the screen. 'Let's see if my guess was right.'

He carefully typed in the address, each keystroke precise and deliberate. As he did, he felt a rush of anticipation, wondering what secrets lay behind that cryptic address. Vanessa seemed to feel the same, leaning forward, the screen lighting up her face. He allowed himself a moment to observe her profile. She was interesting to look at. There was no *blurring* with her. Everything about her was distinct. *Dark* brown eyes. *Bright* red lips. *Sharp* black tattoos.

He turned his attention back to the screen. At first, it did nothing. But then something loaded.

'It's very slow,' Vanessa noted.

'It's the multiple layers of routing,' Ru explained.

When it finally rendered, they were met with a black and green discussion forum interface, the beetle motif from the business card in the corner.

'Interesting,' Ru observed. 'It's a forum.'

'I was expecting an e-commerce site.'

'Me too.' Ru's dark eyes scanned the screen. 'Though I suppose, in a way, this is about e-commerce. Unlike regular internet forums, dark web forums are less about community and more about transactions and information exchanges. Their anonymity makes them a breeding ground for various activities, some more sinister than others. What unites them all is they thrive on the dark web, the ultimate market for things that shouldn't *be* on the market.'

Vanessa shuffled her chair forward, taking an even closer look at the screen. The forum was divided into sections, each dedicated to a specific aspect of the insect world with titles such as 'Rare Specimens Exchange', and 'Preservation Techniques'. Ru noticed there were some prolific posters, such as someone called ByteCraft and another called StickyThought77.

'We can ask Bronagh to try and get these people traced to their IPs,' Ru said as he looked at them. 'Unlikely though, considering this is the dark web.'

Vanessa gestured to the 'Rare Specimens Exchange' section with a 'No Newbies Allowed to Post' rule. 'This might be what we want?'

Ru nodded, clicking into it. A series of threads came up with titles like 'Golden Stag Beetle – Auction' and 'Looking for a Goliath Tarantula.'

Vanessa shook her head in disgust. 'These are *incredibly* rare species.'

'Looks like we've hit the jackpot, then.'

Ru scrolled through more posts.

'This is an interesting username,' Vanessa said, tapping her finger on a user calling themselves ChrysinaResplendens70. '*Chrysina resplendens* are a species of scarab beetle native to the rainforests of Central America.' Ru noted how she smiled as she talked about her favourite subject, her face lighting up. 'They're exquisite. Their exoskeletons turn gold under direct sunlight. What's even *more* interesting is I read an article in *The New Yorker* last month about an academic who is studying these very beetles. His name is Professor Alan Regan and he works at the Urban Wings Insectarium.'

'That isn't far from here.'

'Well, he's a real enthusiast,' Vanessa said. 'So enthusiastic, he might have a username to reflect that?' She shrugged. 'Just a thought.'

'A sensible thought. The leap from academic curiosity to illegal activity is not that far when the lure of financial gain is involved,' Ru commented. 'Let me pull up their posts.'

Within moments, a list of posts by the user appeared, many of which involved conversations with ByteCraft. The posts spanned several sections of the forum, but a significant portion was clustered under the 'Rare Specimens Exchange'.

'These are all the kind of species one might find in a place like the Urban Wings Insectarium,' Vanessa said. 'Zoos like that will receive clusters of insects, making it easy for someone in charge to extract a few to sell.'

'I think this professor is worth visiting,' Ru said, as his phone buzzed. He looked at the screen and put it to his ear. 'Harris?'

'There's another body,' said the detective.

Chapter 15

Vanessa stepped into the grand foyer of the Bowman estate, home of billionaire media mogul, Jerry Bowman. She had read about him: a self-made businessman who started out in the truck business and now owned one of the most influential media outlets in New York. His estate was nestled in the lush folds of the Hudson Valley, a two-hour drive from Manhattan. The mansion loomed over her, and inside, gilded frames housed expensive-looking art in the large foyer.

Detective Harris was waiting for Vanessa in that very foyer. She'd gone back to the lab first to change and collect her kitbag, then headed back out in her truck. 'It's pretty bad,' he said, wrinkling his nose.

Yes, Vanessa could smell the heavy, cloying odour of death already, intensified by the sealed opulence of the mansion.

'You suspect it's the housemaid who's dead?' Vanessa asked as she followed Harris towards the back of the foyer. Harris had told her what they knew of the case when he'd called her to attend earlier. Vanessa noted several species of adult flies buzzing around the window ledges.

'Yep, Bowman is at his ski lodge in Switzerland while his wife is visiting her mother, so it's just been their housemaid here the past two weeks. We're trying to get hold of him. Judging from the, er, insect activity on the deceased, she's been dead as long as Cordelia Montgomery.'

'I see,' Vanessa said. 'May I ask her name?'

'Rhoda Matheson.'

They both walked into a huge kitchen, a vast expanse of gleaming surfaces and professional-grade appliances. Sunlight streamed through the large French doors and windows, framing a view of the snowy landscaped gardens outside. Flies raced around the room as though excited for new company, one landing on Vanessa's cheek. Vanessa stayed very still, moving her eyes downward so she could discern its species. Predictably, *Muscidae,* the common house fly. She watched its proboscis – the appendage it used for feeding – probe her skin, a tasting ritual driven by the scent of the sweat beading on her cheek above her mask. She moved slightly and it flew towards Ru, who stood with his arms folded and his gaze fixed grimly on a figure on the floor – the housemaid. She was in an advanced state of decomposition. Her skin, pallid and marbled with the purplish hue of post-mortem lividity, clung to her frame. Even from where she stood, Vanessa could see larvae and adult flies buzzing around her eyes, nostrils and mouth, multiple levels of colonisation allowed to take place since her death, whenever that was.

Vanessa's eyes found an open door. 'Was this open when the first officer arrived?' she asked.

Harris nodded. 'We found binbags outside. We think Rhoda had just put them out, then collapsed before she had a chance to close the door.'

That would explain the number of flies. Easy access.

A young pathologist was crouched by the body, and alongside Ru stood a woman in a suit, her detective badge attached to her hip.

'I appreciate you calling us with this, Detective Lynch,' Vanessa heard Ru say.

'A death connected to another high-profile figure in this state in forty-eight hours?' the detective replied. 'I don't believe in coincidences.'

Ru looked over at Vanessa. 'This is the forensic entomologist working the case with us. Mind if she takes a look?'

'Mind?' Detective Lynch said. 'I insist. The forensics guys have already checked her over.'

Vanessa walked over the tread plates and crouched down beside the body.

'Oh, Rhoda,' Vanessa whispered as she carefully collected samples from the housemaid's body, 'I'm so sorry.' When she'd finished her task, she focused on capturing a live fly using an entomological net, gently sweeping it through the air around the body to trap it. Once it was in the net, she coaxed it into a vial with a funnel-like top.

'Those insects give you any sense of time of death?' Detective Lynch asked Vanessa.

'I can't provide times of death estimations,' Vanessa said. 'But it's clear she's been lying here, deceased, for some time, maybe a week. I'll know more once I get my samples back to the lab and check the data loggers I've set up.'

As she said that, she noticed a chunky gold bracelet loosely circling the woman's wrist, featuring two species of preserved beetle encased in clear resin. One, a very rare violet click beetle. The other an emerald-green *Chrysina resplendens* beetle . . . just like the beetles revered by Professor Alan Regan. Even more reason Ru needed to speak to the professor, something he seemed poised to do before he'd got the call about another murder.

Vanessa instantly stood up, stepping back. 'I recommend everyone leave the room to avoid contamination.'

The officers in the room all paused what they were doing and looked over.

Ru nodded. 'Do as the doctor said.'

'Judging from the looks you've all been exchanging,' Detective Lynch said as she followed Ru, Vanessa and Harris out into the foyer, 'my instincts are right and this is connected to the other deaths?'

Before Ru could answer, Harris paused by a small table in the hallway. 'Look.'

He was pointing to a black gift box which lay open on the table's surface with a stylised dark green and gold beetle silhouetted against the lid . . . the same logo from the business card *and* the dark web forum. Inside was a grooved area which matched the size of the bracelet Rhoda was wearing.

'There's a note with it,' Harris said, holding it up with a gloved finger so Vanessa and Ru could read it.

To Jerry,
  Happiest of Valentine's Days.
  x

'Rhoda must have decided to try on her boss's gift. A fatal error.' Ru turned to Harris. 'Did we find any such boxes and notes at Cordelia's and Maximilian's places?'

'Not as far as I know,' Harris replied, 'but we're still going through the trash so we might find something.'

'Jewellery of destruction sent under the guise of a Valentine's Day gift,' Ru said.

'How many more of these "gifts" are circulating out there?' Vanessa said.

'And how many more deaths to come?' Ru added. The room seemed to go quiet, officers pausing. 'The clock is ticking. And if we don't get a lead soon, that ticking bomb is going to blow up in all our faces.'

Chapter 16

The briefing room was hushed, a tangible tension hanging in the air as the officers awaited the lieutenant's update. Ru sat at his usual spot, cross-legged on the desk, his expression solemn.

'As you may know, another body has been found,' Haworth began. 'This time, the housemaid of billionaire Jerry Bowman. Now that this case has, sadly, grown even more complicated, Detective Bouchier from the Manhattan South Homicide Squad has joined us, too.' She gestured to a petite, poised detective Ru had worked with before. The Manhattan South Homicide Squad would often be called upon when the complexities of a crime scene hinted at a puzzle that stretched far beyond the ordinary, like this one. Alex Bouchier was a woman in her thirties who'd quickly risen through the ranks and carried herself with a quiet confidence and intuition that had been honed through years of working New York City's criminal landscape.

'Ru, if you can brief us on the latest?' Haworth asked.

He nodded. 'As in the previous two cases, a piece of jewellery incorporating a rare insect was found at the scene – this time, a man's bracelet. There was a new detail to help us with our investigation, too. A gift box and note, suggesting the item was sent as a Valentine's Day gift.'

'The captain needs to do a press conference about this,' Ramos said. 'More gifts like this could be going round.'

Officers around the room, including Bouchier, nodded.

'Agreed,' Haworth said. 'The captain wasn't in when I arrived, but I have briefed the precinct's press office. Now, let's get all our heads clear about where we're up to before the media start sniffing around even more than they have already. Let's continue.'

Ru used the remote control to turn on the screen.

'Jesus,' Harris said. 'It works.'

'You haven't used it yet?' Ru asked.

'Tried but it kept crashing,' Harris replied.

'Plus, the captain's threats to take any damage to it from our wages kinda put us off,' Ramos added.

Ru clicked for the screen to load, showing smiling photos of the three victims. Ru found photos like this helped humanise the deceased for the team, adding to their determination to track down the killer. Cordelia's photo was the one she'd had on her bedside table, with her mother. A reminder that she wasn't just an actress, but a daughter, too. A sister. A friend. He clicked on it and the details he'd prepared came up on the screen:

Name: Cordelia Montgomery
Job: Actress
Age: 25
Last contact: 2 p.m., Tuesday 14 February (phone call confirmed by agent, selfie taken shortly after. Nothing else of note)
Date of discovery: 10 a.m., Tuesday 21 February
Suspected cause of death: Pulmonary oedema caused by exposure to lethal toxins (pending toxicology)
Jewellery item: Hair clip
Mechanism: Miniature injector
Illegal insect: Queen Alexandra's birdwing (also ironclad beetle, not illegal)

'So. Updates on Cordelia, please,' Haworth said, turning to the room.

'I've gone through her receipts,' Ramos said. Ru had placed her in charge of Cordelia's case. 'They confirm Cordelia had multiple stays at the Seraphim Garden Hotel, the last one being on 13 February, the night before she's believed to have died. There are no receipts to suggest she paid for a suite, but there are receipts for things like room service. I questioned the staff who confirmed Cordelia was seen with Nils Thorsen on several occasions in the past three months . . . including the evening of 13 February.'

Murmurs filled the room as the officers absorbed the new information.

'So that scumbag Nils was lying when he said he didn't know Cordelia that well?' Harris said.

'Seems like it,' Ru said.

'That's enough to haul him in for questioning, surely?' Harris asked.

'Let's not rush into things,' Haworth said. 'In fact, while we're on the topic of the Thorsens, did you turn anything up on Jacqueline Thorsen, Harris?' she asked. When Ru told the team what his old friend Souta had said about her being the real person in charge, Harris had offered to look into her.

'Not much to say, really,' Harris said. 'She's a photographer. Bit of a socialite. If she does tangle herself in the crime side, like your contact seems to suggest, then she hides it well.'

'I see,' Haworth replied.

'Anything else found at Cordelia's apartment?' Bouchier asked, tilting her head, her blonde ponytail swinging. 'Any sign of a gift box like the one found today?'

Ramos shook her head. 'Nope. Officers just finished checking her trash, too. Nothing. Talked to family and friends again as well.' She shook her head. 'Man, that was hard. Real nice family, you know?' She frowned. 'Something about her brother, though.'

'Yes?' Haworth asked.

'Can't put my finger on it,' Ramos replied. 'Maybe it's just my dislike of white men in suits. But he seems a bit uncanny valley.'

'Uncanny what?' Harris asked.

'Jeez, you really are a Luddite, Harris,' Ramos said. 'It's when someone has human characteristics but doesn't look quite human.'

'You've been watching too much *X-Files*, Ramos,' Harris said.

'More like reading too much alien romance,' another officer piped up.

Ramos rolled her eyes. 'Fuck you all. I'm just saying,' she continued. 'Mommas have gut instincts and I got a biiig gut.'

Everyone laughed.

'Then follow those instincts,' Ru said.

'I agree,' Haworth said. 'Do some digging into Levi Montgomery. Anything else come up?'

'Nope. People really seemed to love her.' Again, Ramos shook her head. 'Such a damn waste.'

'This digital detox, though,' Ru said. 'Strange thing to do, don't you think?'

Ramos shrugged. 'I don't know. Selena Gomez announces she's coming off social media like, once a week before she's back on again. It's kinda trendy with celebrities.'

'Did you get more details about this detox?' Haworth asked.

'Sure. Her mom said she just needed some time away from all the craziness, you know?'

Haworth nodded. 'I'd like you to keep on it, though, do some more digging. Right. Let's move on to Maximilian.'

Ru clicked on a photo of Maximilian. It had been difficult to find one that didn't involve him being surrounded by beautiful models. But there was one photo from his apartment of him with his cat, who was now in the care of his vapid friend, Laife. Maximilian's details came up:

Name: Maximilian Rossi
Job: Fashion designer
Age: 28
Last contact: Tuesday 21 February
Date of discovery: Tuesday 21 February
Suspected cause of death: Poisoning (pending autopsy and toxicology)
Jewellery item: Watch
Mechanism: Pressure pad with release system
Illegal insect: Lotis blue butterfly

Haworth turned to Adiche, who she'd asked to look into Maximilian's life. 'Updates?'

'I can confirm we still haven't found a gift box,' she replied. 'But officers *did* find some photos with close-ups of models' breasts and crotch areas from his photo shoots.'

The officers around the room shook their heads.

'I know, gross,' Adiche said with a lip curl. 'It corresponds with rumours online about him overstepping the mark with women over the years. I got in touch with a model who I'd heard rumblings about but she clammed up.'

'She denied the rumours?' Ru asked.

'Officially, yes,' Adiche replied. 'But the look in her eyes when I mentioned his name suggested otherwise.'

'Any luck with other women?' Harris asked.

Adiche sighed. 'I've been doing my best. Hopefully, with more time, I'll come up with something.'

'Good,' Haworth said.

'In light of this,' Ru murmured, 'the ripped-up invite at Cordelia's apartment is . . . interesting.'

'Maybe he was handsy with her?' Ramos suggested.

'Maybe,' Ru agreed.

'But it doesn't explain why they were both targeted,' Bouchier added.

'Unless we're talking about a jealous lover,' Harris said. 'They mistake Rossi's touchy-feelies with Cordelia as consensual, so the jealous lover sends them both these gifts on Valentine's Day in revenge?'

'But how is Jerry Bowman's maid connected?' Ramos asked.

'You mean Jerry Bowman,' Ru stated. 'The bracelet was intended for him, judging from the note.'

'Another scenario is that Cordelia was seeing Maximilian *and* Jerry,' Harris said, 'and the jealous lover is her ex.'

'Like Nils Thorsen?' Ramos suggested.

'Let's not get carried away,' Haworth advised. 'It's definitely worth considering, though. Let's move onto Rhoda and Jerry.' Ru clicked on a picture featuring two photos side by side of Rhoda and Jerry. In Rhoda's photo, she was smiling, her short brown hair lifting in the wind, her two grown-up children either side of her, grandchildren at her feet. Jerry's photo showed a moustachioed man with a brilliant tan, pictured with his wife and two daughters on a yacht.

Suspected Target Name: Jerry Bowman
Job: Owner of Vezo Media, publishers of news sites
    including the *Chislington Post*

Age: 64
Actual Victim Name: Rhoda Matheson
Job: Housemaid
Age: 54
Last contact: Tuesday 14 February (via phone call with eldest daughter)
Date of discovery: Thursday 23 February
Suspected cause of death: Poisoning (pending autopsy and toxicology)
Jewellery item: Bracelet
Mechanism: Pending investigation
Illegal insect: Violet click beetle (*Chrysina resplendens* also used)

'Hey, it's a rich man version of Harris!' Ramos declared as she looked at Jerry's photo.

'Minus the money and the hair,' Harris said. 'But same beautiful wife and daughters, though, am I right?'

'Hell, yeah,' Ramos said. 'I always tell your wife when I see her that you're punching.'

'Ramos, she tells me that every day, too,' Harris said.

Haworth smiled and turned to the screen. 'Now, as Rhoda was not the intended victim, our main focus should actually be Jerry Bowman. What do we know about him?'

'I did some research while you were driving back,' Adiche said. 'Turns out Mr Bowman enjoys the company of young ladies.'

'Why can't these men keep their peckers in their pants?' Ramos said, groaning.

'I know, right?' Adiche concurred. 'Anyway, a few years back, the *Chislington Post* – for those of you who don't know, think *Huffington Post* but with more celebrity goss – exposed an affair he was having with a young actress. He denied it, but there are rumours online he paid her off. Then, conveniently, he buys shares in the very news company that outed him.'

'Interesting,' Ru said. 'So he enjoys the company of young actresses.'

'Did you find any connection with Cordelia?' Haworth asked, catching onto what Ru was implying.

'Nothing, apart from the articles written about her in the *Chislington Post*.'

'What kind of articles?' Bouchier asked.

'The usual,' Adiche replied. 'Some good, some outright bitchy.'

'Hmmm.' Ru looked at the screen. 'So we have three illegal insect items. These aren't the kinds of animals you can buy in PetSmart. But Dr Marwood and I did track down a dark web forum potentially related to these items.' He updated the team on what they'd discovered at the funeral – the man with the business card and the dark web forum it led to. 'We think there might be a potential witness in the form of a professor called Alan Regan, who I was planning to visit until I got news of another murder,' Ru said after. 'Interestingly, he is a fan of *Chrysina resplendens* beetles, like the one found in the bracelet Rhoda Matheson was wearing. He looked at Harris. 'The officer you speak to have any luck tracking him down?'

Harris shook his head. 'Just had a call. The prof's on a flight back from Australia as we speak, but he'll be in tomorrow.'

Ru nodded. 'We'll pay him a visit then.'

Just then, the captain walked in, the room going instantly quiet. He stopped before the screen, arms crossed as he read what was on there. 'Amelia in the press office just informed me about the latest developments with the gift box,' he said eventually. 'I'm not convinced.'

The whole room seemed to bristle with tension, all eyes turning to Haworth.

'I don't understand,' Haworth said calmly, 'how the presence of a gift box containing jewellery modified to administer a lethal dose of poison – similar to the jewellery we found on the other two victims – isn't convincing enough for you?'

'Until we get toxicology reports through,' the captain said, 'I still believe drugs are involved, and have briefed the narcotics team accordingly.'

'Brief the narcotics team, by all means,' Ru interjected. 'But you should also be holding a press conference to alert people. If similar gifts are circulating, this is now a public safety issue.'

'Have you found any other gift boxes like the one found at the Bowman estate?' the captain asked.

Ru shook his head. 'No, but—'

'Then there's simply not enough evidence.'

'But—'

'I will *not* turn this investigation into some sensational headline about an outlandish, insect-obsessed serial murderer on the loose,' the captain snapped, interrupting Ru. 'I want more evidence. And what's this I just overheard about Nils Thorsen being implicated again?' His eyes scoured the room, finally landing on Ru again. 'You know more than most how carefully we have to tread when it comes to the Thorsens. I urge caution. In fact, any more developments related to the Thorsens, I need to know, right?'

Ru gave a slight nod of the head. Satisfied, the captain strolled back out.

'For fuck's sake,' Haworth muttered under her breath. 'OK, so if we're going with the theory that Nils Thorsen—'

'Wait, didn't the captain just say not to go down the Thorsen route without checking with him?' Adiche asked.

'This isn't his investigation,' Ru said.

'Agreed,' Haworth added. 'As I was saying, if we're going with the theory that Nils Thorsen did this out of jealousy, he could certainly get access to all the things needed to make such gifts.'

'But surely he'd know we'd eventually link it to the illegal insect enterprise the Thorsens are rumoured to run?' Ru asked. 'There are only so many outfits in this city one could link to the illegal insect trade. Why would he want to risk the business?'

'Come on, Hoshino,' Harris said. 'Surely the fact Nils was seen with Cordelia the night before her death is enough to cast doubt?'

Haworth nodded. 'You're right. Let's bring him in for questioning.'

Chapter 17

Ru sat on one side of the interview room table beside Harris. Opposite them both was Nils and his solicitor. Nils looked calm, on the surface. But his face was ashen. He was clever enough to know Ru must have something on him.

'We have it on very good authority that you knew Cordelia Montgomery,' Ru began, 'despite telling us you didn't.'

'Good authority?' Nils said with a slight laugh. 'Hmmm.'

Ru slid a photo Adiche had managed to find of Nils sitting with Cordelia in the background of a party-goer's photo. 'This was taken on the evening of 13 February, the night before Cordelia is believed to have died. You look very cosy.'

Nils frowned. 'That could be anyone.'

'We know it was you,' Harris said.

Nils fixed the detective with his gaze, clearly weighing up his options.

'Fine,' he conceded. 'We were friends, have been for a few months.'

'Just friends?' Harris asked.

'Might have shared a bed a few times,' Nils replied dismissively. But a flinch suggested there was more to it.

'Why tell me you didn't know her very well?' Ru asked again. 'Clearly you did.'

'I don't *trust* you,' Nils hissed as he leaned across the table and glared at Ru.

'This is a *homicide* inquiry, Mr Thorsen,' Ru replied.

'A triple homicide inquiry,' Harris added.

'Triple?' Nil said, looking surprised. Of course, news of the latest murder hadn't yet been released to the media. Nils's jaw twitched. 'I did *not* kill Cordelia.'

'What was the *exact* nature of your relationship?' Harris asked.

'Like I said, we hooked up sometimes,' Nils admitted, rubbing his hand over his smooth chin. 'We had a . . . connection.'

'How often did you see Cordelia?' Ru asked.

'I don't know, every couple of weeks?' Nils said.

'When was the last time you saw her?' Harris asked.

'That evening,' he said, referring to the photo. 'We had dinner, went to the club then retired to my suite.'

'So you woke up together on Valentine's Day?' Harris asked. 'The day she died?'

Nils closed his eyes briefly and nodded.

'Did you argue?' Ru asked.

Nils opened his eyes. 'Of *course* not.'

'Are you the jealous type, Nils?' Harris asked.

'No! Jesus, no,' Nils said, voice calmer. 'Quite the opposite.'

'What's that supposed to mean?' Ru asked.

'I enjoy open relationships,' Nils replied, 'so no, I've never been the jealous type. I really have no issue with any woman I'm seeing sleeping with others. In fact, I find it a turn-on.'

'Was she sleeping with Maximilian Rossi?' Harris asked.

'She *hated* him,' Nils said, eyes angry.

'Why?' Ru asked.

Nils sank back in his chair, raking his fingers through his hair. 'Haven't you heard, he's the Harvey Weinstein of fashion.'

'Did she confide in you about something he did?' Ru asked.

Nils's jaw flexed. 'Not quite. But whenever he was around, I noticed how she . . . wilted. I didn't ask why, I don't like to pry. But it was obvious, really.'

'That must have made you angry,' Harris said.

'Maybe,' Nils confessed.

'Angry enough to kill him?' Harris asked.

'So let me get this clear,' Nils said, leaning forward with a strained smile. 'I kill Maximilian because he's a pervert but *not* before I kill the woman he potentially abused because . . . what?'

'Did you give Cordelia a present?' Harris asked. 'Seeing as it was Valentine's Day?'

'A first edition of *The Great Gatsby*,' Nils said, picking at the table's surface with his fingernail.

Ru examined his face. 'Anything else?'

'No.'

'What about jewellery made out of real insects?' Harris suggested.

'I've told Detective Hoshino already,' Nils said, 'I know nothing about any insect jewellery.'

'You are lying,' Ru said. It was something Ru had possessed since boyhood, an uncanny knack for uncovering untruths. Like when he was eleven and his mother had heard rumours the new chef at the restaurant was stealing food from the kitchen and selling it on. When she told her boss, the chef had denied it, but a young Ru had detected a falter in the man's voice. His mother had believed Ru over this man – she had seen her son's ability to detect lies all his life – and a week later, Ru's instincts were vindicated when the chef was caught in the act.

'I'm not,' Nils protested.

Ru extracted a photograph from his folder of Cordelia's hair clip, the lethal injector in focus. 'This,' he said, voice sombre, 'is almost certainly what ended Cordelia's life.'

'A hair clip?' Nils asked.

Ru nodded. 'Someone crafted this piece of jewellery with a singular, dark purpose – to kill Cordelia.'

Nils stared at the photo, brow furrowed.

'Imagine Cordelia's final, terrifying moments,' Ru continued. 'She was a clever girl. Graduated with full honours, top of her class. There would have been irritation around the site of the hair clip as the poison was released.'

Nils squeezed his eyes shut.

'*So* I wonder if she put it all together,' Ru continued. 'I wonder if, along with the fear and the horror, she felt a deep sense of betrayal, too. After all, the gift box it arrived in featured a distinctive green beetle logo. Maybe she recognised it?'

A small white lie. They hadn't found a gift box at Cordelia's place yet. But if it was enough to maybe nudge Nils in the direction Ru was hoping he'd go, it was worth it.

'In those last moments, as her chest constricted and she was in unbearable pain,' Ru said, his voice growing softer, 'maybe Cordelia was tormented by the question: *who would do this to me?* Even worse, if she had the slightest knowledge about the trading outfit behind this logo, maybe a certain face came to mind . . . And maybe, just maybe, her last thought was: *is my lover the one who has killed me?*'

Nils clenched his fists, his jaw tightening as a storm of emotions crossed his face. As he observed this, the theory about Nils being the killer began to disintegrate for Ru. He could discern an authentic shard running through Nils's grief, and he couldn't detect any lies now that Nils had confessed to sleeping with Cordelia. But he knew something about these illegal insect items. Ru could tell that.

'I don't think you killed Cordelia,' Ru said slowly, as Harris gave him a surprised look. 'But I think you liked her, very much, and I think you grieve her passing, very much.' Nils swallowed, tears filling his blue eyes. 'There is one way to help her now, Nils. Tell us what you know about these illegal insect items.'

Nils put his head in his hands. 'Shit,' he whispered. 'Fine, I—'

At that moment there was a knock at the door and Ramos popped her head in, giving Nils a disgusted look.

'He's got to be released, Boss,' she said, jutting her chin at Nils.

'Impossible,' Ru retorted.

'Captain's orders,' Ramos replied. 'Sorry, Hoshino.'

Even Nils looked slightly shocked.

'Is there anything you want to tell us?' Ru asked.

Nils blinked, then he seemed to pull himself together, standing and buttoning up his blazer; back to his confident self. 'I would say it's been a pleasure but – well, it hasn't.' Then he strolled out of the room with his solicitor as Ru clenched and unclenched his fists, every muscle taut with fury.

'Fucking captain,' Harris said, when Nils had left the room.

'You said the captain was at a fancy restaurant tonight?' Ru asked. 'Which one?'

'Botany Glaze, for his daughter's eighteenth birthday,' Harris replied. 'Why?'

Ru frowned. 'Don't the Thorsens own that place?'

'No way!'

Ru got up and strolled from the room. 'I'm going to pay the captain a visit.'

Harris jogged after him. 'Hoshino, you can't just crash the captain's private event.'

'He crashed our interrogation.'

'Don't go, Ru. Seriously, this could get you in real trouble. The captain's only just let you back on the squad, do *not* push his buttons.'

Ru ignored him, striding ahead.

Harris grabbed Ru's arm, trying to slow him down. 'I'm serious. You barge into the captain's dinner, and then what? You'll be thrown off the case – what good is that gonna do to the victims? This isn't some puzzle you can solve by tipping the board over.'

Ru stopped and looked Harris straight in the eye. 'If the captain is in someone's pocket, then he's not the one calling the shots. I'm going to find out who is. Don't try to stop me.'

'Fine,' Harris said, putting his hands up and stepping back. 'Not like I've ever been able to make you see sense anyway. As long as you know there's a line, and if you cross it, there might be no coming back this time.'

'Justice isn't served by respecting boundaries that protect the guilty, Harris. The captain made his choice, now I'm making mine.' With that, Ru strode away.

Chapter 18

Vanessa walked into the Botany Glaze restaurant for Bronagh's birthday dinner, immediately enveloped by the lush tranquillity of its botanical garden theme. The walls were covered in greenery and there were hanging terrariums that glowed with soft, ethereal light. Each table was a secluded haven, separated by natural partitions of bamboo and trailing ivy.

She strolled past tables set with glass tops that reflected the delicate fairy lights woven through the foliage above, and caught glimpses of herself in some of the mirrors dotted around the room, realising how much her sleek black velvet dress and vintage crimson-red belt stood out against the verdant surroundings.

She hadn't been in the mood for dinner out after a busy day – the funeral, then Rhoda Matheson's crime scene and the drive back after – but now she was here, she was pleased for the distraction.

'She's here!' Bronagh declared as her husband Joe pulled a seat out for Vanessa.

He was a slender man with salt-and-pepper hair and a warm, intelligent smile, his brown eyes hidden behind reading glasses. 'Our favourite forensic entomologist,' he said as she took her seat.

'How many others do you know?' Vanessa asked.

'Oh, thousands,' Joe joked back.

Bronagh's three sons greeted her with 'heys'. At seventeen, Simeon was Bronagh's eldest, and the one who looked most like her with his messy brown hair. He was followed by fifteen-year-old Cameron, who looked just like his father, and then thirteen-year-old Elon who looked like neither of his parents with his blond hair and green eyes.

As Vanessa observed them all, she suddenly felt a dull ache of yearning. Bronagh was only a few years older than her. She'd fallen pregnant with Simeon just after leaving university. Vanessa could just as easily have a seventeen-year-old too.

She had always told herself, and others, that she didn't want kids. But she hadn't really acknowledged *why*. Deep down she knew. She had never forgiven herself for losing her brother all those years back. If she couldn't look after him, how could she be deemed worthy of motherhood? The mere thought of family was fractured for her, criss-crossed with murder and abandonment and guilt. Now it was even worse.

'Guess who's here, too?' Bronagh said, pointing to a large table nearby. Vanessa looked over to see a familiar face: Captain Williams, the precinct's head. There were at least twenty people on the long table, their table-top laid with what looked like the restaurant's entire menu. She'd seen the captain host a press conference since she'd arrived in New York, and feature on the news. He always came across as very confident.

'Right, let's order,' Joe said, handing the menus out. Over the next hour, the conversation ebbed and flowed naturally. But there was another conversation that silently throbbed between them: the deaths of Cordelia Montgomery and Maximilian Rossi, not to mention the billionaire's housemaid. It wasn't long before Cameron brought it up.

'I know we have a "no work chat" rule, Mom,' he began, 'but can I just say, it is just *so* cool you're both working on the Cordelia Montgomery case.'

Vanessa noticed Joe shift around in his chair uncomfortably. She'd learned at her last meal that he disliked work chat at the table when she'd made the mistake of bringing up a case they were working on. Usually such an affable man, he'd snapped, prompting a telling-off from Bronagh.

'You still can't tell us how she died, Mom?' Cameron asked, leaning forward to stare at his mother and then Vanessa, voice low. 'And is it connected to that fashion designer's death? I *bet* you know.'

'Cameron,' Joe said in a warning voice as he peered towards the captain's table. In truth, their party was so loud, there was no chance they'd be able to hear what any other table was talking about.

'I personally think that hairstylist dude is sus,' Simeon said.

'You mean Laife Ravenna?' Cameron asked his brother.

Vanessa raised an eyebrow. The extravagant man from the news report and the funeral.

Simeon nodded. 'There's this rumour going around that he wanted to start a haircare line with Cordelia, but she pulled out at the last minute.'

'What about Madeline Layton?' Elon asked. 'Apparently, Cordelia started dating her ex about *five* minutes after they broke up. Major ouch!'

Cameron raised his eyes. 'You're saying Madeline Layton killed Cordelia over some dude?'

Elon winked. 'You said it, bro, not me.'

'By ex, do you mean Nils Thorsen?' Simeon asked.

Vanessa noticed Joe grow even more tense.

'My friend's sister works at his hotel,' Cameron continued, 'and she said she saw Cordelia there with the owner and that's him. I looked him up, he's so *dreamy*.'

Bronagh and Vanessa exchanged a look.

'What friend?' Bronagh asked.

'Oh my God, Mom, *please* don't make me tell you,' Cameron pleaded.

'Which friend?' Bronagh pushed.

'Fine. Phoebe Cane.'

'Bronagh,' Joe hissed. '*Not* at the dinner table.'

Vanessa watched as Bronagh gave her husband a hard look back. Was it her imagination or was there some tension there?

'Did you know Nils Thorsen's mother, Jacqueline Thorsen, is a photographer?' Elon said, completely ignoring his dad. 'She fell in love with his gangster father.'

'Oh, how *romantic*,' Simeon said sarcastically.

'*Where* are you reading all this?' Joe asked.

'Not reading, watching,' Elon said. 'TikTok.'

'You're not even on TikTok!' Joe said.

'Simeon showed me.'

Vanessa smiled. 'Guys, you should really consider a career in criminal investigation.'

Cameron took a mock bow. 'Thank you, thank you. We'll be here all week.'

'It's not something to be proud of, Cam,' Joe said. 'This obsession with celebrity isn't good for anyone. It's all so . . . *fake*.'

'Don't be so naïve, Joe,' Bronagh said.

'Yeah, Mom's right. Who do you think you are, Dad?' Cameron shot back. 'AuthenticAegis?'

Vanessa frowned. 'Authentic who?'

'It's a YouTuber who spouts conspiracy theories,' Joe said. 'I told you I don't like you watching their stuff, Cameron.'

'Dad, I watch it because he's funny,' Cameron said. 'Not because I believe anything he says. You know his latest video is about the murders?'

'Show me,' Bronagh insisted as Joe rolled his eyes.

Cameron dug his phone out of his pocket and held up the screen as they all leaned in. The video began with an image of New York City, its skyscrapers standing tall, lights twinkling in the early evening. A voice, distorted to protect the speaker's identity, spoke.

'New York, a city where the facade of grandeur hides the rotten core within. The recent deaths? A cleansing. A chance to rid New York of the evil inauthentic.'

As the voice continued, clips played: a glamorous party with guests laughing, sipping champagne; a panhandler on a street corner, ignored by those passing by; a close-up of an expensive watch, juxtaposed with a child's hungry eyes.

Then serene piano music played, accompanied with more visuals. The first image was of Cordelia Montgomery, dazzling in a red-carpet gown, her smile bright and her posture confident. This was followed by a photo of Maximilian Rossi, who looked achingly trendy in a crocheted suit, a charming grin playing on his lips. However, as the video progressed, the images distorted. Cordelia's radiant smile twisted into a grotesque grin, her eyes hollowed out, making her look almost skeletal. Maximilian's image, too, suffered a similar fate: his confidence turned sinister as his eyes darkened and his smile warped.

The screen then transitioned to AuthenticAegis, a silhouette against a dark, smoky backdrop. Face obscured by a mask, reminiscent of Ancient Greek theatre, split down the middle – one half tragedy, the other comedy. Their distorted voice filled the room, dripping with disdain.

'Witness the luminaries of New York, parading their supposed perfection for all to see,' they began. 'But beneath the sheen, there lies a rot. A decadence that they wear as a mask. Are these deaths tragic? Or are they the universe's way of restoring balance? Of reminding us of the dangers of living a lie – of exploiting the vulnerable to maintain one's inauthentic persona?'

The video ended with the mask, now lying on a table, the two halves separated. The haunting piano tune resumed, playing the video out before ending with the vlogger's logo – a shield with a fractured mask.

'Wow, what a psycho,' Simeon observed.

'More like a philosopher,' Joe said.

Bronagh frowned. 'Philosophy or not, this is dangerous rhetoric. I'll send it to Ru's team.'

'OK, that's enough,' Joe said. 'Let's move on to a more palatable topic. Tell me about school.'

The case chatter was replaced by school gossip, and when they had all finished their dinner, Bronagh let the kids head to the arcade at the hotel across the street.

'I must thank you for recommending *Insects and the Mind: The Psychological Impact of Nature* to Bronagh as a gift for me,' Joe said to Vanessa. 'It's wonderful stuff. In fact, I referred to it today during a session with one of my clients.'

'How so?' Vanessa asked, taking a sip of her rum and Cherry Coke.

'I read in this book how cicadas spend years underground,' Joe said, 'before finally emerging to sing their songs.'

Vanessa nodded. 'Yes, I spent an Australian summer listening to that very song.'

Joe smiled. 'Ah, perfect. Anyway, as I told my client, it speaks to resilience, waiting for the right moment, and making the most of the time we have.'

'I hope you didn't use that information with a suicide watch patient,' Bronagh said, grimacing.

Joe hesitated a moment then shook his head. 'Of course not, darling. I drew attention to it to show the patient their inner strength, and the songs they have yet to sing.'

'Before they then kill new prey,' Bronagh said, winking at Vanessa. She certainly knew how to wind her husband up.

'You're getting praying mantises and cicadas mixed up,' Joe said.

'Oh yes, cicadas are the cute ones, praying mantises are the predatory ones,' Bronagh commented.

'Praying mantises aren't so bad,' Vanessa said. 'They're like nature's little pest controllers. They play a crucial role in protecting gardens and crops.'

'Yes, another praying mantis fan!' Joe said, eyes excited as he leaned forward. 'I particularly admire how a praying mantis waits with incredible patience and focus for its prey.'

'Wow,' Bronagh said with a laugh. 'Who knew my husband was such a fan of predators?'

'You know what I mean,' Joe said, waving his hand about. 'In fact, I'd say it's a reminder of the power of mindfulness. Of being present in the moment. When my patients feel overwhelmed, I often ask them to channel the focus of a mantis. It's no wonder the mantis pose is so popular in yoga.'

Vanessa smiled. 'My mother used to love yoga. She'd teach me and my brother. It was Vincent's favourite pose, the Mantis Pose. Well, he was only four so he didn't quite manage it but he liked the idea.'

She noticed Bronagh and Joe exchange a look at the mention of her brother.

'Bronagh told me about the newspaper article, Vanessa,' Joe said. 'Have you heard anything from the prison?'

Vanessa unconsciously put her hand to her face, fingers tracing the bite mark her brother had left on her cheek that fateful night. 'I spoke to my brother, actually,' Vanessa said.

'Good. I know the pain and trauma he's caused you, Vanessa,' Joe said gently. 'But sometimes, confronting those demons can help bring closure.'

'I apologise for my husband,' Bronagh quickly said. 'Give Joe an inch, and he'll give you an entire therapy session!'

Joe shot his wife a look Vanessa couldn't read. She shrugged. 'It's fine, really. It's something I struggle with.'

Joe nodded. 'That's only natural. Uncertainty has a way of festering. I find—' He paused, eyes crossing to the front of the room. 'Is that Detective Hoshino?'

Vanessa followed his gaze to see Ru standing at the front of the restaurant, a bike helmet in his hands. His eyes scanned the crowded room before settling on the captain's table. Captain Williams was in the middle of a toast, his cheeks red. Ru slipped past the distracted restaurant host and strolled up to the table, and lowered himself into an empty chair, folding one leg over the other, studying the family like an intricate puzzle.

'I didn't know Detective Hoshino was a family friend,' Bronagh whispered to Vanessa.

The captain paused mid-toast when he noticed Ru's presence, but then continued, eyes flitting back and forth between his daughter and his detective.

'I'm not sure Ru is supposed to be there,' Vanessa noted.

Bronagh topped up her wine glass. 'Oooh, exciting. Let's see what happens.'

When the captain was finished with his toast, he stormed up to Ru. Vanessa and Bronagh leaned closer to the table so they could hear.

'What the hell are you doing here, Hoshino?' Vanessa heard the captain hiss. 'Ever heard of a phone?'

'Apologies for the intrusion,' Ru replied. 'I just wanted to ask you why you'd arranged for Nils Thorsen to be released.'

'This is neither the time nor the place,' the captain muttered through gritted teeth.

'Some might say it's the perfect time and place to discuss the intersection of law and power. After all, this is a Thorsen restaurant, isn't it?' he asked, looking around him.

'You booked a *Thorsen* restaurant?' Bronagh hissed at her husband. 'I didn't know!' Joe insisted.

'I didn't think a family connected with crime would be so keen to host a police captain, of all people,' Ru said, loud enough for most people to hear now.

Bronagh's mouth dropped open. But Vanessa just frowned. This was not a good move by Ru. It surprised her, too. He'd struck her as being very controlled, very calm. But maybe she'd got him all wrong.

The captain's eyes narrowed. 'You're walking a fine line, Detective.'

'No, Captain,' Ru said. '*You're* the one who has crossed the line. Imagine if this got out to the press? I can see the headlines now. POLICE CAPTAIN DINES IN MURDER SUSPECT'S FAMILY RESTAURANT.'

The captain looked like he was about to explode. 'Have you forgotten who brought you back into the fold on this goddamn case, Hoshino? Leave. Right now. Or I swear, you'll regret it.'

The last words were delivered like a growl, right in Ru's face.

Ru rose calmly, lifting a half-drunk glass of champagne as he looked at the captain's daughter. In the background, the host started walking over, a look of alarm on his face. 'I wish you a happy eighteenth birthday,' Ru said. 'May you come to understand the world you're stepping into – a world where your father may have to choose between upholding the law and continuing the tradition of family dinners.'

'Jesus,' Vanessa whispered under her breath as Bronagh shook her head.

With that, he walked away from the table. As he passed their table, Vanessa noticed the tormented look on his face. It reminded her of how Paul had often looked during the investigation last year. She impulsively excused herself from the table and went after him. When she got outside, the world was muted by snowfall. She found Ru by his bike overlooking the Hudson River, a dark silhouette against its freezing expanse. She approached him, her footsteps muffled by the snow as she crossed the road.

'You OK?' she asked.

'It's like the city's elite have a different set of laws,' he said, his voice betraying a simmering frustration. 'The thing I've never been able to wrap my head around is how the Thorsens have always been a step ahead.'

'And now you think that's because the captain's in their pocket?'

Ru's gaze drifted to the icy water below. 'I don't know, but it's hard to ignore how much they get away with. Ebbe Thorsen . . . he was a ghost when he first came here in the seventies. No one could trace his money, but he started buying up property like he was playing Monopoly.'

'And the crimes?' Vanessa asked.

'Everything you can think of. Drugs, cover-ups, illegal trades . . . high-end stuff, like art.' Ru's hand clenched into a fist. 'That's how I finally managed to hook something on him. I used his own arrogance against him, baited a trap with a fake buyer interested in a particularly rare and stolen piece he couldn't resist flaunting. We caught him red-handed, with enough evidence to put him away for life.'

Vanessa knew what happened next but let Ru continue.

'On the way to the station,' he said, his dark hair in his eyes as he looked down at the river, 'our car was ambushed, and Ebbe was killed. Never found out by whom. It was professional, clean. No traces. Someone didn't want him talking, didn't want those secrets to come out.'

'You're saying the Thorsens are just the tip of the iceberg, then?'

Ru nodded, his eyes meeting hers. 'Exactly. Ebbe's death . . . it wasn't justice. It was someone tying up loose ends. And now, seeing his son walk because of a call from the captain? It's not right. He was on the point of telling us about the illegal insect trading. It could have been the breakthrough we needed.'

Vanessa sighed, wrapping her coat around herself. 'You did what you could, Ru. And you're still fighting. That's more than most can say.'

He looked at her, and for a moment, the detective mask slipped, revealing the man who carried the weight of unfinished business on his shoulders.

'True,' he murmured. 'This city . . . it deserves better. And I won't rest until the truth comes out.'

The intensity of his vow hung in the air, and Vanessa felt a surge of respect for the man beside her. They were both quiet for a few moments, the snow lacing the air around them.

'So, how do you think the captain will react to what just happened in there?' she asked.

Ru sighed. 'Unpredictable. He needs me, though.'

'True,' Vanessa acknowledged, her tone sharpening with curiosity. 'What's your move now?'

'I'm paying a call to the zoo,' he said. 'It's time to have a chat with your so-called *Chrysina resplendens* acquaintance.'

'He's no friend of mine, not if he's trafficking in stolen life for profit. Make sure he's acutely aware of just how displeased we are with his side business – if that's what he's up to.'

Ru's eyes met hers. 'Oh, he'll get the message,' he assured her. He looked at his watch. 'I have to go. But . . . thank you. It was good to talk.' With that, he pushed off from the rail, placed his helmet on his head and jumped on his bike, his silhouette merging with the night.

Chapter 19

'An insect zoo in the middle of hipster central?' Harris remarked early the next day as he took in the zoo's minimalist glass exterior against the background of the bohemian neighbourhood of East Village. 'I guess even bugs need their artisanal coffee fix.'

The two officers walked through the main doors and both approached the reception desk.

'We're here to see Professor Alan Regan,' Harris said, flashing his ID to the young woman working there.

The receptionist's eyes widened. 'Oh. I think he's giving a talk at the moment to children.'

'Where?' Ru asked.

'The amphitheatre.' She looked at the clock. 'If you can just wait here for five minutes, he'll be finished soon.'

The two men took seats nearby, Harris looking nervously at Ru's phone as they did. 'Still no word from the captain, then, after last night?'

'Nothing.'

'That's good . . . I guess.'

'Haworth texted me, though.'

'Oh yeah. What did she say?'

'Three words. *You fucking idiot*.'

Harris smiled. 'Yeah, that doesn't surprise me.'

Ru knew confronting the captain had been a risk – a calculated intrusion born from necessity, not impulse. Nils's premature release was unacceptable.

'You can't get kicked off this case, Hoshino,' Harris said. 'We really felt the gap when you weren't around.'

'You seemed to manage fine.'

'No, remember the Whitman homicide?'

Ru remembered reading about it. It had been a complicated affair involving a series of burglaries along one of New York's most prestigious streets, culminating in the murder of a prominent judge, Ronald Whitman.

'Well, it was a complete mess.' Harris ran a hand over his bald head, a gesture Ru had come to associate with his frustration. 'No clear motive, no witnesses, and the judge's crime scene was contaminated by first responders. It was like trying to piece together a puzzle blindfolded without you.'

'You're doing yourself a disservice,' Ru said. 'You figured out who did it in the end. The cleaner, right?'

As all the burglaries took place just after three in the morning, it was eventually tracked down to a former boxer turned cleaner who worked the early hours shift at a hotel at the end of the street.

'Yeah, about three months after you would've,' Harris said. 'You would've seen the patterns we missed. Haworth said the same.'

'I'm not so sure.'

'Come on! Remember those arsons a couple of years back? We were stumped until you dug up those ancient city planning documents.'

Ru remembered spending nights poring over dusty maps and crumbling blueprints until a pattern emerged – a network of forgotten tunnels snaking beneath the city, perfectly aligning with the arson sites.

'Anybody can read old maps,' he said.

'It wasn't just *old maps*,' Harris said. 'It was understanding the arsonist's psychology, his need to leave a mark on history. You used it to predict his movements. Man,' he said, smiling as he shook his head, 'I still remember that, waiting for him in the dark, underground . . . like something out of a movie.'

Ru remembered that night, too, the damp air of the tunnels, the sound of their own breath echoing off the walls. They had intercepted the arsonist moments before he could strike again.

'We couldn't have done it without you,' Harris said.

'*You're* the one who tackled him to the floor,' Ru said.

'Look, all I'm trying to say is, we need you. These victims need you. But now you've gone and messed things up by playing the rebel, just like you did last time. You need to get it in your thick skull,' he said, gently tapping Ru's head, 'that you're a police detective, not a James Dean wannabe.'

Ru remained silent, his gaze steady and thoughtful. He wanted to tell Harris that sometimes acts of rebellion were also acts of policing. But he knew it would be futile. Harris, for all his experience and insight, viewed the world through a different lens.

So Ru just nodded. 'Understood, Harris,' he said. 'I promise to behave. Now, let's find this insect professor, shall we? I think our five minutes are up.'

They both stood back up and the receptionist quickly pressed a button, allowing them to walk through the turnstiles. As Ru strolled down the corridor, he absorbed every detail. He had enjoyed visiting such places as a child, a chance to add layers to his inner knowledge library. It seemed zoos had changed in his time, though. The place was laid out with open-concept habitats and interactive displays. Glass terrariums hung suspended from ceilings, each a self-contained world of crawling, fluttering life. Neon lighting illuminated the pathways, lending an avant-garde feel to the place.

'Fuck me, look at that one,' Harris exclaimed, pointing at a giant centipede in a glass container suspended above his head. 'Looks like something out of a horror movie! The way it moves,' he added, shuddering as he watched the centipede slowly slink along.

Ru watched in fascination, taking in its multitude of legs which moved in a mesmerising, undulating wave. 'Amazing, how nature creates such diverse forms and functions. Every pattern, every movement has a purpose.'

'Purpose or not, I wouldn't want any in my house,' Harris said.

Ru stopped in front of a terrarium housing a colony of ants. 'Such social insects,' he mused. 'Each individual might seem insignificant, but together they create complex societies, not unlike humans.'

'Maybe you can learn something off 'em. Like coming for drinks Saturday night?'

'You mean tomorrow?' Ru asked. Harris nodded. 'You know how I feel about social gatherings, Harris. In fact, they remind me of ant colonies: noisy and chaotic with everyone scrambling for a piece of the cake. I've always found solitude to be . . . more enlightening.'

Harris shook his head, smiling. 'A simple "no" would be fine, Hoshino.'

They continued walking until they found themselves at the edge of a small amphitheatre. A gathering of schoolkids sat on the steps, their eyes glued to a figure at the centre: Professor Alan Regan, Ru presumed. The professor was a predictably eccentric-looking man, with a shock of unruly silver hair, round glasses perched precariously on his nose, and a vibrant bow tie adorned with beetle motifs. He was holding a large, shiny beetle in his hand as the schoolchildren stared at it in fascination.

'Now, children,' he said in a southern accent, his voice booming around the theatre, 'this here is Arnie the titan beetle, one of the largest beetles in the world. He can grow up to six and a half inches!'

Harris leaned over to Ru and whispered, 'That thing's bigger than the hotdogs they sell at the Yankee Stadium.'

Professor Regan continued, oblivious to the detectives' presence. 'But what's truly fascinating is their jaw strength. Arnie's jaws are so powerful they can snap a pencil in half or even cut into human flesh!'

The kids gasped, some in horror, others in awe. Harris winced, rubbing his fingers together unconsciously.

'Did you also know that adult titan beetles don't eat?' the professor went on, his eyes gleaming. 'They spend their larval stage – that's when they're young – eating and growing underground. But once they become adults, they have only one purpose: to find a mate.'

'Sounds like half the guys at the precinct after payday,' Harris murmured to Ru.

As the talk concluded, the kids clapped enthusiastically, clearly enraptured by the doctor's words. Ru watched as Professor Regan interacted with them, answering questions and showing off various specimens. The man's passion for these beetles was clear, which made the idea of his willingness to *sell* the object of his passion on the dark web all the more infuriating.

As the last of the schoolchildren exited, Ru and Harris descended the auditorium steps, their footsteps echoing around the space. Professor Regan was meticulously packing away his specimens as they approached.

'Professor Regan?' Ru asked.

The professor looked up with a smile. 'Yes?'

'I'm Detective Ru Hoshino, and this is Detective Harris. We're leading the investigation into the murder of Cordelia Montgomery.'

The professor blinked in shock. 'Cordelia Montgomery? The – the actress? What a tragedy! She had such talent. But why are you two here, speaking to *me* about it?'

'That's what we're hoping you can help us with, Prof,' Harris chimed in. 'We've got a few questions that need answering.'

Professor Regan's eyes darted between the two detectives. 'I'm not sure how I could be of any assistance, but please, ask away.'

Ru drew his phone out from his pocket and presented the doctor with the screen grabs he'd taken of his forum posts. 'These look familiar to you?'

Professor Regan's face paled. 'I – I've never seen these before,' he stammered.

Ru could tell he was lying. He sighed. If only humans possessed the straightforwardness of beetles. Their lives, driven by instinct and purpose, lack the convolutions of deceit and moral ambiguity people so often grapple with.

'Interesting choice of username, don't you think?' Harris asked. 'ChrysinaResplendens70, I mean?'

The professor shifted uneasily on his feet. 'Well, of course, they're a fascinating species of scarab beetle.'

'Funny that,' Harris said, crossing his arms over his chest. "Cause the kind of insects this ChrysinaResplendens70 fella seems to offer are suspiciously like the types of creepy-crawlies you'd find in a zoo like this. In fact, someone in your esteemed position would have easy access to these kinda bugs, wouldn't they?'

'And with the financial allure of such a trade,' Ru added, 'it's not a stretch to imagine someone on an academic wage being tempted.'

The professor's face turned bright red. 'I have dedicated my life to the study and preservation of these creatures. To even *suggest* such a thing is absurd.'

Ru had to give it to the professor. He was holding on tight to his obvious lie. Maybe the dark web's ability to shroud users in layers of anonymity was giving the professor a false sense of security, like he was in a unique, protected bubble.

Ru wanted to burst that bubble.

He took a step closer to the professor, his posture relaxed, but his eyes sharp. 'Have you heard of NovaScope Forensics?'

The professor shook his head. 'No, should I have?'

'It's a brand-new forensic firm we're working with,' Ru explained. 'The lead there is the best in the business when it comes to digital forensics. With people like her, and advances in artificial intelligence, it's not possible to hide yourself behind layers of encryption anymore. Every piece of data, every byte transferred leaves a trace, like a beetle leaving behind its tracks.'

Professor Regan's face paled as he listened, revealing that he was clearly out of his depth with the intricacies of digital technology.

Harris put his large hand on the professor's shoulder. 'Let me translate for you. What Detective Hoshino is trying to say is by cooperating now, it might mean the difference between several years in prison and just a few ... or hell, if you're lucky, maybe even probation.'

The professor's eyes widened in shock and he was quiet for a few moments. Then he took in a deep sigh. 'I ... I never thought it would come to this,' he said quietly. 'I just wanted to share my passion, to make a difference in the world of entomology. It was never about money, I swear.'

Ru and Harris exchanged a look.

'So you are ChrysinaResplendens70, then?' Harris asked him. The professor nodded.

'So you *illegally* stole insects from your employer,' Ru said, 'to then *illegally* sell on the dark web?' He thought of what Vanessa had said the evening before. 'You're essentially trafficking in stolen life for profit?'

'I – no,' the professor stammered unconvincingly.

'Let's start with who your broker is,' Ru said.

The professor swallowed nervously, looking around the theatre. 'His name is Edgar Trent. But please, this can*not* come back to me.'

The two detectives glanced at one another. The name didn't ring a bell.

'When does Mr Trent usually do business with these rare specimens?' Ru asked.

'They have auctions,' the professor said in a low, shaky voice.

'When?' Harris asked.

'Well, we are told not to—'

'When?' Harris pushed.

The professor sighed. 'On the last Friday of every month at a Red Hook warehouse in Brooklyn, 7 p.m. sharp.'

Harris raised an eyebrow. 'So that's tonight, then?'

The professor nodded. 'But please, do *not* reveal to anyone I told you.'

'You seem fearful,' Ru observed. 'Is this because you fear those who run these auctions?'

'I promise you, I have absolutely no idea who runs them,' the professor stuttered. 'There is never anyone of any seniority at these things, from what I can tell. But it would seem reasonable, considering the—' he swallowed, 'the more *underground* nature of these things that one wouldn't be *wrong* to fear consequences of sharing the date and time of an event patrons have very specifically been advised *not* to share.'

'I think we need to attend this auction,' Ru said.

'Brooklyn baby,' Harris said as he got his handcuffs out to bring the professor in, 'here we come!'

Ru pushed through the glass doors of the precinct with Harris after they'd checked the professor in. He'd probably be released on bail the same day, but that didn't mean he wouldn't face some time for illegal insect trading. As Ru and Harris walked into the squad room, a conspicuous silence fell over the area. Heads popped up from behind monitors, conversations dwindled into whispers, and the clack of keyboards softened. It was the kind of reception that made it clear news had travelled fast; they all knew about Ru gatecrashing the captain's dinner.

'Oh, great, you're back,' Ramos said when she noticed them. 'Just had a call. Maximilian *did* receive the watch as a gift. We found a gift box just like the one from the Rhoda Matheson scene. It was in a bin by his apartment block's shared pool. We found a note too. *Exactly* the same as the one from Bowman's place, apart from the name.'

'Good work,' Ru said.

'Also, Bronagh Thompson sent an email over about some YouTuber called AuthenticAegis?'

Ru nodded. 'I saw the email.'

'I had a look and it's interesting, for sure,' Bouchier said, joining them. 'But probably just one of many nutjobs.'

'Understood. Thank you both for looking into it.'

'Another thing—' Ramos began.

'Christ, Ramos,' Harris said, 'you eaten Duracells for breakfast?'

She rolled her eyes. 'No, just trying to get in as much work as I can before going into early labour because of the stress of *you*,' she said, glaring at Ru.

'Agreed,' another voice chimed in. It was Haworth, brown eyes sparking with anger. 'What the hell were you thinking, pulling a stunt like last night, Hoshino? I put my neck on the line bringing you in on this case and this is how you repay me?'

'None of that is important,' Ru said. 'What's important is the auction tonight.'

'What auction?' Captain Williams had just stepped into the room, his arms folded over his barrel chest as he watched Ru. Ru's impassive gaze met the captain's.

'An illegal insect auction,' Ru explained. 'There's one taking place this evening.'

'And you're planning to send Hoshino?' Williams asked Haworth.

Haworth hesitated a moment then nodded. 'Yes.'

He shook his head. 'Absolutely not.'

A few eyebrows went up around the room. Ru took a breath to calm himself. The captain still seemed convinced there was nothing to the insect angle.

Williams pointed towards Bouchier. 'Why not send another officer? Like that pretty little thing over there?'

There was a brief silence, the young officer's face flushing as she tried to figure out how to respond.

'Pretty little thing. Quite an archaic perspective, Captain,' Ru said. 'And that happens to be Detective Bouchier from the Manhattan South Homicide Squad.'

The captain's face reddened, a vein on his forehead becoming more pronounced. Harris flinched as Ramos pinched the bridge of her nose, shaking her head.

'But you're correct,' Ru continued, 'it probably shouldn't be me. There is someone else who might be suitable.'

'Who?' the captain asked.

'Dr Vanessa Marwood,' Ru said. 'The insect expert we've brought in to work the case. It's unlikely the Thorsens themselves will be there, so she won't be recognised, and her knowledge of insects will allow her to make note of any illegally obtained insects.'

'It does make sense, actually,' Haworth said. 'By pinning the Thorsens down with the illegal insect trading, it gives us more power to *question* them in relation to the murders, too.'

'As long as we're not interrupted mid-interrogation,' Ru said.

Haworth groaned, looking up at the ceiling in exasperation.

The captain took a long, deep breath through his flared nostrils. 'Detective Hoshino,' he said. 'My office. *Now.*'

Captain Williams marched out into the corridor with the fierce stride of a charging rhinoceros beetle, commanding every inch of space around him. Ru followed him, Ramos mouthing 'be good' as he passed her. Officers glanced up as they passed, a mixture of curiosity in their eyes. Some even offered a nod to Ru, maybe a gesture of solidarity.

Ru eventually reached the captain's office at the end of the corridor. Its walls were adorned with photos of handshakes with the city's elite, plaques of commendation, and memorabilia from high-profile cases. The captain's irritation was clear as he sat on his chair and faced Ru from across his large desk. 'Bursting into my daughter's celebration, Hoshino?' His voice was a controlled rumble, the anger simmering just below the surface.

Ru met his gaze evenly. 'There were concerns that needed addressing, Captain. About the release of Nils Thorsen.'

Captain Williams snorted, leaning back against his desk. 'Concerns? Based on what? You have no concrete evidence against Nils Thorsen, and I had his law firm's director – rumoured to be a future Attorney General – on my back. What would you have me do, Hoshino? Jeopardise the precinct's standing on a hunch? You can't possibly understand the complexities of my job. The careful balance I must maintain.'

Recalling Harris's cautionary advice, Ru chose his next words carefully. 'I do understand the pressures, Captain. However, dismissing . . .'

The captain cut him off with a wave of his hand. 'That's enough said about last night except for one thing.' He leaned forward, hard eyes squarely on Ru. '*Never* pull that act again. If you do, your career in the NYPD really will be over. I have been *more* than patient with you because – as much as it frustrates me to admit it – you are a superb detective. But frankly, my patience is wearing thin. *Very* thin. Understood?'

Ru nodded. 'Understood.'

He leaned back, satisfied. 'So this auction. It seems your insect theory might have legs, if you excuse the pun. Once again, Hoshino, you've made yourself frustratingly indispensable after the stunt you pulled last night. It's clear from what I've seen in NovaScope's report about the hair clip, and the watch, that whoever's doing this has some kind of insect fetish. But are you convinced this bug doctor is the best person to send?' the captain asked. 'Plus, it could be dangerous for her.'

Ru thought about that impulsive suggestion of his for a moment. Part of him recognised a desire to keep Vanessa close to this case. Why did he have such a need? Maybe he recognised something in her – a kindred spirit, perhaps, a relentless pursuit of truth that mirrored his own. Or maybe it was her unique perspective, her ability to see beyond the surface details to the intricate patterns beneath. Or perhaps it was just that hunch – something instinctive about where this case was leading. Whatever it was, Ru couldn't deny that Vanessa's involvement brought an invaluable dimension to the investigation. She wasn't just another detective or scientist; she was a catalyst, transforming every piece of evidence into a significant lead. 'Yes, I am convinced.'

Chapter 20

That evening, Vanessa found herself sitting in an unmarked police car parked a block away from the auction venue. Ru was sitting in the driver's seat while Harris sat with Vanessa in the back, attaching a small, inconspicuous microphone under the lapel of Vanessa's dark spider-patterned blouse. 'Speak softly when you communicate; the mic is sensitive,' he said.

'Will do.'

'Remember, you're there to observe and gather information,' Harris continued. 'If you feel uncomfortable at any point, say the code word, and we'll get you out of there.'

'Can I say it now?' Vanessa asked.

'Of course,' Ru said. 'We can stop this now if you wish and you can go home.'

Vanessa thought of all the insects she might be helping and, of course, the three victims of whatever the hell was going on.

'I'm joking, it's fine,' she said, smoothing her hands over the knees of her pencil skirt. 'Right, let's do this.'

She stepped out of the car, and took in a deep breath, before letting it out as a mist in the cold night air. Then she walked down the dark street towards the warehouse where the auction was being held. As she approached the metal-gated entrance, a burly man with an impassive face halted her.

'Password?'

'*Forma insectum*,' Vanessa replied, using the password that had been shared on the dark web forum.

The man nodded and stepped aside, allowing her entrance. She crossed a dark concrete car park. Three luxury cars were already parked up, the pale faces of their drivers looking out from the windows. Another security man stood at the entrance to the warehouse. Again, Vanessa gave the password when prompted. He stepped aside, and she walked in.

She'd been expecting a huge space considering these units were known for being storage warehouses, but it was actually quite intimate inside, with tall, circular tables arranged in a semi-circle. On each table's surface were glass terrariums filled with items she couldn't quite see from where she stood. Mounted spotlights focused on the displays, casting the room in a surreal mix of shadow and light. A bar lined the back of the room and servers walked around with canapés and drinks on trays.

Dozens of people were already there, an eclectic mix of different ages and styles. Vanessa raised an eyebrow when she noticed the influencer Madeline Layton among them, her multiple ear piercings glinting in the dim light of the room; her plump lips looking even more expansive, shrouded in pink lip gloss.

Vanessa walked through the throng, observing some of the items up close, her heart sinking. The first she came to was a clutch bag made from the bodies of what looked like jewel wasps, a species renowned for its vibrant metallic blue and green sheen, and now under threat because of habitat loss. They were placed delicately over the high-gloss, black leather clutch that highlighted their alien beauty.

Next to it was another forbidden treasure: an Asian long-horned beetle which was encased, alive, in a large crystal cube about two inches by two inches in size which hung as an extravagant pendant from a chain. Its jet-black exoskeleton was adorned with random white spots and the long, curved antennae were a spectacle in themselves, twisted like wrought iron in a gothic mansion. These insects had been banned and nearly eradicated all over the world, an invasive species that wreaked havoc on other creatures and in forests. And yet here one was, alive, one wrong move meaning it could easily begin its trail of destruction again. So it seemed these illegal traders weren't just interested in the protected and the vulnerable, but also the banned and the dangerous, too. The irresponsibility made Vanessa's blood boil.

'Beautiful, isn't it?' Madeline was beside her now, looking down at the necklace.

'Yes, very,' Vanessa murmured, trying to keep her anger and disgust in check.

Madeline tilted her head, regarding Vanessa. 'Weren't you at Cordelia's funeral yesterday?'

'I was,' Vanessa replied.

'Sorry, I was a bit of a mess, I absolutely detest funerals. How did you know Cordelia?'

'I'm an entomologist.'

'Oh, wow, you must have met her on the del Toro horror she was working on.'

'Ah-huh,' Vanessa lied.

'Your eye make-up is bomb, by the way.' Madeline dug into her designer bag, pulling out a moody eyeshadow palette of deep, smoky hues and metallics. 'Here, this one's on me. It's from my new range.'

Vanessa looked at the palette. To be fair, it was absolutely the kind of make-up she'd use. She tucked it into her bag. 'That's really kind of you. So, what brings you here?'

'When I was a kid, I was a *total* bug nerd.'

Vanessa smiled. 'Snap.'

'I used to run around like a wild child, looking under rocks, checking out bugs.' She frowned slightly. 'I guess they were like a substitute family. I was stuck on a farm in Wyoming with my aunt after my dad and brother went to prison.'

Vanessa had a fleeting image of her own brother. 'I'm sorry to hear that,' she said.

'Oh, it was a long time ago. Anyway,' Madeline said, forcing a smile onto her face, 'anything you have your eye on?'

'Not yet,' Vanessa said. 'Do you often attend auctions like this?'

'This is my second. It's fun,' she said with a shrug. 'A bit of a secret hobby, you know? A little *illegal* hobby,' she added in a whisper. 'Must be in the blood.'

Vanessa leaned in slightly, lowering her voice too. 'Have you ever met Edgar Trent?' she asked, using the name the professor had given to Ru for the broker.

'*Nobody's* met him. It's just a name people whisper. Who knows if he's even real?'

'Any idea who runs these things?'

Madeline's lively demeanour dimmed a fraction. She busied herself with rearranging a bracelet on her wrist. 'Just rumours. Names float around, but no one really knows. It's *super* hush-hush.'

Vanessa was about to ask if Madeline had heard rumours of people getting gifts from the organisers on Valentine's Day. But then the auctioneer – a tall, rail-thin man with a booming voice – took his position at the front of the room. 'Ladies and gentlemen, please take your seats. The bidding shall shortly commence.'

Vanessa found a spot at one of the tables with Madeline as a screen displayed enlarged images of the items, which showcased their extraordinary features. The room was electric with anticipation, the air humming like the wings of a dragonfly. Each auction item was presented with a flourish, bids flying like sparks in a frenzied fire.

Vanessa felt nauseous. Didn't these people understand the harm they were causing?

As she thought that, a sudden, unnerving hush fell over the room, as if the air itself was bracing for impact. Then, in the blink of an eye, the room exploded into chaos. From both entrances, armed law enforcement agents burst in, FEDERAL OFFICER emblazoned across the back of their bulletproof vests.

Panic fluttered in Vanessa's chest. Was this part of the plan? Surely Ru would have told her.

'Federal agents!' one of the officers shouted, a man in his mid-thirties with a handsome, stubbled face. 'Everybody on the ground, *now.*'

People scattered, trying to flee, but the exits were quickly blocked by officers. Madeline was visibly trembling, her face ashen.

The stubbled officer began moving through the crowd like a panther, his team following his lead. 'Under the Endangered Species Act,' he called out in a clear, commanding voice, 'you are all under arrest for the purchase and distribution of illegal insects.'

One by one, people were forced to their knees, their hands being cuffed behind their backs. Some tried to protest, claiming innocence, while others like Madeline merely sobbed, fearing the gravity of the situation.

Vanessa's heart raced. It was clear now that Ru knew nothing of this. As the leading officer approached her, anxiety swirled in the pit of her stomach.

'Hoshino,' she hissed into her hidden microphone. 'Get in here, NOW!'

Chapter 21

Harris tucked into a homemade sandwich, while Ru jotted down observations in his notepad as he listened in to the auction from the front seat of his car, impressed by how Vanessa was handling herself.

'My wife seriously needs to up her sandwich game,' Harris said, wrinkling his nose as he looked at the contents.

'You could always make your own, you know.'

As Harris was about to reply, a commotion filled their headphones, a loud voice cutting through it all. 'Under the Endangered Species Act, you are all under arrest for the purchase and distribution of illegal insects!'

Harris's eyes widened. 'Oh shit.'

Without a second thought, they flung the car doors open and sprinted towards the warehouse entrance, passing a security guard who was being questioned by an officer. Ru noted the emblem on the officer's arm as they passed: the US Fish and Wildlife Service.

'Wasn't Adiche supposed to contact them about the case?' Harris asked.

'I'm sure she tried,' Ru replied. 'But if they've been focused on a raid here, they may not have picked it up.'

Ru and Harris flashed their badges then jogged into the warehouse, finding Vanessa kneeling with others on the floor, her hands behind her head. She looked surprisingly serene given the situation. Though that serenity soon turned to anger when she caught sight of Ru and Harris.

'This just gets worse,' Harris whispered as he watched an officer with cropped dark hair stride over to Vanessa with handcuffs. 'That's Agent Valdez. I know someone who trained with him. He's tough as they come. Damn ambitious, too.'

Ru walked over swiftly, flashing his badge at Agent Valdez. Valdez regarded the badge with an expressionless look. 'Detective Hoshino, this is Detective Harris,' Ru said. 'I need to talk to you, *now*.'

'I'm a little busy right now, Detective,' Agent Valdez said.

'This is important,' Ru said.

'Yeah, you're gonna wanna hear this,' Harris added.

Valdez took in an irritated breath then jerked his thumb towards the quiet bar area.

'What?' Valdez snapped when they were out of earshot. 'And make it quick.'

'That woman you're about to arrest is part of our investigation team for a triple homicide case,' Ru explained.

He looked over at Vanessa. 'She a cop, then?'

'A doctor,' Ru replied. 'Specifically, a doctor of forensic entomology.' Valdez tilted his head, giving Vanessa an interested look. 'She's working undercover for us here. We believe the deaths we're investigating may be linked to illegal insect trading.'

Valdez forced his eyes away from Vanessa and back to Ru. 'Why the *hell* weren't we notified of this?'

'I suggest we discuss that later, out of earshot of people,' Ru replied. 'It's a very . . . sensitive case.'

'It better fucking be,' Valdez said. 'Stay here and watch how the big boys do it. We can talk when I'm done.'

'Big boys,' Harris muttered as Valdez strolled off, puffing his chest out. 'Who'd he think he is?'

'A federal agent – so in theory, he *is* senior to us,' Ru stated.

'No need to be so literal, Hoshino.'

After all the guests were led out, Vanessa was allowed to join Ru and Harris.

'I am trying to remain professional,' Vanessa hissed as she smoothed her hair back. 'But what the *hell*, Detective Hoshino? You didn't check these auctions weren't already on the radar of the US Fish and Wildlife Service?'

'We only found out about the auction today,' Ru said.

Vanessa pinched her nose, shaking her head as Agent Valdez walked over, the displeasure on his tanned face matching Vanessa's.

'Detective Hoshino,' he said when he reached them, 'you do realise you could've jeopardised months of covert work?'

'We only received the intel about the auction this morning,' Ru replied calmly, 'and your office was notified. We are in the midst of a triple homicide case. Time is of the essence. It was a judgement call.'

'*Poor* judgement,' Valdez snapped. 'We're trying to bring down a global illegal trading ring. Notified my ass . . . You should've *consulted* us, or did you think that New York's finest could single-handedly tackle international wildlife smuggling?'

Their eyes met in a charged stand-off, each sizing the other up. Then Valdez's gaze momentarily flitted over to Vanessa. 'And what are you doing using a doctor to carry out undercover work for you?'

'As Hoshino said, she's an entomologist,' Harris offered. Valdez gave him a look that seemed to make the officer regret speaking.

Vanessa's eyes met Valdez's squarely. 'I would never have agreed to this if I had known we'd be stepping on the toes of the US Fish and Wildlife Service.' She shot Ru an icy glare that didn't require elaboration.

Ru noticed a softening around Valdez's brown eyes. 'Don't worry, this is not on you. I've heard Detective Hoshino has a penchant for playing fast and loose with the rules.'

Ru didn't counter him. He was right, after all.

'Well, now you're here and you've trampled all over my case with your Converse,' Valdez said, eyeing Ru's trainers disapprovingly, 'I might have something for you.' He pulled his phone out, Ru noticing his nails were perfectly rounded and manicured. 'We've been tailing the person we suspect has been running these auctions for some time now.'

'And that is?' Ru asked.

'Jacqueline Thorsen.'

Ru frowned. So it seemed the real power behind the Thorsens *was* its matriarch.

Chapter 22

Vanessa strode down the street not far from where the auction had taken place. Ru had offered to give her a lift back, but she needed some fresh air. Or, more accurately, an excuse not to spend more time with Detective Hoshino after the mess he'd just caused. And yes, maybe she needed a drink, too. A strong one.

The fact was, Ru had put her in an awkward position. She was no stranger to bending the rules – sometimes the situation demanded it. But she preferred to make those deviations on her own terms, not to have them thrust upon her by someone else. Paul Truss wouldn't have done that to her. In fact, he would be furious right now.

As she mulled over her irritation, a light in the distance spilled out onto the street like a beacon. She couldn't believe it. It was a British-themed pub, the sign above swaying in the breeze: The Queen's Arms. Well, this queen needed a slice of home. It was clearly fate.

With a smile, she headed towards the pub and straight inside. It was busy, people red-faced from drink and laughter. Whoever was running it, Brits she supposed, had done a decent job. It felt like it had been plucked straight out of a cobbled London street and dropped into this alien city with its tightly packed skyscrapers, rowdy bars and sidewalks pocked with grates and lined with garbage bags. Vanessa closed her eyes for a moment and left all that behind as she exhaled. The walls in here were adorned with classic British pub decor – dark wood panelling, antique brass fixtures, and a dartboard that had seen better days. A muted TV in the corner was even showing a Premier League match. The scent of fish and chips wafted from the kitchen, mingling with the aroma of ale, triggering a sense of nostalgia and homesickness in Vanessa that almost overwhelmed her.

Vanessa headed to the bar and ordered herself a rum and Cherry Coke, settling on one of the stools. As she sipped her drink, a man

Tracy Buchanan

dressed all in black with multiple piercings took the stool next to her, his thigh pressing against hers. 'Hey, honey, you're a breath of fresh air. Can I buy you another drink?' he breathed.

Vanessa paused, the rim of her glass still pressed to her lips. She set her drink down, ice cubes chiming as she looked the man over; he was decent enough to look at, but she wasn't in the mood for company tonight, especially the kind of company that invaded her personal space without permission. 'I'm afraid I'm more a tempest than a breath of fresh air tonight. Best not to get too close,' she said, moving her thigh away from his.

The man's eyebrows knitted together. 'You saying no to a free drink?'

'It won't be free, though, will it?'

Annoyance flickered across his face. 'Just trying to be friendly. Jesus Christ, you Brits.'

'Yeah, we're the worst, aren't we?'

He huffed, then turned on his heel and stalked off. As he did, Vanessa noticed a figure watching her from nearby.

Nils Thorsen.

He was near the entrance, completely out of sync with the pub's rustic charm in his sharply tailored suit and steady gaze. His eyes locked on hers, and unease unfurled in Vanessa's stomach as she thought of the oddly intimate gift she'd received from his family.

Nils strolled over and took the stool the other man had just vacated. She could smell alcohol on his breath.

'If you're going to say something like "fancy seeing you here" or "small world", forget it,' she said. 'I know this is no coincidence.'

'Now, Dr Marwood, why *would* you say that?' he said, voice slurring slightly.

'You're really trying to suggest you frequent places like this?' she asked, gesturing around her.

'Even a club owner needs a break from his own kingdom. Besides,' he leaned in closer, 'there's something exhilarating about anonymity, don't you agree?'

She moved away from him. 'Yes, I do. Like how I prefer random people not to know my personal address *or* be aware of where I'm drinking at any given moment.'

Nils frowned. 'Personal address?'

'The plant delivery.'

'What do you mean?'

Vanessa reached for her phone, showing Nils the photo she'd taken of the plants and the note that came with them. Nils was quiet for a few moments then he shook his head. 'My mother uses that florist. She's the one who sent them to you, not me.'

'Why would your mother send *me* a gift? We've not even met.'

A flicker of anger crossed his blue eyes. 'Much like God, my mother works in mysterious ways. You've clearly captured her attention, you poor thing.'

Vanessa stared at the photo of the plants, a new unease spreading over her. How strange.

Nils gestured to the barman, ordering a single malt scotch. 'I heard rumours you were caught up in a raid just now,' he remarked.

Vanessa said nothing. She didn't want to jeopardise the case. Another few sips and she'd leave, she told herself. But then she thought of the insects she'd seen, helpless *and* dangerous. 'The people who run those auctions can't truly comprehend the damage they're doing to our ecosystem. It *disgusts* me.'

He shot her a wry smile as he downed the shot, then ordered another. 'There is far worse being done to our ecosystem, trust me.'

'Is that an admission of involvement with the trade?' Vanessa could not stop herself from asking, as she pinned him with a hot gaze.

Nils didn't answer. Just stared ahead of him.

'Why are you even here?' Vanessa asked.

His face grew serious. 'I need you to know I had *nothing* to do with Cordelia's death.'

'Isn't that something you should be telling the NYPD?'

'No, you're more of a rational individual than the rest of those NYPD imbeciles. Cordelia deserves better than them. Better than Hoshino.'

His voice cracked when he uttered Cordelia's name. 'You and Cordelia were close, weren't you?'

'We were friends . . . with benefits,' Nils admitted, his fingertips whitening as he pressed them into the glass, taking a long sip of his drink. 'Maybe it was going to be more, I don't know. She had authenticity, a rare quality. She wasn't crafted from pretence like so many others.' His blue eyes flared with anger. 'Despite what the likes of "AuthenticAegis" might suggest.'

'I've seen those videos,' Vanessa said. 'I have to say, some of the sentiments, like "evil inauthentic" and "facades of grandeur hiding the rotten cores within", came to mind at your auction earlier.'

'Not *my* auction,' he hissed.

'Then whose?'

More silence.

'If you really cared about Cordelia,' she said gently, 'you'd cooperate fully with the police.'

'Cooperate? With Detective Hoshino?' he spat. 'I wouldn't trust him if I were you.'

'What do you mean by that?'

'Aren't you curious why he chose to remove himself from the NYPD for a year?'

'Is that what happened? It was his choice?'

Nils held her gaze then shook his head. 'It doesn't matter.'

'Fine,' Vanessa said. 'If you don't trust Detective Hoshino, then talk to me.'

He was quiet for a few moments then his shoulders slumped. 'What really bothered me when Hoshino showed me a photo of the hair clip Cordelia was wearing is she hated *any* kind of animal cruelty. It was something we argued about. She didn't like the way collectors like me treated creatures as though they were mere objects. So to have a hair clip like that just didn't make sense. Then he mentioned the *gift* element.'

Vanessa leaned forward. 'And?'

'My mother's PA mentioned receiving an email from a client last week, thanking them for some Valentine's Day gift,' Nils said. 'The client had received a ring featuring a rare ruby-tailed wasp set in amber.'

Vanessa flinched. Another creature wasted.

'The box,' Nils continued, 'and even the note with it, featured our branding. Hence why the client linked it to us. But it wasn't from us.'

'I need this person's name. They could be in danger.'

'Don't worry, I did my due diligence after the detective revealed the nature of the hair clip. They're fine.'

'So you've checked with your *entire* client list?'

There was a flicker of hesitation on his face. 'Obviously, we have a rather extensive client list, but our team are continuing with their enquiries.'

'So more could be out there without you knowing?' Nils didn't answer. '*Jesus*, Nils,' Vanessa said, 'this is serious. Three people have already died, someone you adored being one of them. This could be some sick attempt to sabotage you and your family . . . your business. What's stopping you sharing the list?'

'My mother.'

'Then you need to talk to your mother, stat.'

Nils took in a shuddery breath. 'I know. She won't be happy.' He stood up. 'Do not mention this to Detective Hoshino.'

'I have to.'

Nils shook his head. 'No. He will rush in and make contact with my mother. *She* needs to be the one to make the first move.'

'Are you serious? It's like watching the courtship of the peacock spider.'

'You're quite right,' Nils said, face very serious. 'One wrong move from the male spider and he'll get his head bitten off. Literally.'

Chapter 23

Ru sat at the breakfast bar in his kitchen, tucking into his favourite breakfast: a very colourful and incredibly unhealthy bowl of Froot Loops. The buzz of his phone cut through the morning's quiet. It was a message from Souta.

> I'm gonna be King of the Pirates . . . and your mom's katsudon. See you at the restaurant tonight, usual time?

Ru smiled. The *King of the Pirates* quote was from their favourite manga when they were kids: *One Piece*. It was good news his old friend would be meeting them. Maybe he'd see more of him from now on?

He was about to reply when his phone started vibrating with a rare call from the captain. A jolt ran through him – was it another body? Or maybe the captain had changed his mind about keeping Ru on. He picked it up.

'Detective Hoshino,' the captain's voice boomed down the phone. 'I just had a call from Jacqueline Thorsen. She has asked you to come to her offices to talk.'

'Did she tell you why?'

'No, but this is what *I'm* telling you: you better behave yourself, Hoshino.'

'Always, Captain.'

Half an hour later, Ru was standing in front of the building from which the Thorsens ran their more legitimate businesses. Sitting between the glass and steel titans of Lower Manhattan, its carved stone and Art Deco facade set it apart from its more modernist neighbours, a sign of the Thorsen family's long-standing influence in the city.

Stepping inside, Ru was ushered through a lobby that was all marble and hushed tones, and past security that seemed more suited to guarding a fortress than a business office. The elevator whisked him to the top floor, doors opening to reveal an office with floor-to-ceiling windows, the Hudson River gleaming in the distance.

Jacqueline Thorsen awaited him, seated behind a mahogany desk. In her mid-sixties, she carried her age like armour, her hair a mane of silver that framed a well-maintained face etched with the lines of a thousand negotiations, betrayals and victories. Her suit was impeccable, her eyes sharp as she watched Ru enter. Cold, too, which didn't surprise him considering the Thorsens blamed him for her husband's death.

The last time he'd seen Jacqueline had been at her husband's death scene. She had arrived from a yoga class so was still wearing her yoga pants, her silver hair pulled back from her pale, make-up-free face. She looked different now. Like the boss he'd learned she was.

'Detective Hoshino,' she began, a hint of Scandinavian in her cold voice. 'Let's not waste time, shall we? I understand my son has been of interest to you in connection with the unfortunate demise of Cordelia Montgomery.'

'Yes. Your son's connections to Miss Montgomery are . . . intriguing.'

She sighed. 'My son has always enjoyed a diverse social circle. She will be one of many actresses he knows.'

'But how many of those actresses have ended up dead the day after he was with them?'

Her gaze turned even colder. 'And how many witnesses under your care have ended up dead?'

He held her gaze, refusing to be drawn into the past. This case was what was important right now.

She moved on. 'I believe you're also delving into a rather peculiar aspect of this case. Something about . . . insects?'

Ru nodded. 'Indeed. How do you know about this?'

Her smile was thin, almost imperceptible. 'I make it my business to know things, Detective. Especially when it concerns my family and our enterprises. So, to confirm, one of our enterprises is, indeed, a jewellery line that incorporates insects into its designs.'

So this *was* her game, then. Coming clean. Nearly. 'Rare insects?' he asked.

'Some.'

'I'm not convinced the US Fish and Wildlife Service would take kindly to rare insects being used for embellishment.'

'It's not a crime to use deceased insects as art,' Jacqueline replied calmly. 'I can assure you that all the insects we use are sourced ethically and all deceased before they ever become part of our collection.'

He scrutinised her face. All the evidence told him she was lying. How easily deception seemed to come to the Thorsens.

'But this is not why I have called you here,' she said. 'You're a homicide detective, after all, not an agent for the US Fish and Wildlife Service. And anyway,' she added, leaning forward, her elbows on the table, 'wouldn't Dr Vanessa Marwood be the one to deal with any insect-related aspects of this investigation?'

'You know Dr Marwood?'

'I'm familiar with her.'

'How?'

She didn't answer that question, instead saying: 'Let's move on to what I want to share with you. Something *interesting* happened recently that I believe might be pertinent to your case. Two of our clients got in touch just after Valentine's Day to thank us for the gifts they'd received from us . . . Gifts we didn't send.'

Now *this* was interesting. 'What kind of gifts?' Ru asked.

'Insect jewellery. A ring, and a pair of earrings. As I said, we did *not* send these items.'

'I need the names of those two people,' Ru said, 'and your whole client list.'

'The two names, I can supply you with. But the rest is not possible.'

'Why? If everything's above board?'

'We pride ourselves on discretion,' Jacqueline said.

Ru detested the way people used discretion as an excuse for dubious morals. 'This is a multiple homicide case. A case where items delivered in *your* packaging, featuring the kind of jewellery *you* create, play a huge role. You understand that I will have to question your staff, and I will get a court order to subpoena your records if you don't hand them over willingly. Which approach do you think will help with the image you so carefully curate? Cooperating with the police . . . or blocking an investigation? How will it look to your clients – to the world – if you failed to prevent further deaths? Listen,' he added, leaning forward, 'I imagine you, too, must be as desperate as we are to uncover who is doing this under your name. Let's work together to find out.'

Jacqueline was quiet for a few moments. Then she nodded. 'It seems,' she said, 'we find ourselves with aligning interests, Detective Hoshino, if only momentarily. You are free to question our staff. I will also have our client list sent to you today. As for the two names.' She got a pen out and scribbled them down onto a plain piece of paper, sliding it across the desk. 'We have made contact with Kendra, but not Madeline.'

Kendra Grey (wasp ring)

Madeline Layton (spider earrings)

Kendra Grey didn't ring a bell, but Madeline . . . Wasn't that the influencer who'd been at the funeral and the auction, too, the night before?

'Thank you for your cooperation, Mrs Thorsen,' he said, taking the piece of paper and slipping it into his coat pocket, keen to track these two potential victims down.

'Oh, don't worry,' Jacqueline replied. 'It won't come without a price.'

Ru frowned. What did she mean by that? It didn't matter. He didn't have time for the Thorsens' games. His priority now was to locate these two women. He marched out of Jacqueline's office, calling Harris as he walked. By the time he left the building the team were already hard at work tracking down the names.

'So,' Ramos said, falling into step beside him as Ru arrived at the precinct, 'I got an address for Madeline Layton from the system, but when officers went around, her roommate said she'd moved into a new place a few weeks back. Looks like she hasn't registered that address, and the flatmate only knows it's somewhere in SoHo. The number she has for her just goes through to voicemail, and she's not replying to my messages via her social media platforms. *But* judging from the TikTok live she did an hour ago, she's fine.'

Ru nodded. 'That's a relief. But it's crucial we keep trying to track her down. What about Kendra Grey?'

'Better luck with her. I managed to speak to her on the phone and guess what? She's a journalist for the *Chislington Post*, one of the publications Jerry Bowman owns.'

'Interesting.'

'Luckily, she never wore the ring that was sent to her. Said the only reason she was on their client list in the first place was because she was investigating illegal insect trading.'

'Do you believe her?'

Ramos gave Ru a look. 'She writes about celebrities for a living, Boss, I'm not sure investigative reporting is her thing. Either way, we've sent some forensic guys to collect the ring from her place and I'll go talk to her tomorrow.'

'Why tomorrow?'

'She's out of town until then. But she said her landlord had a key he'll share with us and she told us exactly where the gift box with the ring is.'

'Good.'

They walked into the squad room where the lieutenant was already waiting with Harris, Bouchier and a few others.

'I hope you have your phone voices ready,' Ru said to a group of six junior officers in the corner of the room. 'As soon as I receive that list from Jacqueline Thorsen, you'll be making calls to their clients, seeing if they received any gifts and ensuring they are safe.'

'We will also be conducting interviews with their staff,' Haworth added. 'I'll ask for extra officers to help with this. As for the rest of you: briefing room, please. I believe Detective Hoshino has done another one of his presentations for us.'

They all followed her into the small room. Ru went up to the laptop attached to the presentation screen and began to type the word 'Method', his words reflected on the screen.

'Let's further our profile of this killer,' he said, looking up at the faces in the room, 'by drilling down into what they needed to carry these acts out. Looking at their *method* will open up multiple routes that could lead us to them.'

'Well, if you're a Thorsen, you have it all in your back pocket,' Harris said. 'The gift boxes, the jewellery, the insects, the addresses.'

'Yes. But I'm not sure I believe the Thorsens are behind this,' Ru replied. 'The fact Jacqueline cooperated speaks volumes. And why would they sabotage their brand and business?' Ru clicked on the remote control and photos of the insects found with the jewellery items appeared. 'How would these insects have been procured? Rare, expensive, illegal.'

'The dark web seems obvious,' Bouchier said.

Ru nodded. 'Indeed. Which will make it difficult to pin down, as the dark web operates on anonymity. But Bronagh at NovaScope is looking into this.'

Another series of images popped up, this time close-ups of the jewellery pieces. He turned to Ramos who was sitting down, rubbing her belly. 'You OK?' he asked her.

'You should go home,' Haworth added.

'Not a chance,' Ramos said. Ru had known Ramos for ten years now, since she'd joined the force as a young recruit. There was no point trying to talk her into doing something she didn't want to do.

'Stubborn as always,' Haworth said with a small smile. 'I hear you've been checking out websites to see if there are any similar pieces, based on the likely scenario that our killer has modified jewellery they've acquired rather than creating pieces from scratch. How's that going?'

'We've got five pieces now to research: the hair clip, man's bracelet and watch that were all worn by the victims,' Ramos replied, 'and the ring and earrings Jacqueline Thorsen informed us about. So far I've found a couple of Etsy shops that sell jewellery in a similar style, minus the insects and injectors and so on. I'll be getting in touch with them today.'

Another series of images appeared, with close-ups of the items used to harm the victims: the minuscule injectors and pressure pads.

'Where would someone source this kind of equipment?' Haworth asked.

'Not easily,' Adiche said. 'I've been chatting to various suppliers – especially medical suppliers – to get a sense of where these items could be accessed.'

'So we're talking medical staff?' Harris asked.

'Potentially.'

Another click of the remote control, and this time a photo of the gift box appeared.

'Packaging,' Ru said, adding this to the growing list under 'Method' on the screen. 'As part of our investigations, we will be talking to anyone connected with packaging the Thorsens' items. In the meantime, Adiche, any luck tracking down packagers to get a sense of where this thing might be bought in bulk?'

'Nothing yet,' Adiche said. 'But I'll keep at it. And to confirm, on the delivery side, it's likely this killer paid by cash in a USPS post office. I did think about going through footage, but the package size is so common and thousands of people go through these post offices each day. I just feel like it wouldn't be worth it.'

Ru nodded. 'Agreed.'

Harris looked at his watch. 'Probably best we cancel the drinks we've already cancelled a million times, then. Can get some pizza in instead?'

'I won't hear of it,' Haworth said. 'If we get these calls done, a couple of drinks won't harm. Delay them anymore and you'll all be retired. Anyway, it's good for morale, especially at a time like this. I can hold the fort here. I'll call you if I need you.'

'I'll stay behind, too,' Ru said.

'Not a chance, Hoshino,' Haworth insisted. 'Anyway, if I recall, you did some of your best work from the Lock-Up bar last year.'

'Yeah, remember when you had that breakthrough after two beers and had to hotfoot it back to the office?' Harris said with a laugh.

Ru shifted uncomfortably in his chair. It was that 'breakthrough' that had led to him taking a sabbatical, something Haworth was aware of, too.

She turned to Ramos, keen to change the subject. 'While the others make phone calls, I want you to continue focusing on tracking Madeline down. Whatever it takes.'

'Sure thing, Boss.'

As she said that, Ru noticed two officers whispering as they looked at one of their phones.

'Care to share?' Haworth asked.

The officer holding the phone gave her a quick, uncomfortable look. 'Spill, Lariso,' Harris said to the officer.

'There's an article that's just gone live in the *Chislington Post*, Detective Hoshino,' the officer said hesitantly. 'About you.'

Ru got his phone out and googled his name and the *Chislington Post*.

Leaked Blog Post of Detective in Charge of Montgomery and Rossi Case Raises Ethical Questions in Current Investigation.

The real identity behind an anonymous article written for online blogging platform, Medium, has been revealed as Detective Ru Hoshino – the very lead detective working on the recent deaths of actress Cordelia Montgomery and fashion designer Maximilian Rossi. In a post last year, under the pseudonym of 'Grit City Guardian', Hoshino revealed his unorthodox views on society, social media, and the very nature of humanity. The post, titled 'The Unseen Stage: A Critique of Modernity', depicts New York City as an 'unprecedented theatre' where, in Hoshino's words, 'reality and illusion blur. It's a place where the truth is often masked by the performances we put on daily.'

Though the post is believed to have been removed over a year ago, screenshots have emerged online from anonymous sources, including content management tags linking it to Hoshino's NYPD email address. Hoshino's text raises particular alarm bells in light of the recent murders, especially passages where he describes influencers as 'modern-day jesters', engrossed in a 'carnival of ego', painting a bleak picture of a society obsessed with vanity and superficiality.

The leaked material provides a compelling glimpse into the mind of Detective Hoshino, and could explain why the officer is believed to have taken a year off from his duties. While it is intellectual and thought-provoking, it also raises questions about the detective's approach to his work, particularly in his current case.

As the city continues to reel from the impact of a spate of high-profile murders, Hoshino's words gain an eerie relevance.

'Jesus, Hoshino,' Harris said as he looked up from his phone. 'The captain is going to lose his mind.'

But Ru wasn't concerned about that. Instead, he was thinking about what Jacqueline had said an hour ago: *Don't worry. It won't come without a price.*

Chapter 24

Vanessa stepped inside the Lock-Up bar for Egbo's birthday drinks that night, pleased to escape the mini snow blizzard outside. She'd been to the bar a few times before. Based just a ten-minute walk from the NovaScope offices, it was popular with the team. It was also a favourite of NYPD officers with walls adorned with vintage mugshots and memorabilia, sounds of blues and classic rock echoing off the steel-barred faux jail cells, and 'criminally' good cocktails. Bronagh had told Vanessa it used to be a normal bar until the high number of police and forensic officials who attended made the new owner decide to play on the theme.

'Vanessa! Over here!' Egbo waved from a table surrounded by several people, some Vanessa recognised, some she didn't. To her surprise, among them was Agent Valdez. Vanessa smoothed down the soft material of her black and red flared skirt, and headed over to the table, the agent's deep-set brown eyes surveying her as she did. His skin tone was deep olive like hers. His hair, neat and meticulously styled, was a rich shade of chestnut, each strand seemingly in its rightful place. He was wearing a navy cable-knit jumper revealing subtly muscled arms.

'Dr Marwood,' he said as she took the seat across from him.

'Agent Valdez,' she replied, giving him a nod. 'I didn't expect to see you here.'

'Egbo and I go way back. Oh, and call me Dariel.'

'Vanessa.' She turned to Egbo. 'Happy birthday. Sorry I'm late, there were no taxis.'

'Taxis,' Dariel said. 'You Brits sure have a whole different language.'

Vanessa shot him a look. 'Yes, that language is known as the English language . . . from *England*.'

Everyone around the table laughed, including Dariel.

'OK,' Dariel said, standing up, 'I'm getting this round and *you*,' he added, pointing at Egbo, 'get a double.'

As Dariel took drink orders, Vanessa was enveloped in the chatter. Tom, the trace evidence analyst, was passionately debating the value of hair strands versus blood samples in a murder investigation with the birthday boy. Jamie was flirting with Sophia, the young forensic documents expert, while Bronagh teased his flirting technique. As Vanessa joined in with the chat, she felt the tensions of the past few days dissolve a little. She glanced around the table at her colleagues, all immersed in their own worlds of forensic intricacies, and felt a momentary sense of belonging. It was a strange career, one that straddled the line between life and death, and Vanessa felt grateful to be with people who understood that tension.

'No way. Is that Detective Hoshino?' Sofia asked, watching as a tall man slunk across the room. Vanessa followed her gaze. It *was* Ru. He made his way to a nearby table where some other officers she recognised from the case were sitting.

'I can't believe *he's* out,' Sofia said in a low voice. 'That blog post of his that was leaked is intense.'

'What blog post?' Vanessa asked.

Bronagh did a search on her phone and handed it to Vanessa. As Vanessa skimmed the article her eyebrows rose with each line. She glanced up, watching Ru as he stood in the middle of the bar, looking awkwardly around him. Was this what Nils had meant the night before when he'd warned her she couldn't trust him?

'Did you hear he gatecrashed the captain's daughter's birthday dinner the other night?' Jamie asked.

'We were there,' Bronagh said. She filled them in on what she'd witnessed with Vanessa.

Dariel knocked back his beer, eyes narrowed as he watched Ru. 'I'd go mental if someone did that at my daughter's birthday.'

Vanessa watched Dariel with interest. So he had a daughter? No wedding ring, though.

'Maybe he had a good reason to gatecrash the dinner,' Jamie said with a shrug. 'If the suspect was using his influence to get released and the captain just bowled over and let him do it, I get why Detective Hoshino would be annoyed.'

'I don't know,' Dariel said. 'I've heard he's difficult to work with.'

'I wouldn't agree with that,' Bronagh said. 'I worked with him on cases back when I was at the NYPD labs and I'd say Hoshino is the best detective in New York. A bit of a genius, in fact.'

'The quirky genius vibe doesn't make him a skilled detective,' Dariel said. He turned to Vanessa. 'What do you think about him?'

Vanessa watched Ru as he folded himself into a chair with his colleagues, looking incredibly uncomfortable. 'I think his brain is wired a bit differently from other cops,' she observed, 'and that might be what makes him such a good detective.'

And could make him a danger? a small voice within her asked. She reprimanded herself. Is this what her brother had done to her, made her suspect even the most unlikely of people?

'Hey, Bug Lady!' a voice called out. It was Harris, who'd finally noticed their presence. Ru's dark eyes glided over to her, then to Valdez. 'Look, it's Bronagh, too,' Harris said. 'Let's put our tables together.'

Everyone got up and started shuffling the tables together. Vanessa noticed the pregnant officer, too, her stomach straining against the white top she was wearing. Over the next hour, the conversation was a lively one between the police and forensic officers as they shared various cases they'd worked on together. Only Ru was silent, watching on quietly as he sipped what looked like water.

Jamie, emboldened by alcohol, eventually nudged the conversation towards Ru. 'We were talking about your blog post earlier, Detective Hoshino.' Bronagh gave him a sharp look. 'I hope you don't mind me bringing it up,' Jamie quickly added.

'Of course not,' Ru replied. 'Discussion is the first step towards understanding, Jamie.'

Vanessa observed Ru from across the table, noting how his voice remained calm, but his fingers tapped an irregular rhythm against the side of his glass – a Morse code of anxiety.

Dariel leaned back in his chair. 'Dangerous game, though, Detective, especially considering your position.'

Harris laughed. 'You wildlife types scared of danger?'

'Not scared. Just professional,' Dariel replied. 'As someone who heads up a department, I'm aware of the pressures your captain faces. It's a delicate ecosystem.'

'Tell me, Agent Valdez,' Ru said, 'does that delicate ecosystem involve having dinner at a restaurant owned by a known crime family implicated in an ongoing murder case?'

Dariel raised a dark eyebrow. 'That's where the captain's daughter's birthday was?'

Ru nodded.

'Then fuck the ecosystem,' Dariel said, 'that's just plain wrong.'

'Hell, yeah!' Harris exclaimed, clanging his bottle of beer against Dariel's.

Ru downed his water. 'I must go now.'

'You've only been here an hour,' Harris exclaimed.

'Sixty-eight minutes,' Ru said, looking at his watch. 'I showed my face. I have a dinner awaiting me, then more work.'

'Too much peopling for the night?' the young pregnant officer asked Ru as he stood up.

He smiled down at her slightly. 'Something like that, Ramos.' With a quick nod to Vanessa, he headed straight out.

The two joint tables settled back into easy banter. After a while, Jamie picked up the topic of Ru again, voice low enough that Ru's colleagues couldn't hear. 'Do you think Detective Hoshino's too close to it all, especially as the Thorsens might be involved?'

'How's he involved with the Thorsens?' Sofia asked.

'He was the one transporting Ebbe Thorsen to the precinct when he was shot,' Bronagh explained. 'The Thorsens blame the detective for it.'

Sofia's eyebrows shot up. 'Shit. I read about Ebbe Thorsen's death. He was like a proper drug baron, wasn't he?'

'He definitely had a lot of money,' Jamie said, 'and now he's passed it to his wife. My friend works in real estate – he just sold her this apartment on Fifth Avenue, right near Central Park. You should *see* the place.' He pulled his phone out and flicked through the photos, holding one up to show them. 'This is just the hallway. My friend's there tonight, actually, as Jacqueline's hosting a housewarming and invited her.'

Vanessa couldn't help but lean in to look at the photo like the others, drawn into Jamie's enthusiasm and the three glasses of rum and Cherry Coke she'd already sunk. The photo showed a hallway – understated yet undeniably opulent. A plush carpet runner lined the floor, leading through the corridor towards a huge window which offered a panoramic view of the iconic Central Park.

'Very nice,' Vanessa agreed. She was about to turn away when something caught her attention: a sculpture positioned prominently on a sleek table. A chill ran down her spine as she took in the abstract swirl of metal and wood. It bore an uncanny resemblance to one of her mother's creations. What were the chances Jacqueline Thorsen had purchased a sculpture by a small-time artist like Vanessa's mother, of all people?

'You OK?' Dariel asked as he noticed the way her expression changed.

'Fine. Just need another drink. Who's in?' She took her purse from her bag and headed to the bar. But over the next hour, what she'd seen played on her mind, that fleeting glimpse of her mother at the club and the fact her mother had lived in New York for a while beating inside her like a drum.

As she stepped out at the end of the night, the evening air was freezing cold, a welcome relief after the warmth of the crowded bar. Vanessa, Bronagh and Dariel stood on the snowy street, their voices a murmur against the distant city sounds as they waited for their taxis.

'Ergh,' Bronagh slurred, massaging her temple as she swayed slightly. 'I just know I'll have a hangover tomorrow and Mr Grumpy Pants Thompson will be angry at me.'

'You mean Joe?' Vanessa asked.

Bronagh nodded. 'Honestly, he's been sooo irritable lately. Super distant, too. I don't know *what's* going on with him.'

Vanessa and Dariel exchanged a look. The alcohol was clearly making Bronagh overshare. She had drunk a *lot* of red wine. But then Vanessa didn't exactly feel sober.

'Where are you staying, Dariel?' Vanessa asked, changing the subject but making a note to check in on Bronagh the next day.

'Just some hotel uptown. Nothing special,' he replied. 'Better than a four-hour drive home.'

'Where do you live?' Vanessa asked.

'Cortland, near the offices.'

Bronagh smiled. 'Gorgeous area.'

'Yeah, it's not bad,' Dariel agreed. 'Actually, come visit the office sometime, Vanessa. We've got this whole section of insect exhibits. I think you'd like it.'

Behind his back, Bronagh raised an eyebrow. Vanessa's gaze lingered on Dariel. If her mind wasn't still filled with that hauntingly familiar sculpture, she might suggest they stay for one more drink, and see where it led. But she suddenly had an urgent need to go home and find that photo again.

A taxi pulled up then, its yellow light cutting through the darkness. 'Ladies first,' Dariel said. 'I'm in the opposite direction.'

'Take care, handsome,' Bronagh slurred, giving Dariel a kiss on the cheek as he looked at Vanessa, bemused.

'Good to see you outside of a raid,' Vanessa added, helping Bronagh into the taxi.

'Yeah, hopefully see you again,' he replied meaningfully.

Vanessa stepped into the waiting taxi, casting one last glance at Dariel.

As soon as she got back to her apartment, she found the photo again. It really *did* look like one of her mother's sculptures. She googled Jacqueline Thorsen, finding plenty of pictures of her at various social events, characterised by her striking, silver-streaked hair and power suits.

Then she noticed an older photo featuring a young-looking Jacqueline standing in front of a bar with four other women . . . one of which looked just like Vanessa's mother.

She gripped the edge of the table. Was it really her mum?

It wasn't the best photo, blurry and taken from a distance. But she had the same centre-parted curly hair her mother had in the photos Vanessa had seen of her time studying art in New York. As

Vanessa studied the photo more, she realised one of the other women bore an uncanny resemblance to Helena Oberlin, the mother of her ex, Damon. But Vanessa's mother hadn't met Helena until she'd moved to Greensands a couple of years after she returned from New York . . . right?

Vanessa grabbed her phone and scrolled through to a number she'd been tempted to call many times since arriving in New York: Damon Oberlin. It was past ten in New York, which would make it the early hours in the UK. Would he even be awake? She dialled his number anyway, and he eventually answered.

'Vanessa Marwood,' he said, his voice oozing down the line in all its British aristocratic smoothness, 'to what do I owe this unexpected pleasure?'

She imagined him leaning up in his bed in the middle of his family's country manor, a sardonic smile on his handsome face. Vanessa's heart fluttered, the remnants of their unresolved history making her slightly uneasy.

'Sorry, I know it's late – or early, even,' she said.

'No, no, it's fine, I'm up reading about the empress cicada for my new show. *Fascinating* creature. Did you know the female is known for her selective and, let's say, *decisive* mating rituals? She draws in the males with her song, but only the most persistent and resilient get her attention. And once she's done? She's off, leaving a trail of broken-hearted admirers in her wake.'

Vanessa shook her head. 'Nice try, Damon. I'm no heartbreaker, though.'

'Well, worth a shot.' He let out a yawn. 'How *is* New York?'

'Fine. Very busy. Look, I need to ask you something. I'm sending you a photo. Is that your mother at the back?'

There was a brief pause as he checked his email. 'Yes, that's her. And yours, too. The fact they're both with the incomparable Jacqueline Thorsen confirms it.'

'You *know* Jacqueline Thorsen?'

'Yes, and in fact, you would have met her, too. She attended quite a few soirees at the manor back in the day.'

Dread filled Vanessa's stomach. Her father had worked for Damon's father, the owner of the now closed Greensands Butterfly Farm. The Oberlins used to host a variety of events at the manor, some of which she attended with her family.

Vanessa chewed at her lip, mind racing. 'You know the Thorsens are dodgy as hell, right?' she said eventually.

'I know that *now*. I didn't have a clue then. Honestly, Vanessa, my father knows all kinds of people. Well, I say *know*. I mean how anyone "knows" anyone in high society – vaguely, superficially, and always with a raised eyebrow.'

'But my mother didn't know your parents until she moved to Greensands *after* she was in New York. After I was born! And yet here she is, in a photo with your mother.'

'Well, then, it seems our mothers knew each other for longer than we thought. What can I say? I didn't keep track of my mother's friendships.' He paused. 'Is Jacqueline Thorsen tied up with the Cordelia Montgomery case? I'd place a fair wager you're involved, too.'

Vanessa kept quiet.

'Look, truth is,' Damon said with a sigh, 'I really don't know much about this woman *or* her connection with my family. My father seemed to know anyone and everyone back in the day, from saintly Buddhists to gang leaders like this. I'll ask him. Will that make you happy?'

'Thanks, I'd appreciate it.'

'How's the Big Apple treating you otherwise?' Damon said. 'Do the larvae talk in thick Bronx accents?'

Vanessa couldn't help but smile. 'Damon, I think you need to retake your zoology master's. Larvae do *not* possess vocal cords.'

'But wouldn't it be exciting if they did? You know, I was considering a little new year jaunt . . .' His voice trailed off. She very nearly offered to host him at the apartment. Again, damn that rum. But then she remembered things invariably ended badly when she spent time with Damon.

'Let me know if you do,' she said instead, 'I can take you on a tour of the Smithsonian to up your knowledge of larvae.'

'That sounds delightful.' He grew serious. 'This has been nice, hearing your voice, even if it's slurred. Let me guess? Rum?'

Vanessa sighed, rubbing at her temples. 'Yes, too much rum.'

'Feel free to call me next time you have too much rum. I'm always here for you. And good luck with your maggots and mysteries. I'm sure you'll figure it out. I always think of you like a dung beetle.'

Vanessa's mouth dropped open. 'I don't know how to respond to that.'

'It's a compliment! What I mean is, you've got that same focus and strength, pushing through until you uncover the truth, no matter how messy it gets.'

Vanessa smiled. 'Fine, I'll take that. Look, I better go. But . . . look after yourself, OK? And good luck with the next show.'

He sighed. 'Will do. Take care, my little dung beetle. Always remember, I'm just a phone call away.'

Vanessa hung up, smiling. While her past with Damon was complicated, knowing he was a phone call away *did* provide a strange comfort. She strolled to her drinks cabinet, pouring herself more rum before putting on some Nick Cave and the Bad Seeds. She settled into her plush green velvet armchair, glass of rum in hand. The amber liquid flickered in the dim light as she swirled it around, lost in thought. Her laptop sat open on the coffee table, its screen awash with tabs of various articles, social media posts and photographs – all painting a vivid yet opaque picture of Jacqueline Thorsen.

She took a sip of her rum, feeling the warmth spread through her body. Jacqueline seemed to be everywhere and nowhere, a woman woven into the fabric of both New York's high society and the UK's elite. What were the odds that her mother knew her too? And the Oberlins? That she'd even been to Greensands?

She wished she had all the answers.

She thought of what Damon had said about her pushing through until she uncovered the truth, no matter how messy it got.

Didn't Jamie say Jacqueline was hosting a party that night? Maybe Vanessa would get her answers there.

Impulse overtook her. Perhaps it was the rum, or maybe the accumulation of stress and curiosity. She swiftly downed what remained of her glass and strode along the hallway, pausing to look at herself in the mirror. *Who are you doing this for, Vanessa?* she thought. *And what are you hoping to find?*

Then she stepped out into the night, ready to find answers.

Chapter 25

Hoshino Restaurant was situated in St Marks Place in the East Village, its facade a welcoming mix of sleek, modern glass and traditional Japanese woodwork. Ru made his way through the maze of tables, the scent of traditional Japanese cuisine blending with the soft murmur of conversation. It instantly brought back memories of being there as a child, his homework sprawled out in front of him as his mother glanced over every now and again with a frown on her face.

He imagined he'd get a similar frown soon, turning up late. Maybe worse if she'd read about that blog post of his. But then, she wasn't one to read the news.

One person who did know was the captain, who'd already left him several messages to call him. Messages Ru was choosing to ignore. Ru thought back to when the captain had first called him in, confronting him with the blog post. When he'd asked how he knew it was him, the captain had kept quiet. But now he wondered if Jacqueline Thorsen had told him.

'Maybe it's time you took a couple of weeks off, Hoshino?' the captain had said. 'Reading this makes me realise there's been a lot of pressure on you after you were shot. You came back too soon.'

'A piece of writing offering my views – *anonymously*, I might add – on New York shallowness does not make me unfit to work, Captain.'

The captain had tilted his head. 'I'm not advising you, Detective Hoshino, I'm *telling* you. Take the time.'

After that talk, Ru applied for a year's sabbatical. The very fact he'd drunkenly posted his manifesto from a NYPD computer had shown him he'd grown sloppy. He needed time out to regroup.

'Ru! *Suwatte kudasai. Shukudai o shi nasai.*' His reverie was broken as his mother's voice called out to him to sit down. Ru obliged, taking a seat at his usual spot at the back of the restaurant, a two-seater table so tucked into the corner it was virtually part of the wall. As he sank down, he felt the day's worries dissipate a little. A day spent trying to track down all the Thorsens' clients with the rest of his team. Some names he recognised as notable figures: singers, writers, directors. Many, unsurprisingly, didn't answer their phones. Those who did insisted they had not received any insect-related gifts on Valentine's Day. He was particularly concerned about Madeline, who still hadn't responded all day to phone calls, and messages via social media. Next step would be to put a call out on the force's social media platforms, which he was currently talking to the media team about.

Ru forced his mind off work and watched as his mother attended to a nearby table of businessmen, a plate of fugu the centre of their attention, its translucent slices fanned out like the petals of a dangerous flower. The preparation of fugu – pufferfish, as it was better known – was an art form and a dance with death. Only chefs certified through rigorous training could prepare it, removing the lethal toxins that resided within with precision, leaving just enough thrill behind.

Ru remembered his own grandfather meticulously preparing fugu in the family kitchen, his skilled hands moving with exactitude and reverence, a silent dance of tradition and expertise. His mother, young and eager, would watch intently, waiting to taste the dish that symbolised both danger and good fortune, a rite of passage wrapped in family legacy.

Ru watched one of the businessmen lift a piece of fugu to his lips now, the other men observing with smiles playing on their lips. As the man savoured the bite, Ru pondered the allure of risk in culinary traditions. For the Japanese, eating fugu was connected to a deeper cultural narrative. Pufferfish were revered by the Japanese, regarded as a symbol of good fortune and often served at celebratory events to bring luck and prosperity.

As he thought that, Ru noticed a familiar figure walk in. Souta, his old friend. He made his way to the table, eyes darting about. Ru's mother hadn't noticed him yet and maybe that was for the best. She would only tell him he looked too skinny, like a drug addict, without realising he was one.

'Dude,' Souta said as he took the seat across from Ru.

'Dude,' Ru replied.

'You look tired, man.'

'You look even more tired.'

'Yeah, well, nothing that a bowl of your mom's katsudon won't fix.'

One of the servers, a young girl who looked more like a ten-year-old than the twenty-year-old Ru knew her to be, approached their table.

'Detective Hoshino,' she said, bowing her head. 'The usual?'

'Yes, two bowls of katsudon instead of one,' Ru said, gesturing to Souta.

'Of course.'

When the server walked away, Souta leaned back in his chair, watching the businessmen. 'It's like unprecedented theatre,' he said, 'where reality and illusion blur.' So he'd seen the news article, considering he was quoting from it.

'Big words,' Ru said. 'Wonder where you picked those up from?'

'You, as always. *So* funny, considering you used to write the same stuff for your essays at school. Seriously, man, isn't it time you grew up?' The flicker in Souta's brown eyes showed he was joking. He leaned forward, face suddenly serious. 'Don't let them pull you down. You're obviously getting close to something. They don't like it.'

'Who's this *they* you refer to?'

'The Thorsens. The Deep State. The Powers That Be. All of them. They all blend into one.'

'You and your conspiracy theories.'

'Am I wrong, though?'

'Maybe not.'

'How's the case? I heard about the actress.'

'You know I can't tell you.'

'You did when you first started out.'

'I've grown up since, contrary to what you believe.'

Souta rolled his eyes. It was true, though; when Ru had first become a police officer, he'd shared small snippets with his friend, feeding him the drama over shared gaming and takeout sessions. They had both dreamed of becoming investigators as kids, Ru's uncanny ability to home in on truths and read people paired with Souta's charm and talent for infiltrating groups. At school, they'd confronted bullies together, found stolen items. In the end, though, Souta took his ability to fit in too far, falling down the slippery slope of drug-taking after a sporting injury got him addicted to opiates.

Their food was brought over, the familiar aroma of the crispy pork blending with the subtly sweet and savoury sauce. Ru took a blissful bite. This was what he needed, what they both needed, judging from the huge smile on Souta's face. When they were halfway through the dish, Ru's mother finally made her way across to them, her movements swift and graceful. This was the way of their regular dinners. Snatches of time.

'Souta!' she declared when she saw him.

She settled across from him and next to Ru, her hands folding neatly on the table. She was a woman who had aged like fine art, her beauty transcending the years. Her hair, peppered with silver, was styled elegantly and her deep brown eyes held much wisdom. Was that why he had never truly fallen in love with a woman? No one had come close to his mother's model of womanhood. There had been lovers. But they all felt cursory. A way to tick a box: *yes, I can be normal. Yes, I have needs.*

He thought of Vanessa Marwood. She was unlike any other woman he'd met. He hadn't been able to read her expression when the talk turned to his blog post.

'Ru, you were late,' she noted.

'I am always late, Mom.'

'Late and sickly-looking,' she said. 'Both of you boys! Souta, you look even worse. You feeding yourself properly?'

'Too busy to eat,' Souta said, the way he was spooning down his food suggesting he wasn't lying.

'Busy with your work?' Ru's mother asked. 'Pharmaceuticals, isn't it? That's what your grandmother told me the last time I saw her.'

'Sure, pharmaceuticals,' Souta said, avoiding Ru's hard glare. 'Hey, enough about me, though. Your son's working on a big investigation at the moment. It's been on the news.'

'*Pah*,' she said, waving her hand about. 'You know I watch little news these days. Too depressing. As for my son's work.' She leaned over and yanked down the top of Ru's T-shirt, trying to get a look at his bullet wound. 'How's that wound healing?'

'Mom, come on, I'm fine,' he said, batting her hand away.

'How's business, Mrs Hoshino?' Souta asked.

She clucked her tongue. 'Bad.'

Ru looked at the busy restaurant around him. 'Doesn't look bad.'

'Prices are ridiculous,' his mother snapped. 'Gone through the roof.'

'Since lockdown?' Souta asked.

'No, since last year.'

Ru frowned. 'Can't you change suppliers?'

'It's very specialist, Ru. Grasshoppers, bee larvae, the pufferfish, too,' she said, gesturing to the table of businessmen.

Ru paused just before the next helping of katsudon reached his mouth. Of course, many popular Japanese delicacies included insects, like inago no tsukudani, a traditional dish where grasshoppers were cooked in a sweet soy-based sauce.

'Who's your supplier?' Ru asked his mother.

'Kaiyo Delicacies. Real professional outfit. Always been meticulous about their deliveries. Just so expensive now!'

Ru noticed Souta frown.

The restaurant's host for the evening, a short, neat man with side-swept hair, discreetly walked over to Ru's mother then, whispering something in her ear. 'Damn it, that goddamn toilet,' his mother said as she stood up. 'We have a flood. I need to call a plumber . . . again. Yes, another expense.' She reached down and stroked Ru's cheek then Souta's, like they were still the two young boys who'd come to the restaurant after school each day. 'Find me before you leave,' she instructed, before she swept away.

'Hey,' Souta said, lowering his voice as he leaned across to Ru. 'You know the Thorsens own Kaiyo Delicacies, right?'

Ru sighed. Was this how they'd been getting back at him since last year? Target him, fine. But his mother?

'Jacqueline Thorsen is having a party at her new pad tonight, you know,' Souta said. 'Man, you should see it.'

'How do you know?' Ru asked.

Souta scrolled through his phone then held it up to Ru, showing the latest picture from Anja's Instagram account. She was pictured arm in arm with Madeline Layton, the very person they were trying to trace. Even worse, as Ru took the phone and zoomed in on the picture of Madeline, she was wearing what looked like spider earrings.

'Damn it,' Ru said. 'I have to go. Tell my mother I have urgent work business.'

Then he ran out, putting his phone to his ear and making calls, dispatching a team to Jacqueline's apartment, including an ambulance. He just had to hope they'd be in time.

Chapter 26

Vanessa had been in the city for six months and yet she still hadn't visited Central Park. Now she was getting dropped off right beside it, to attend a party she hadn't been invited to. It was nearing eleven at night, so the park was cloaked in darkness save for the occasional glint of moonlight reflecting off the freshly fallen snow. It felt like a world away from the urban pulse that bordered it. That part of Fifth Avenue reeked of money, apartment blocks lining the street like columns of privilege. Vanessa peered up at the glass and steel marvel that housed Jacqueline Thorsen's new penthouse. She adjusted her blouse and took a deep breath before catching up with a well-dressed couple making their way into the building. She was hoping she could slip in with them. But the man stopped, looking her up and down. 'Do you live here?'

'No,' she admitted. 'I'm attending an event in the penthouse suite.'

'Then you'll have the code for the elevator,' he said, letting her in. 'The elevator doors won't open without one.'

Vanessa hesitated. Should she just walk away? But that would make her look even more suspicious.

'Well, are you coming in?' the man asked.

'Of course.'

She walked in and headed over to the lift, pleased to see the couple disappear down a corridor. In the corner, a security man sat behind a counter, reading. She paused before the doors of the lift. There was a number pad on the side. She peered up at the cameras.

God, this was stupid. Bloody stupid. Damn that rum. She was about to turn on her heel and leave when the lift doors slid open. She frowned, looking over her shoulder at the security guard. Hadn't the man she'd followed in said the doors wouldn't even open without a code? But hey, who was she to question it? She stepped in and held her breath as the doors slid shut behind her. Then the lift began its journey upward. Maybe she'd be prompted for a code when she got up there? Oh well. She'd talked her way out of worse.

The lift came to a stop, and she breathed a sigh of relief as the doors slid open to reveal the very hallway she'd seen in the photos Jamie had shown her of city skyline views and hints of a snowy Central Park below. A large man walked towards the lift and looked her up and down. Then he nodded, letting her through.

Was it sheer good luck, or was someone watching, *wanting* her to enter?

Either way, Vanessa didn't care at this point. She just needed answers. She walked down the hallway, music mingling with laughter and snippets of intense conversation. As she scanned the room, her eyes fell on the sculpture she'd seen in the photo. Perched on a table, almost shrouded in the shadows, it was an intricate piece crafted from metal and wood. Of course, it was an insect – a praying mantis, poised in an attack stance. The wooden elements seemed to give it an organic texture, an almost lifelike quality, while the iron provided a contrasting mechanical harshness. Its eyes, made of amber glass, glinted eerily in the soft light of the room. It was hauntingly beautiful, incredibly detailed . . . and it looked *unmistakably* like one of her mother's works. Vanessa would know. She had spent her childhood surrounded by similar creations, continually amazed at how her mother could transform raw materials into something so vividly real and yet dreamlike.

Vanessa felt a surge of emotion; nostalgia mixed with confusion as she thought of what Damon had told her. Her mother *knew* Jacqueline Thorsen. This fact made it even more possible the woman Vanessa had seen at the Thorsens' club was her mother. A thought suddenly occurred to her: what if her mother was *here*, at the party? She felt queasy and grabbed a glass of champagne from a passing waiter to steady her nerves.

Venturing further into the depths of the penthouse, she encountered an increasing number of art pieces. Among them, a painting of a moth undergoing metamorphosis caught her eye, its eerie resemblance to the symbol she had observed painted on the wall of a secret room belonging to Benjamin Oberlin – one of her brother's victims – unmistakable.

She also passed some familiar faces from TV and film. Nearby, a well-known singer was engaged in animated conversation with a group of fashionistas. Across the room, a former hotshot Olympic swimmer whispered into a pretty young woman's ear, hands not quite where they ought to be in polite company. Vanessa looked around her at the vaulted ceilings adorned with intricate frescoes, and marble floors polished to a mirror shine. But what quickly caught her attention were the decorative details. From a distance it looked like the usual expensive tones and lines of luxury interior decor, but once you looked closely you saw them. Insects. *Everywhere.* They featured in ornate centrepieces on tables and were intricately depicted in the artwork on the walls. Even the chandeliers seemed to borrow their elegance from the iridescent sheen of beetle shells.

Arthur Oberlin had been obsessed with insects. And her mother, whose art was inspired by her favourite class in the animal kingdom: Insecta. Jacqueline, it seemed, shared this passion . . . A fascination she'd passed down to her son, Nils.

As Vanessa's eyes scoured the room, she caught sight of the man she'd seen at the funeral with the business card. Tonight, he was unmistakably tipsy, holding a glass of champagne as if it were an extension of himself. He noticed her watching him and slunk towards her.

'I recognise that face,' he slurred. 'You were at dear Cordelia's funeral.'

'I was. Enjoying the party?' Vanessa asked, taking another sip of her drink.

'Immensely.' He lifted his glass, champagne sloshing over the rim. 'You know this is a special edition Dom Pérignon Vintage? Only the best for our Jacqueline.'

'How do you know Jacqueline?'

The man laughed. 'Come now, you know that's one of the rules. Not to ask the hows and the whys.'

'Oops,' Vanessa said, pretending to pull a zip across her red lips. 'I can tell you my name, though, if you ask nicely.'

She shot him a seductive smile. '*Please* may I have your name?'

'Why yes, beautiful. It's Edgar Trent.' Vanessa quirked an interested eyebrow. He was the auction broker. She thought, for a moment, about slapping him to avenge the lives of the insects he'd taken.

'I see you're a fellow insect lover,' he said, gesturing to her gold butterfly necklace.

'Absolutely. But I can't share where I got it from,' she said, tapping the side of her nose.

'Oooh, sounds deliciously illicit. I think you and I might be friends. It's *very* important,' he said, moving closer to her and slipping his business card into her pocket, 'that *very* close friends share the *very* same deliciously illicit taste, don't you think?'

She slipped the business card into her bag. That would be useful for Ru. Then her eyes alighted on the sculpture, still visible from where they stood. 'Yes, like that beautiful piece over there.'

The man giggled, putting his hand to his mouth. 'Surely you know the story behind that?'

'That's exactly why I mention it.' Vanessa leaned in close. 'Only those in the know *know* . . . if you know what I mean?'

The man smoothed his hand over Vanessa's arm. 'I *like* you.'

Vanessa resisted the urge to shove him away.

'It *is* amusing it being here, though, isn't it?' he continued. 'Like a *fuck you* to the NYPD, displaying one of the very items used to smuggle our marvellous little bugs into the country.'

Vanessa went still.

'You know,' he said, rubbing his chin with his finger, 'I was actually thinking about commissioning Delilah to do a similar piece for me. If you pass your number to me, I could do the same for you?'

Delilah. Her mother's name.

It hit Vanessa like a sledgehammer. Sculptures. Her mother. *Smuggling.* She felt the room spin around her, the weight of this knowledge threatening to bring her to her knees. Somehow, she managed to steady herself and looked the man straight in his eyes, finding the strength to ask the next question: 'Remind me of the sculptor's surname?'

'De Souza. She's very well respected in art circles, which makes it *all* the more wonderful.'

De Souza was her mother's maiden name. So that was it. Confirmed. Horribly, indelibly confirmed. She felt sick to her core. Of course, she had come here for answers. But now that she had them, she wished she had never come at all. She wished she could rewind and go back to an hour before, when she didn't know her mother was a criminal.

At that very moment, the air outside was split by the piercing sound of sirens.

'What's going on out there?' Edgar asked with a curious drawl, sauntering towards the expansive window overlooking Central Park. Vanessa joined him, looking down towards a chaotic scene of red and blue lights as police cars and ambulances pulled up on the road below.

But even worse was the sight of a woman in the park, sprawled out in the white snow, her hair fanned out around her head.

Chapter 27

Ru jumped off his bike and ran towards the officers just stepping out of their police cars. 'Madeline's upstairs,' he said to them, 'top floor.'

'Not anymore,' one of the officers said sombrely. Then he gestured into the park, where Ru could see paramedics working on a prone form laid out in the snow.

'That's Madeline Layton?' Ru asked as a wave of cold dread washed over him.

'Yes, she—'

Before the officer could answer, Ru was running through the snow towards Madeline. She was dressed in a glittering short dress, the fabric shimmering as if in defiance of the darkness that was trying to claim her. It appeared the offending earrings had already been removed, SOCOs in protective coveralls and masks carefully placing them into a sealed evidence box nearby.

When he arrived at Madeline's side, she turned her head slightly, her eyes finding his amid the blur of falling snow and flashing lights. In her gaze, he saw a spark of fear, and confusion.

'Is she going to be OK?' Ru asked the paramedics.

'I hope so,' one of them replied. 'She's lucky we arrived when we did, and that we were informed she may be poisoned. It means we've been able to take the right steps to stabilise her and administer the right meds. Without all this, things wouldn't be looking so rosy.'

'Who was with her when she collapsed?' Ru asked a nearby officer.

They gestured to a distressed man who was sobbing on a nearby bench. Ru instantly recognised him as Brett Chambers, a former Olympian swimmer, and went over.

'I'm Detective Hoshino.'

'Is she going to be OK?'

'We believe so,' Ru said. 'I'm hoping we got to her just in time.'

'How – how did they know?' Brett asked. 'I called 911 and the ambulance was here within seconds.'

'They were dispatched ten minutes ago,' Ru said. 'We were aware Madeline might be in danger.'

'Thank God,' Brett said, his lips – blue from shock – trembling.

'Tell me what happened.'

'Sh-she was fine. We were having such a good time. We'd decided to take a walk through the park and—' he swallowed, eyes flickering towards Madeline who was being gently manoeuvred over to a stretcher, 'we fooled around a bit, you know? And then she just started acting . . . strange.'

'Strange how?' Ru asked.

'Shaking and blinking and saying she was feeling dizzy. I suggested we head back but then she—' he squeezed his eyes shut, 'she fell backward. I tried to lift her but I – I could see she was in a bad way. That's when I called 911.' His voice was getting more and more high-pitched. 'I only just met her properly tonight. Jesus, I'm married. I have kids.'

Ru showed him a close-up of the earrings Madeline had been wearing from the Instagram photo Souta had shown him. 'Was she wearing these all evening?'

Brett looked at the photo and nodded. 'Yes. She said she got them as a gift, that they were made out of real spiders. She'd only put them on in the cab ride over as she was so paranoid about damaging them.'

'I see. And how long were you with her?'

'She only arrived about an hour ago.'

So Madeline would have been wearing the earrings for an hour. Enough time for whatever they were tainted with to seep into her bloodstream.

Ru nodded. 'Thank you. One of my officers will need to take an official statement from you.'

Ru looked towards the edge of the park where a small crowd had gathered, their breath forming misty clouds in the cold air. Already, some press were there, too, somehow aware of the unfolding tragedy, cameras hungry for a glimpse as their flashes punctuated the night like distant lightning. Behind them, from the steps leading up to her apartment building, Jacqueline Thorsen watched the scene with a hard expression as other party guests in all their finery looked on from the window at the top of the building. She caught Ru's eye, then quickly turned away.

Officers began to set up a cordon around the ambulance, pushing the crowds back. Ru followed the paramedics as they carried Madeline's stretcher to the vehicle, the thin layer of snow squelching beneath the soles of his trainers as new snow began to fall. It wouldn't be long before the city would be quilted in it. But the headlines wouldn't be about the snowpocalypse. They'd be about yet another high-profile person targeted in just five days. But at least Madeline had been saved from death ... Ru hoped.

He paused as he noticed Vanessa Marwood dip under the cordon and approach him.

'You managed to get here quickly,' he said.

'I was at the party already,' Vanessa explained. 'Can I have a private word?'

He frowned. 'Of course.'

They moved beyond the harsh glare of the crime scene lights, into an area where the snow lay undisturbed and the trees formed a white canopy above them. Ru noticed Vanessa was shivering, her breath visible in the cold air. She wasn't wearing a coat, probably discarded in the drama of the moment. He took off his own and draped it over her shoulders, the adrenaline enough to keep him warm.

'It sounds like she might be OK?' Vanessa said as the police disbanded the cordon, and they stepped back to watch the ambulance set off, blue and red lights illuminating the white snow.

'I hope so.'

'I found out something tonight,' she said, 'about my mother. It seems she knew – maybe still *knows* – Jacqueline Thorsen. There's a sculpture of hers in the hallway,' she added, peering towards the apartment block, 'that's why I came here. And – and I spoke to Edgar Trent.'

'He's here?' Ru asked, eyes scouring the crowds in the distance.

'Not anymore, he scarpered as soon as this all happened,' Vanessa said, 'but I got his business card.' She sighed. 'I can't believe I'm having to say this but he told me the Thorsens use my mother's art pieces to smuggle illegal insects into the country.'

Ru was quiet as he digested it all.

'Just to make it clear,' Vanessa continued, 'I haven't seen my mother in many, many years. She walked out when I was a kid. But from what I *do* remember of her, I'm beyond shocked she'd be involved with illegal insect smuggling.'

Ru remained lost in thought for a few moments, his brown eyes scanning the night sky. 'This must be very unsettling for you,' he said after a while. 'People like us, we delve into the darkest corners of humanity, but we never expect to have that light shine on ourselves, our own families.'

Vanessa nodded. 'Very true.'

'I will make some discreet enquiries. Your mother's role, if indeed there is one, doesn't need to be revealed until we uncover the full truth.'

Vanessa shook her head. 'No, I *have* to disclose it. I'll speak to Bronagh.'

An officer walked over then, holding out a phone. 'Sorry to interrupt, but the captain's on the phone. He wants to speak to you, Hoshino.'

'Better get back to it, Detective,' Vanessa said with a sad smile.

Ru paused a moment, examining her face. Usually so composed, so professionally detached, it had been clear to him she was navigating an unfamiliar emotional landscape with the revelation about her mother. He felt an unexpected tug, a disruption in the ordered universe of facts and clues that usually commanded his focus. But then the facts and the clues returned. He nodded, taking the phone.

'Captain?' he said, ensuring the tone of his voice delivered the message loud and clear: he lay part of the blame for this at the captain's feet.

'I just heard the news about Madeline Layton, and that your fast work possibly saved her life?'

'That's the hope. She was wearing earrings made from spiders.'

There was an audible and very heavy sigh. 'I will do a press conference tomorrow,' the captain said. 'And Hoshino? To put this blog post chatter to rest, you're going to be leading it with me.'

Chapter 28

In the quiet of her lab, Vanessa peered through the microscope at some tiny, glistening eggs she'd collected from Cordelia's crime scene nearly a week ago. She'd placed these ones in cold storage, which had delayed their hatching. It was something she liked to do with all her samples, if there were enough, so she could watch the miraculous event unfolding under her gaze. One egg quivered subtly, its surface stretching until, with a delicate persistence, a minuscule larva emerged. The newborn, almost translucent against the white backdrop of the petri dish, wriggled slowly, its form minute yet full of life. Vanessa watched, mesmerised by the tiny creature's first foray into existence.

She thought of Madeline Layton, so young herself. A news item that morning had implied she might make it. That was some good news, at least.

'Good, you're smiling.' She peered up to see Bronagh watching her, a cup of coffee in her hand, no doubt to ward off her hangover.

'I was just thinking about the news that Madeline Layton will make it,' Vanessa replied. 'Oh, and the birth of invertebrates always makes me smile.'

'I suppose that's another decent reason for coming in on a Sunday. I presume you got Egbo's text about wanting to share his preliminary toxicology results?' Vanessa nodded. 'Hey, you know I'm here if you need to talk, right? You just discovered your mother might be involved with an illegal insect smuggling ring *and* you were in the middle of a crime scene last night. It must be tough.'

'Yep, it sucks,' Vanessa admitted. 'But please, I'm British. I prefer your jokes to your sympathy.'

'I suppose contraband smuggling does beat my mother's hobbies: crocheting and the Kardashians.'

Vanessa laughed. 'Honestly, that sounds *amazing*.'

'I'll invite you to dinner at hers in a couple of weeks. You might change your mind.'

Vanessa grew serious. 'I still think I should recuse myself from any direct involvement in this investigation,' she said.

'I told you when you called last night, not a chance. There's no proof yet your mother's involved with smuggling these insects, just hearsay from one random dude trying to get into your pants. But you should give Agent Valdez a call.'

Vanessa nodded. 'I'll call him once Egbo shares his results. How about you?' Vanessa asked, examining Bronagh's face. 'Was Joe as grumpy as you suspected he'd be?'

'Oh, you know, men will be men,' Bronagh replied dismissively. 'He made me his famous hangover smoothie, so that's something.'

'You know the offer to talk goes both ways? I'm here if you ever need to chat.'

Bronagh frowned and went to open her mouth but then Egbo's assistant appeared at the see-through window, gesturing for them to come.

'Egbo must be ready,' Bronagh said. 'He even brought in Bourke Street Bakery cinnamon rolls. And I'm fine,' she added, giving Vanessa's arm a squeeze, 'but thanks for checking in.'

They both walked into the conference room, and Vanessa grabbed one of the cinnamon rolls, taking a seat with Bronagh as Egbo sat across from them. Vanessa lifted the cinnamon roll to her nose and breathed in its scent before taking a huge bite, moaning with pleasure as she did.

'You got the toxicology results back quickly,' she said to Egbo. 'It's been less than a week.'

'You're playing with the big guns now, Vanessa,' Bronagh said. 'Plus I got a call from Captain Williams in the night to put a rocket up our asses. He wants preliminary results for his press conference today. Fire away, Egbo.'

Egbo walked to the front of the room and perched on the edge of the table. 'Let's begin with Cordelia Montgomery.' A close-up of the hair clip Cordelia had been wearing appeared on the screen. 'As we learned from Vanessa on Tuesday, this clip featured a sophisticated injector mechanism attached to a minuscule vial. We carried out tests on the parts and have discovered traces of botulinum toxin.'

'Botox?' Bronagh said in a surprised voice.

Egbo nodded. 'And before you ask if it's simply the case Cordelia had Botox fillers, the traces we found were concentrated to a degree that would cause instant death if a small amount was injected into the skin.'

'Botulinum toxin *is* actually one of the world's most poisonous substances,' Vanessa said.

'That's right,' Egbo said. 'In cosmetic procedures, highly diluted quantities are administered in controlled doses. This means the toxin only affects the specific muscles into which it's injected. But if concentrated enough, even a small dose can cause death within minutes, especially if injected. I suspect it may have been used in the earrings worn by Madeline Layton, too.'

'Interesting,' Vanessa said. 'And is a toxin like this reasonably easy to get hold of, considering its use in the beauty industry?'

Egbo nodded. 'It is. Now, let's move on to the watch worn by Maximilian Rossi.' A photo appeared on the screen of the watch. 'We found traces of a cyanide compound in a compartment hidden beneath the back of the watch. As you know, the back panel of the watch was designed to sit flush against the skin and engineered to respond to pressure, expelling a fatally concentrated dose of cyanide that was absorbed into the skin. I imagine this is what we'll find in Rhoda Matheson's bracelet, too.'

'The procurement of cyanide is tightly regulated, though, right?' Bronagh asked.

Egbo nodded. 'Yes, but unfortunately, no such regulation exists in the digital underworld. It's highly plausible that the killer used the dark web to acquire the cyanide.'

Vanessa stared at the screen. Illegally procured insects and poison. Faked notes and elaborate gifts. Whoever did this had gone to great lengths to cause as much terror as they could.

'Right, I better update Detective Hoshino and the captain before the press conference,' Bronagh said. 'And *you* better call Agent Hotsville, Vanessa.'

Vanessa rolled her eyes then headed into her office, picking her phone up and calling the mobile phone number she had for Dariel.

'Agent Valdez.' It sounded like he was in his car, the noise of traffic in the background. Perhaps on his way back from the city.

'Hi, Dariel, it's Dr Vanessa Marwood.'

'Hey, good to hear from you. Or maybe not so good. I heard about Madeline Layton. At least it looks like she'll pull through.'

'Yes, I was relieved to hear that, too. There's something else.' She told him about her mother's possible connection with the Thorsens. Dariel was quiet as she spoke. He was quiet a little time after as well.

'Wow, that's a lot, Dr Marwood,' he said after a while. 'So, you say she's called Delilah de Souza? I don't think I've come across the name. Do you have any idea where your mother might be now so we can chat to her?'

'No,' Vanessa replied, eyes homing in on the photo of her mother on her desk. 'We've been estranged since I was a girl. I didn't even know she was in New York – if she is. She studied art here many years back, though. I think that might be how she met Jacqueline.'

'I see. I'll make some enquiries for you.'

'I'd appreciate that.'

'Of course, I'm happy to help. Where did she live when she was studying here?'

'East Village. She was studying at the Cooper Union in the early seventies.'

'Ever any indication she might be involved in the black market?' Dariel asked.

Vanessa frowned. 'During a case I worked on last year in my childhood village in the UK, one of the suspects suggested my mother was involved in an illegal insect trade there. The detective on the case uncovered a bit of an illicit ring.'

'Interesting. Could all be connected. Can I have his name?'

'Detective Paul Truss. I'll send you his number.'

'Just looking at your mother's sculptures,' he said. 'They're interesting. Insects, broken apart.'

'Yes, it's her theme.'

'So this insect fascination runs in the blood, then?'

Vanessa sank down into her chair. 'My father was a butterfly expert. He *loved* insects. That's the thing, though,' she said, shaking her head, 'my mum loved them too. She always treated insects with respect, never used them *in* her art. So her involvement with illegal insect trading just feels . . . *wrong*.'

'We don't really know our parents, though, do we? The role of nurturer and creator can form a block to really needling out the truth of their souls, you know?'

'So you're a philosopher, a dad *and* a USFWS agent?'

He laughed. 'What I'm trying to say is, my kids definitely don't know everything about me and I sure as hell didn't know the reality of what my parents were.' He was quiet for a few moments. 'This might sound crazy but why don't you come visit my offices in Cortland? You could learn more about the illegal insect trade to help with the case, and maybe we can do some research together to track your mom down? It's only a four-hour drive . . .'

'I don't know, I'd need to check with Bronagh.'

'Come on. It'd do you good to get out of the city. Cortland is a pretty town. Mountains. Trees. Even a lake or two. Might even remind you of the UK.'

Vanessa's gaze drifted to the window, watching the city hustle by. Maybe it would be good to escape for a couple of days?

Chapter 29

Ru stepped away from his bike, leaning down to rub at his heels, which were sore from wearing a pair of leather brogues he only usually got out for weddings and funerals. But the media relations team had been insistent he at least swapped his trainers for shoes for the press conference later. They also emphasised the importance of being 'approachable yet authoritative, confident yet humble'. When Ru had pointed out the contradictions, they'd looked at him like he was mad.

Before the press conference, though, he had one task: to update Cordelia's mother, Felicity, on the latest developments. Harris was handling Maximilian and Rhoda's families, and Ru had already been to the hospital to visit Madeline, where the doctor confirmed she would recover, especially now they had an idea of the kind of toxin that may have been used on her, following work carried out by Bronagh's team.

'If we hadn't got to her when we did,' the doctor had said, 'it's likely she wouldn't be alive right now. Time is of the essence with any toxin, but particularly with something as potent as botulinum toxin, if that is indeed what was used on her. We'll need to see how her body responds to treatment in the coming days and weeks. But she's young and healthy. I'm confident she will make a good recovery. For now, though, she needs peace and quiet . . . and she's certainly not ready for questions,' he'd added pointedly.

Ru was fine with that. He was just relieved she'd survive. He wished he could have done the same for the other victims, including Cordelia. Instead, he was visiting her grieving mother.

Felicity lived in a smart-looking apartment building in the Lower East Side of Manhattan, between a synagogue and a family-run deli. Ru imagined Cordelia would have earned enough money for her mother to live somewhere a lot flashier, and yet it seemed Felicity had chosen to remain where she had brought up her family. Ru's own mother was the same, still in the Astoria apartment she had bought from proceeds from her restaurant.

He pressed the buzzer and waited. Levi answered.

'Detective Hoshino, do you have news to share?' Levi said through the speakerphone in his usual clipped tones.

'I do,' Ru replied, wondering if he'd seen the news about Madeline's poisoning. It would have been hard to miss.

'I'll let you in,' Levi said.

With a soft buzz, the door clicked open. Ru pushed through into the lobby and across a floor of black and white tiles, worn down by the comings and goings of the building's residents. He took the lift to Felicity's floor to find Levi already waiting for him at the open door of the apartment, wearing smart trousers and a white jumper. His eyes, sharp and assessing, flicked over Ru.

'Please, come in,' he said, holding the door wide.

Felicity was already waiting for him in the small hallway. She looked even more worn down since the last time Ru had seen her, as though she had been holding herself together for the funeral. Her greying hair was in disarray and her face was make-up free, revealing sallow and tear-drenched skin.

'Detective Hoshino,' she said. 'Is this connected to that poor girl's collapse in Central Park?'

'Yes, plus a few other developments.'

'Please, come through.' She led him down a corridor. The apartment was spacious and homely all at the same time, featuring bookshelves lined with a mix of literature and Judaica art, and family photos gracing the walls – snapshots of birthdays, bat mitzvahs, and other celebrations, Cordelia's pretty face beaming out at Ru from different stages in her short life with family and friends.

'Can I offer you tea or coffee?' Felicity asked Ru.

'Tea would be good, thank you,' Ru replied, following Felicity into the large kitchen.

Levi took a seat across from Ru at a small table, as Felicity busied herself with making tea. When she was done, she brought over three mugs and sat next to her son.

'Mrs Montgomery,' Ru began, trying to inject some warmth into his voice. This victim family liaison side of things wasn't his strength. 'As you are aware, an associate of your daughter's, Madeline Layton, collapsed last night. Luckily, we're hopeful she will make a full recovery.'

'Do you think her collapse is linked to Cordelia's death?' Levi asked. 'And Maximilian Rossi's and Rhoda Matheson's, too?'

'We do,' Ru said, 'and I'm afraid it's looking even more likely that Cordelia's death is part of a larger campaign of deaths. We now have strong reason to believe someone deliberately set out to harm not only Cordelia and Maximilian Rossi, but also Madeline Layton and Jerry Bowman.'

Felicity clutched her hand to her chest, face paling, while Levi looked down into his mug.

Ru explained about the insect jewellery, the gift boxes and, finally, the preliminary toxicology report he'd received from Bronagh a few moments before his visit.

Felicity stood up and walked over to the sink, clutching the edges as she gulped in breaths.

'Are you OK, Mrs Montgomery?' Ru asked. 'Do you need anything?'

'She's just trying to wrap her head around it all,' Levi said, going to the sink and pouring his mother a glass of water, encouraging her to take a sip.

'Are there any leads?' Levi asked. 'Maybe a stalker? Cordelia had some trouble over the years.'

'We're following many avenues,' Ru replied. 'The reason I wanted to tell you today is because the police captain will be making a statement at midday. We preferred you heard it from us than on the news. I understand this is a shock to you both.'

'To be honest,' Felicity said with a sigh, 'nothing can shock me as much as seeing Cordelia on her bed last week.'

As she said that, the intercom buzzer went. 'That will be my wife,' Levi explained.

Felicity excused herself briefly to answer it, her voice a soft murmur as she spoke to her daughter-in-law. Moments later, the apartment door opened and Levi's wife walked in, bringing with her a waft of powerful perfume. She looked rather shocked when she saw Ru.

'Here, let's put this in the fridge,' Felicity said, taking a large bag from her.

As the two women unpacked food, Levi turned to Ru, using the inch in height he had over the detective to full advantage as he loomed over him.

'I'd rather have it that I were the main contact for this investigation from now on, Detective Hoshino,' he said in a quiet voice. 'This is *really* taking a toll on my mother. She may look like she's coping but she really isn't.'

'Understandably,' Ru said. 'But I'll need to check that with your mother.'

'She'll be fine with it.'

'Still, I'd rather check.'

Levi's nostrils flared then he nodded. 'Fine.' He looked over at his mother. 'I was just telling Detective Hoshino that I should be his main contact from now on.'

'I think that's a very good idea, don't you, Felicity?' Levi's wife insisted, squeezing her mother-in-law's shoulder.

'Well, if you think . . . ?' Felicity began, looking between her son and daughter-in-law.

'I do,' Levi said, walking to his mother and rubbing her arm. 'I think you're taking too much on. Planning the funeral last week, and now the memorial gala.'

'Memorial gala?' Ru asked.

'Yes,' Levi said, 'the organisers of an annual winter gala taking place on Wednesday have offered to include an element celebrating Cordelia's life while raising money for a charity dear to her heart. My mother and my wife are helping.'

'You should come, Detective Hoshino,' Felicity said.

Levi and his wife exchanged disapproving looks. 'Mother, we can't just give tickets away willy-nilly,' Levi said. 'And I'm sure you are a very busy man, Detective Hoshino. Thank you for the update.' He gestured towards the door. Ru watched Felicity, wondering if she was really happy about her son being the main contact. Then he looked at his watch. It wasn't something he had time to push. He needed to get back to the precinct in time for the press conference, something he was dreading.

Ru's fingers tapped an arrhythmic pattern on the surface of the lectern. In front of him, journalists jostled for the best position, their cameras flashing in rapid succession. Next to him, the captain was a bastion of composure. 'Ladies and gentlemen of the press,' he began in a deep, authoritative voice, 'I am here with Detective Ru Hoshino to update you on the ongoing investigation into the recent and tragic deaths of Cordelia Montgomery, Maximilian Rossi and Rhoda Matheson and the recent collapse of Madeline Layton who, as you know, is expected to make a full recovery thanks to the excellent work carried out by Detective Hoshino and his team.' The captain paused, scanning the eager faces in front of him. 'First and foremost, I would like to convey condolences to the families and friends of the deceased and injured, and ask that their privacy is respected at this time. I would also like to assure the public that my officers are working around the clock on this case.' He paused, looking directly into the glare of the camera flashes, before continuing. 'Preliminary toxicology results have confirmed Cordelia and Maximilian were both poisoned.' There was a sudden burst of surprised murmuring in the room. 'We suspect we will discover the same when the toxicology results come through for Rhoda and, more recently, Madeline. Now let me pass over to the lead detective in charge of this case, Detective Ru Hoshino.'

Ru pulled at the collar of his T-shirt and coughed into his fist. He wasn't quite sure he'd ever forgive the captain for making him do this. But it was happening and there was nothing he could do to change it. On the screen behind him, an image appeared of the gift box and the card that came with it.

'We believe all four victims received a box like this in the post on Valentine's Day, with this note,' he said, clicking the laptop in front of him to move onto the page with the note. 'Inside each box was a piece of jewellery featuring illegally imported insects. Jewellery which was manipulated to deliver a lethal dose of poison to all four victims.'

There was more murmuring in the room, shocked glances, and camera flashes which made Ru blink. 'It is of paramount importance that anyone who comes into contact with a gift, or indeed any jewellery item, made with real insects, immediately move themselves to safety and call this number.' A number flashed up on the screen.

The captain nodded, looking relieved. Frankly, Ru was relieved, too. He'd done just as asked: 'approachable yet authoritative, confident yet humble'.

'In a moment,' the captain said, 'the New York City Department of Health and Mental Hygiene will make a statement. In the meantime, we'll take a few questions.'

A young female reporter immediately shot her hand up. 'Tina Denman from the *New York Daily*. Reports suggest Cordelia was in a relationship with the owner of the Seraphim Garden Hotel, Nils Thorsen. It can't be a coincidence that Maximilian Rossi then collapsed in his club, and Madeline Layton collapsed just outside Jacqueline Thorsen's penthouse?'

'No one is ruled out,' the captain replied, 'but our findings will be based on evidence, not speculation.'

The captain pointed to a well-dressed man, notepad in hand. 'Jimi Kensington, the *City Chronicle*,' the journalist stated. 'Are the FBI involved?'

The captain nodded. 'I am in conversation with our friends at the FBI due to the federal nature of some of the crimes committed.'

A blonde female reporter shouted over the murmurings: 'Jenny Powell, *New York Daily*. Is it true Cordelia was seeing a therapist?'

'Isn't every celebrity?' Jimi Kensington murmured as the other journalists laughed.

'What I mean is,' the young journalist said, irritated, 'there are rumours she was experiencing quite challenging mental health issues in recent weeks.'

The journalists raised their voices as Captain Williams put his hand up, signalling for calm. 'We urge the public and the media not to jump to conclusions. Every piece of information is being carefully examined.'

Another journalist raised her hand, a woman in her twenties

with brown hair in a blunt bob and bright red lips. 'Kendra Grey, the *Chislington Post*.'

It was the same journalist Ramos was due to visit that afternoon; the one who'd received the second item on Jacqueline's handwritten note to Ru.

'This one's for Detective Hoshino,' she said. 'Your recently leaked blog post painted a dark image of society, particularly pointing out the roles of influencers like Madeline Layton as "modern-day jesters". Given the nature of this case, there's a growing concern on social media about your ability to remain impartial.' Ru felt the captain bristle beside him. 'In fact, some people are suggesting that YouTuber AuthenticAegis is you. How do you address these speculations, and can you assure the public that your personal philosophies have not influenced your conduct in this investigation?'

Ru thought of the advice the media relations officer had given to him should he get a question like this: Basically, 'fluff' – the kind of benign, noncommittal responses that could never be misconstrued or turned into sensational headlines. But fluff was the farthest from what Ru considered the truth – a concept he held in higher regard than his own comfort.

'My writings reflect a personal philosophy I'm sure many normal New Yorkers share,' Ru began, his voice calm. 'They do not cloud my judgement as an officer of the law. In fact, they serve to sharpen it. After all, "modern-day jesters" are as much a part of our society as any, deserving of protection and justice. My commitment to protect and serve is unwavering.'

Beside him, the captain groaned under his breath.

'I'll take over from here,' he hissed to Ru. The journalists continued their barrage of questions, each trying to get that exclusive angle, that one piece of information that would set their report apart. Through it all, Captain Williams stood firm, revealing nothing more than he intended. Ru had to admit, the captain was good at deflecting the press with non-answers.

When the New York City Department of Health and Mental Hygiene took over, Ru quickly left the podium and found Kendra before she walked out.

'Isn't my colleague due to visit you this afternoon?' he said. 'Can you assure me that your personal experience has not influenced *your* conduct in this press conference?' he said, copying what she'd said about him.

'Nice,' Kendra said, 'very nice. Oh, and thank your forensics team, by the way, for royally messing up my apartment.'

'I think a messy apartment is preferable to a contaminated one. I hear you were writing an exposé on the illegal insect trade,' Ru said, 'hence why you connected the packaging with the Thorsens, having bought items from them before which used the same packaging. Interesting topic for a showbiz journalist, illegal insect trading.'

'Clearly not,' she said, 'considering the number of celebrities who wear these things.'

Ru observed Kendra's demeanour, the defensive cross of her arms, the tilt of her head – classic tells of discomfort. She was lying. Even more noticeable as she moved under the window and into the afternoon light were the distinct tan lines – or, as they were sometimes referred to, 'skier's tan' – where her ski mask would have sat.

'You've been skiing recently,' Ru observed. 'Wasn't your boss, Jerry Bowman, skiing too?'

A flicker of unease crossed her face. 'Maybe,' she said, trying to seem casual. 'It's ski season, what can I say?'

'I'd say,' he said, 'as a *serious* journalist, that it's better to control the narrative before someone else takes that control away from you.'

'I don't know what you're talking about,' she said, looking at her watch. 'I better go.'

Then she made a sharp exit. As Ru watched her, he thought about those who had so far been targeted by this killer:

An actress.

A fashion designer.

A billionaire.

An influencer.

A journalist . . . and the billionaire's lover?

A circle of people connected by . . . what?

'What was that about?' Harris asked as he strolled over. 'Good job up there, by the way.'

'Thanks. And that was Kendra Grey, the journalist who received the wasp ring. Something tells me she might be Jerry Bowman's mistress.'

'Interesting. So,' Harris said as they watched the last of the journalists leave, the captain talking in low voices with the New York City Department of Health and Mental Hygiene team, 'wonder what this press conference will bring crawling out of the woodwork.'

'More deaths, maybe,' Ru replied. 'Suspected heart attacks and drug overdoses will take on more sinister possibilities now that news has started to spread about these gift boxes. This could be just the beginning.'

Chapter 30

Turned out Dariel had been right. The long, snowy drive from NYC to Cortland was just the therapy Vanessa needed – as she left behind the towering skyscrapers of the city and entered a serene winter wonderland of sprawling fields and lush woodlands.

It was good to spend some quality time in her cherry-red Mitsubishi, too. It had cost her a small fortune to have it shipped over, and a few weeks for it arrive. But she'd got that vehicle with money her father had left her in his will. It felt like part of her. Part of *him*.

How would he feel about his ex-wife's involvement in this criminal gang? His heart had been broken in two when she had left him. Then it had been shattered into pieces after Vincent went missing and she hadn't even visited. It pained Vanessa to dwell on how devastated he'd be at the developments over the past year: first, the horror Vincent had unleashed on a village her father had so loved. And now this, his ex-wife's involvement in the illegal trading of the creatures he so adored.

Vanessa felt tears threaten to ruin her mascara. She blinked them away and a few minutes later, pulled up outside the offices Dariel had directed her to. The one-storey building sitting among a copse of trees looked just like the small museum that it was, with a sign welcoming her to the USFWS CONSERVATION MUSEUM. She stepped out of her truck, stretching. She'd stopped an hour before for some lunch and to freshen up, but still her limbs ached and her emerald-green blouse felt stuffy and creased. She checked herself in the window's reflection, reapplying some red lipstick and smoothing her black hair down. Then she walked towards the building through the snow.

When she got inside, she was greeted by a basic yet welcoming reception area, natural light filtering through the long, horizontal windows. Behind the reception area was a timeline of the USFWS, from its creation by Congress in 1871 to the signing of the Great American Outdoor Act in 2020. A female receptionist regarded Vanessa with interest as she introduced herself, eyes crawling over the tattoos on her arms, and her winged eyeliner. After a couple of minutes, Dariel emerged, his presence immediately filling the small reception area. A slight smile touched the corners of his mouth, softening the intensity of his gaze.

'Isn't this a treat?' he said as he shook Vanessa's hand, his long fingers callused against hers. 'A forensic entomologist travelling all this way to see us.'

'The treat's all mine,' Vanessa said. 'Cortland is beautiful, especially in this weather.'

'It's not bad, is it? Coffee?' he asked, gesturing to a coffee machine.

'No, I'm fine.'

'Journey OK?'

'Not bad. My truck can handle anything. I drove past the actual USFWS HQ on the way. Why aren't you based there?'

'I convinced the Powers That Be I needed my own place,' he said. 'Half offices, half museum to highlight the wrongs of illegal wildlife trading. Speaking of which, let's start with the museum.' He gestured to the museum and she followed him through.

'How you doing?' he asked as he opened the door for her.

'Oh, you know, how you'd expect after discovering your mother's involved in an illicit insect trading ring.'

He laughed. 'That's one way to put it. The media's reacted predictably after the captain's press conference yesterday. Our press office has gone crazy.'

'I bet they have,' Vanessa said, as she took in the small museum with polished wooden floors below and exposed beams overhead. Modern, glass display cases punctuated the space with written guides. Vanessa's eyes immediately fell upon a display housing several deceased insects. A beautiful Luzon peacock swallowtail, an endangered butterfly native to the Philippines. A giant African millipede. A magnificent Hercules beetle, its chitinous exoskeleton glinting even in death. All extraordinary but illegal specimens worth a small fortune on the black market. Vanessa felt a pang of sadness. These creatures, so fascinating and vital in their natural ecosystems, were now lifeless curiosities.

'What a waste,' she said.

'Sure as hell is,' Dariel agreed with a sigh.

Next was a display adorned with an array of fashion items, all crafted from now deceased insects.

'Jesus,' Vanessa said.

'Jesus definitely had nothing to do with the people who sell these. A lot of these creatures would have still been alive when worn.'

'Any of these linked to the auctions run by the Thorsens?' she asked as she continued to look around.

'No, the first time we've managed to seize any items specifically linked to the Thorsens was at the auction last week. Even then, there's still no evidence to link it all to the Thorsens, just hearsay.'

Vanessa shook her head. As she did, she remembered her mother was part of this. She tried to align that version of her with the mother she remembered, who would sit so still on summer days just so butterflies would land on her.

'OK, this is too depressing,' Dariel said. 'Let me show you the good stuff.'

He led Vanessa to another room which hummed with the low, rhythmic sounds of various insects. Inside, rows of carefully labelled and secured terrariums lined the walls, some empty, most housing a species of insect.

'Think of this like a waiting room,' Dariel explained. 'We try our best to get wildlife rescues out to any locations we raid, but with funding the way it is, it's not always possible. So we keep some here for a day or two until they can be collected.'

Vanessa's eyes were drawn to a small enclosure where a majestic Blackburn's sphinx moth fluttered weakly. Its five-inch wing span and the five vibrant orange spots that paraded down each flank of its abdomen really made it stand out.

'We found this one during a raid in the Southtowns,' Dariel said. 'It was about to be turned into a brooch.'

'It's remarkable, what you do here,' Vanessa said.

Dariel smiled, a hint of pride in his eyes. 'It's a constant battle. But every life we save, every illegal trade we stop, I feel like it makes a difference.'

'It does.' As he continued to show her around, Vanessa enjoyed his enthusiasm for these animals and his obvious passion for his job. He really wasn't just a pretty face.

'Hey, I think I need a drink and some lunch after my tour guide gig,' he said as he looked at his watch later. 'I know a decent bar that does more than decent food. You up for it?'

'Sure, why not?'

Vanessa sat with Dariel in a corner booth at the Rusty Lantern, a quaint bar with polished wooden beams, antique bronze fixtures and a crackling fireplace. It was just a five-minute walk from Vanessa's hotel, where her truck was parked, so was the ideal place to relax. Even better was the window above their booth which looked out over a creek that meandered through a snowy expanse. Not so great was the TV in the corner of the bar, rerunning Captain Williams' press conference from the day before on mute, the images of each poison-laden item appearing on screen.

Vanessa took a sip of her rum and smiled. Dariel had been so right. She needed this. Even more, she needed the company. Since they'd arrived at the bar an hour ago, the conversation had flowed effortlessly between them. As Vanessa talked, Dariel listened intently, always a good sign in a man. And when *he* talked, he was funny, interesting, passionate. He may have given a tough guy aura during that raid, but the *real* Dariel was cheeky, funny . . . and *very* sexy.

'So, what about you?' Vanessa asked. 'How'd you become a special agent for the USFWS?'

Dariel leaned back, his gaze drifting towards the scenery outside. 'My *abuelo* – that's my grandpa – he was a big influence. He taught me that every creature has a role, a purpose. It's just what I grew up understanding. He was a damn good man.'

'Was? Is he no longer with us?'

'Who knows? I sometimes feel like he's still around, you know? Like right now,' he said, looking at the space next to her. 'I can imagine him sitting next to you, and sizing you up, asking me who this strangely beautiful *señorita* sharing a table with his grandson is.'

'He sounds like he has impeccable taste,' Vanessa said, winking. 'So where did you grow up?'

Dariel took a sip of his beer. 'Miami. My dad was Cuban, mom from Miami. I trained to become a cop there.'

'What made you specialise in wildlife?'

'In my first year, we received an anonymous tip. Someone had noticed crates being transported at night and was pretty sure they were dogs. I was pulled in to help a search of the property. Seriously,' he said, shaking his head in dismay, 'the condition those spaniels were kept in. It *sickened* me.' He took another quick sip of his beer to calm himself. 'Anyway, I got talking to one of the USFWS law enforcement officers and it was like a lightbulb came on.' He paused, tracing the rim of his glass with his finger as Vanessa watched him. 'I realised I could make a difference, trying to protect what can't protect itself, you know?'

'And you came all the way to New York to do it?'

He shrugged. 'That's where the ex-wife comes in.'

'Ah. You moved for love.'

He rubbed at his stubbled jaw. 'Something like that.'

'You mentioned having kids? How old are they?'

'Six and eight.' He smiled. 'I get to have them for an entire week soon, my ex is going skiing. What about you? Any kids? Or . . . husband?'

'Nope and nope.'

'Too busy watching larvae hatch, hey?'

'Larvae over humans any day. Not that I don't like kids, or humans. Some of them, anyway.'

The waitress came over and they ordered some lunch.

'So,' Dariel said as the waitress walked away, 'what are your impressions of Cortland so far?'

'It hasn't bored me yet, so I guess Cortland isn't all that bad.'

Dariel raised an eyebrow, a playful smirk forming. Vanessa found herself captivated by the way the afternoon light accentuated the contours of his face and the slight roughness of his jawline.

'Only "not bad"?' he said, his voice a soft rumble. 'I might have to try harder to impress you.'

'I like to push people to be their best.'

As Dariel sipped on his beer, Vanessa's eyes lingered on his lips touching the glass. He paused, his own gaze briefly dropping to her lips before meeting her eyes again.

She knew where this was leading and she didn't mind one bit.

As the afternoon progressed, their conversation turned to deeper topics – their pasts, aspirations, and the complexities of the current investigation. Vanessa appreciated Dariel's insightful comments and the way he listened, his gaze never wavering. She appreciated even more when he tore his tie off, unbuttoning the top of his white shirt to reveal a hint of dark hair and his bronzed skin. She imagined moving her lips across that skin.

'So what about your mom?' Dariel asked. 'What's she like? Or *was* she like? I guess it's been so long since you saw her.'

'She was a good mum . . . at first,' Vanessa admitted. 'She loved cooking for us and would prepare these elaborate curries on the weekends – the whole apartment smelling of spices and coconut milk.' Dariel listened intently, his dark eyes never leaving her face. 'But then . . .' Vanessa's voice trailed off. 'She changed,' she said eventually. 'It was subtle at first. She grew more distant. Her art turned darker, almost morbid.'

'Sounds like something was going on with her. What was your parents' marriage like?'

'I mean, I was a child. I didn't really take much notice but as far as I knew, they were happy.'

'And yet she just left one day?'

Vanessa nodded. 'I was only seven. I came home from school, and my parents were waiting for me in the living room. Vincent was out in the garden, playing. I could tell it was serious. The looks on their faces. Both of them seemed so devastated. It was like Mum didn't want to go but—' She took in a deep breath. 'Anyway, they both explained they were separating and that Mum would be moving to Brighton. No explanation why. I knew kids at school with divorced parents, but I never dreamed it would be *my* parents. And Mum being the one to leave? To move so far away? I guess I was in shock.'

Dariel sighed.

'Sorry, I'm being insensitive,' she said, suddenly remembering he was divorced.

'Nah, it's cool,' Dariel said. 'So, did you see your mom much after?'

The buzzing started up in her head. That bee, fluttering around in the crevices of her mind. Vanessa shook her head, hoping the buzzing would dissipate with the motion. 'Haven't seen her at all since.'

'I'm sorry, Vanessa,' Dariel said, placing his hand over hers. 'And now all the latest stuff you've discovered . . .'

'Just another turn in the twisty tale of the Marwoods. It'd be nice to have a normal family, you know?'

'But you're anything but normal. It's what makes you.'

There was an intensity in Dariel's gaze as he said that. The air between them crackled with an electric tension.

'Can we talk about something more fun?' Vanessa said, the buzzing too much now, her hand slipping from his as she took another long sip of her rum and Cherry Coke. 'I need a reprieve from the chaos of my life at the moment.'

Dariel raised an eyebrow. 'I can do fun.'

They ended up ordering more drinks, and by the time they poured out of the bar two hours later, they were drunk from the alcohol but also with each other, as the winter sun shone over them and the surrounding snow-laden valley.

'Wanna walk a bit?' Dariel suggested as he buttoned up his thick winter coat.

'Sounds good.'

They both walked towards a secluded stream below, the tension between them tangible.

'I know about your brother, by the way,' Dariel suddenly said out of the blue.

Vanessa blinked.

'Shit, sorry,' Dariel said. 'I have a habit of ruining the moment.'

'It's fine. But yeah, I have a serial killer brother who I don't enjoy talking about.'

Dariel examined her face. 'I really have ruined the mood, haven't I?'

'What mood was that, then?' she asked, stepping closer to him.

'The same mood I've been in since the first time I laid eyes on you?' he said, voice husky. 'The kind of mood that makes me want to see and feel what hides beneath those unique clothes of yours.'

She took his hand, placing it palm down beneath the collar of her coat and on the skin exposed beneath. 'This is how it feels,' she whispered.

Dariel glided his thumb across her collarbone. 'You're something else, Dr Marwood.'

He pulled her towards him, his lips meeting hers, soft, questioning, the scent of his cologne and the roughness of his stubble making her feel heady. She hesitated a moment then kissed him back, wrapping her arms around his neck. Their kisses grew more intense, Dariel gently pushing her against the tree behind her, both laughing as snow fell on their heads from the branches above.

He kissed her neck again and she looked up at the blue sky. She knew what she was doing, patching up the broken wings of herself like her dad used to with his butterflies. Muffling the noise with touch and sensation. Maybe Dariel had known it, too, when he'd invited her here. Maybe he saw her like one of the creatures he protected who couldn't protect themselves. That was fine. She'd let him think that. Sometimes the truth – that she could protect herself, always would – drove men like him away. And right now, she needed him right there, making her feel good.

'As much as I'm enjoying every moment of this,' he whispered to her, 'I'm not sure getting frostbite was on my list of New Year resolutions.'

She smiled. 'You going to walk me back to my hotel room, then?'

'Sure.'

When they got to the hotel, they paused outside. 'You can come in, you know,' Vanessa said.

'I was hoping you'd say that.'

When they got into the hotel room, there was barely a moment before their lips were meeting again, both stumbling onto a velvet sofa, Dariel's hand gliding up her back. It wasn't long before they made their way to the bed, Vanessa sinking down onto the covers and watching as Dariel undressed before her, her eyes taking in his tanned, toned body, enjoying the mischievous glint in his eye.

She had a brief flashback to the night she spent with Damon before she moved to New York. The urgency and the tug and pull between them. As Dariel slowly undressed her, too, softly kissing her skin, part of her yearned for Damon's teeth on her, the nibbles and the hard fingers pressing into her flesh.

But no, she couldn't bear more darkness. She needed light, she needed good, she needed *secure*. Later, as Dariel dipped his head between her legs, she wondered to herself if this would ever be enough for her. If, like her brother, maybe her mother, she could never be satisfied with anything but *complicated* and *dangerous*. But then all sensation took over and any lingering questions disappeared into the way Dariel was making her feel.

Later, as she lay in Dariel's arms, he examined her face. 'You could be a TV star like your ex, you know.'

'My ex? You know about Damon?'

'I may have done some light googling. Seriously, though, you got that hot scientist vibe going on.'

'*Please* don't put me in the same category of tanned, perky anthropologists from *Indiana Jones*-type films. I'm a size fourteen perimenopausal mess who needs a truckload of make-up to look half decent.'

Dariel smiled, stroking her cheek. 'You look great without make-up.'

She laughed. 'Dariel, I'm still wearing make-up. In fact, when I went to the loo just now, I did a little touch-up.'

'I love your honesty. I still think you'd make a great TV star.'

Vanessa rolled her eyes. 'You sound like Cordelia Montgomery's agent.'

'Heidi Stone?'

'You know her.'

'*Of* her.'

'She accosted me in the loos at Cordelia's funeral, promising to make me a star.'

He leaned up on his elbow, a serious expression on his face. 'I would *not* trust her. My cousin is an actress. Heidi Stone has quite a reputation.'

'What kind of reputation?'

Dariel shook his head. 'Very shady. Known for losing it if a client drops her, which was quite a few after her drug issues.'

Vanessa raised an eyebrow. 'Drug issues?'

'Yeah, it's an industry secret.'

'I wonder if Ru and the team know about it?'

'I'm sure they do, but I'll drop him a message just in case.' He reached for his phone then frowned. 'Shit.'

'What's up?'

He held the phone up to her, showing a breaking news headline:

Another suspected poison victim.

Chapter 31

Ru looked at the photo of Jimmy Tandy, the latest victim – though he was not the latest to die, given he had actually passed away the day after Valentine's Day, of a suspected heart attack. He'd had heart problems for a decade, so when his daughter found him dead in his bed, she'd presumed it was that. It appeared the coroner had, too.

But then Jimmy's daughter had recognised the gift box on the news. It was the same one she'd found at her father's house with a pair of cufflinks discarded on the side made from metallic spotted beetle shells.

And now here they were in the producer's luxury high-rise apartment in Manhattan's Upper West Side, on the other side of Central Park from Jacqueline's apartment, in an area known for its museums. The apartment was modern, with high-end finishes, a spacious open-plan living area and state-of-the-art technology.

'Tell me about Jimmy,' Ru said to Harris as the forensics team bagged up the gift box and cufflinks in the bedroom.

'He's a producer,' Harris said, checking his notes. 'Worked on a tonne of films.'

'Another victim linked to the world of entertainment and celebrity.'

Harris nodded. 'Yep.'

'Any connection with the other victims?'

'Nothing obvious from a quick search but his daughter said he knew anyone and everyone.'

One of the forensics team walked past with the gift box Jimmy had received in a see-through evidence bag. Ru frowned as he noticed something.

'Stop,' he said to the officer. 'Hold it up to the light, just like you did a second ago.'

The officer obliged, holding the gift box up under the light streaming in from the main window. Ru leaned in closer. Yes, there appeared to be a barely noticeable watermark on the side of the box. Specifically, the same Japanese symbol he'd seen on the envelope in Heidi Stone's office.

He got his phone out, his fingers working deftly as he opened his browser and entered the symbol along with the word 'packaging'. The results brought up a host of content related to luxury packaging with Japanese design elements. Ru combed through them, looking for the distinctive kanji that matched the watermark. But he could find nothing.

When they got back to the precinct, Adiche was waiting for him. 'We've had another person come forward as a result of the captain's press conference,' she said.

'Alive, I hope?' Ru asked.

'Yes, thank God,' Adiche replied. 'It's the actress, Ali Perkins.'

Ru frowned. 'Who?'

'She's no Cordelia,' Ramos called over. 'She's in that Netflix series about dog groomers.'

'He still won't know,' Harris said. 'Hoshino's allergic to his TV, remember?'

'Whatever, it's not really important,' Adiche said. 'What *is* important is she sold the item she received to someone at a craft fair in Williamsburg two days ago.'

The officers in the room exchanged looks.

'Shit,' Harris said.

'Does she know who?' Ru asked.

'No,' Adiche said. 'She got a photo of the item, though, as she tried to sell it on eBay first. I'll get our press team to circulate it. Plus I'm trying to see if there's any CCTV at the venue where the craft fair took place.'

'We need to be all over this,' Ru said.

'I know Williamsburg,' Bouchier offered. 'I'll head there with some uniforms, get canvassing and track down any other fair stall holders and attendees. We'll alert the media, too.'

Haworth nodded. 'Perfect.'

Ru got his notepad out and looked at the names he'd written down of the victims so far. 'So far we know the following received gifts: Cordelia, Maximilian, Jerry, Kendra, Madeline, Jimmy and now Ali Perkins. They key is learning what connects these people. Why have *they* been targeted? We have an actress, a fashion designer, a billionaire, a celebrity journalist, a producer, an actress. All New York natives from what I can see, all high-profile.' He frowned. 'I keep coming back to AuthenticAegis. All these people will represent these "luminaries of New York" that AuthenticAegis refers to. This "decadence that they wear as a mask". He mulled over it for a moment, and nodded. 'I'm going to look at these videos again, try to find some clues to who this person is.'

An hour later, Ru was hunched over his computer in the squad room as he re-watched AuthenticAegis videos, jotting down notes. The timing of the video uploads tended to happen after 4 p.m. on weekdays, and clustered around weekends and school holidays. It was a pattern that suggested the creator had other primary commitments, like attending school, or maybe they were a teacher. It also suggested they lived and breathed New York, someone who saw its beauty and its flaws up close.

He noticed one scene looked like it had been filmed from a window. But it was hard to make out the view properly, overlayed as it was with effects and text. He downloaded the video then uploaded it to a video editing tool he had. With a few clicks, he began the meticulous process of stripping away the layers of digital manipulation, reducing the video to its raw form. As he did, the cityscape became clearer. He zoomed in, noticing the unmistakable outline of One World Trade Center and the Empire State Building, angled in such a way that they appeared almost side by side, a perspective not possible from most parts of the city. This unique juxtaposition, coupled with a sliver of the Brooklyn Bridge peeking into the frame, suggested the video was shot from an elevated position to the south-west of these landmarks. Only a few neighbourhoods could offer such a view where these icons aligned so distinctly – areas like Red Hook, Gowanus, or . . . Park Slope.

Wasn't that where Bronagh Thompson lived?

He frowned, slumping back into his chair as he steepled his hands together, leaning his chin on his fingertips.

Haworth walked over then, an excited glint in her eyes. 'You're not going to believe this,' she said. 'Guess who Cordelia's therapist was?'

'Who?'

'Joe Thompson. Dr Bronagh Thompson's husband.'

Chapter 32

Vanessa grabbed her post from the floor and kicked her Dr. Martens off, pleased to be out of them. She padded into the bathroom and turned on the bath taps. She needed a long soak after her drive from Cortland. Didn't help she'd hardly got any sleep the night before.

The night before . . .

She thought of Dariel. It had been nice. Really nice, despite the awful news about another victim. They'd had a long breakfast, overlooking the snowy valley, talking about their families. He'd mentioned a wedding of an old friend he'd been invited to the next month and had jokingly suggested she come. Well, he pretended it was a joke, anyway, but she could see in his eyes there was a serious note to it. When they'd said their goodbyes, he told her he'd be in the city again in a week's time, suggesting dinner. He'd even messaged to check she'd got home OK. She smiled to herself. There was something about Dariel Valdez. There was something about the inkling of an idea that maybe, maybe, she didn't always have to be alone.

She flicked through her post, then paused when she noticed an envelope with the NovaScope logo on. She quickly opened it to see another envelope inside with her name handwritten on the front along with the NovaScope address.

Strange.

She slit it open, unfolding a handwritten letter. 'Dear Nessy', it began.

Vanessa sank down onto the sofa.

It was from Vincent. He wasn't supposed to write to her, but then she supposed it was easy enough to slip a letter to a soon-to-be-released prisoner to send from the outside. She took in a deep breath and read it.

Dear Nessy,

I've been sitting here in my cell, thinking about our call just now. I realise now how much I upset you, and for that, I'm deeply sorry. I've always been good at pushing your buttons, haven't I? Remember when I used to wind you up by singing 'Cotton Eye Joe' non-stop? Old habits . . .

You reaching out, after all this time, just to check on me . . . it means more than you might think. It's funny, isn't it? How we can still care, despite everything. I guess some bonds are too deep.

What I was trying to tell you during our call is I've been doing a lot of thinking lately. About us, our childhood, the paths we've taken. I know I've made choices that have led me down this dark road, but talking to you, even for just a moment, was like seeing a sliver of light in this endless night.

I'm not asking for forgiveness, Nessy. I know the things I've done are unforgivable. But I hope, maybe, we can find some common ground. Remember how we used to talk about everything? Maybe we can find a way back to that, in some form.

Please, don't worry about me. Focus on your work, your life. But if you ever find it in your heart to reach out again, know I'll be here, waiting to hear your voice. It's the one thing that still feels like home.

Take care of yourself, Nessy. You're all I have left that matters.

Vincent

Vanessa's fingers trembled slightly as she folded the letter back up, her brother's words echoing in her mind. She saw it for what it might be: a masterful play of emotions, tapping into their shared past and the deep-seated bond they shared. But despite her best efforts, she couldn't fully sever that bond. Instead, she felt a desperate need to speak to her brother again. So she quickly opened the prison video-calling app, noticing a time was available in the next hour. She took a deep breath and selected it. The bath could wait.

* * *

Forty-five minutes later, Vanessa was looking at her brother's face on screen. He was squinting slightly as he looked at her. 'Your screen is fuzzy.'

'It might be your Wi-Fi. I got your letter,' she said. 'Now I have "Cotton Eye Joe" running on repeat in my head. That song haunted my dreams for years, thanks to you.'

Vincent's face broke into a grin, the kind of genuine smile she remembered from him. 'Ah, but you loved the dance moves, admit it. You were quite the dancer back then.'

Vanessa laughed. 'Only because I wanted to outdance you. Which, let's be honest, wasn't hard.'

'Hey, I had moves. We had some good times, didn't we, Nessy? You were a good sister, building forts out of couch cushions for me, staying up late during summer breaks in a tent in our garden.'

Vanessa nodded, the memories vivid in her mind.

Vincent frowned. 'I didn't want to give you the impression I never appreciated you. I understand, when we spoke last year, after . . . everything, I may have been harsh on you. But the truth was, you were good after Mum left, really good.'

As she took in what he was saying, Vanessa realised just how much she had needed to hear that. That maybe, it would help ease some of the guilt she felt at Vincent running away when he was only twelve.

'Do you ever think about why she left the way she did, Nessy?' he said. 'I used to think it was me. I was always so clingy, wasn't I? So demanding?'

'She didn't leave because of you.'

'Are you sure?' He leaned back in his chair, brow creased. 'Now I look back, I wonder if she saw it in me – the darkness. Maybe it scared her away? They say nobody knows you like your own mother does. But then I wonder whether I would have turned out the way I did if Mum hadn't left. Do you ever wonder the same? Like, why you haven't followed the usual path for a woman your age? No husband? No children?'

Vanessa took in a sharp breath. This was a mistake, calling her brother. Her head throbbed; temples buzzing, buzzing, buzzing.

'Sorry,' he quickly said, 'let's change the subject. How's the case? We all watched the press conference. Fascinating, isn't it, how someone is out there, killing them with insects? Have you seen the items up close?' he asked, eyes hungry for information. *Too* hungry.

Her phone started ringing then. It was Bronagh. 'I'm sorry, Vincent, but I have to go.'

'But we've only been talking for a few minutes!' Vincent whined, reminding her of how he would complain to her as a child: *But we've only been playing for ten minutes, Nessy!*

He wasn't that child anymore, though. And she wasn't his Nessy. He'd ruined that with the lives he'd taken. 'Seriously, I'm getting an important phone call.'

'More important than this? Than us?' He was shouting now, all that anger she'd seen the year before coming out.

'Goodbye, Vincent.' She logged off, noticing her hands were trembling, then quickly picked up her phone. 'Bronagh?'

'Did you hear? There's another victim. A producer. I emailed you a photo of the cufflinks that were found with him.'

Vanessa's heart sank. 'Oh no, I didn't know.' She quickly checked her laptop, finding Bronagh's email and the photo with it. 'Yep, those are Salt Creek tiger beetles in the cufflinks, one of the rarest insects in the US.'

'How was Cortland?'

'Yes, it was . . . fine,' Vanessa replied.

'Everything OK? You don't sound right.'

Vanessa sighed. 'I just had another video call with my brother.'

'Ah, I see. Bring you down, did it?'

'Just a bit.'

'Why don't you come over for a drink? That was actually why I was calling.'

Vanessa looked around her empty apartment. Yes, she needed company tonight. 'That sounds good. Thanks. Though will taxis be running in the snow?'

'Joe's in your area dropping something off, so he can pick you up.'

Chapter 33

After a tough journey through the snow, Ru pulled his motorbike up alongside the Thompsons' three-storey home in Park Slope. He'd been there once before, for Bronagh's fortieth birthday drinks when she'd worked at the precinct. And now here he was again, at Bronagh's insistence when he'd called her about Joe. Fresh snow had begun to whirl around him during his journey, turning the streets into a canvas of untouched white. He cut the engine and dismounted, the crunch of snow under his trainers the only sound in the early evening winter air. He took his helmet off and walked up the stoop which bore the telltale signs of some diligent shovelling, remnants of the day's efforts clinging to the edges.

Before he could knock, the door swung open, revealing a teenage boy whose eyes immediately fell on the motorbike, a gleam of admiration in his gaze. 'Cool bike. Was it tough riding in this weather?'

'Just a bit trickier than usual,' Ru replied.

'Mom said you'd be coming. Apparently, we all have to hide in our rooms. Come in,' he said, opening the door.

Ru stepped in, shaking off the snow that had gathered on the shoulders of his leather jacket as he followed the boy's lead. The hallway was a warm artery, the wooden floors creaking a welcome beneath his feet, the eyes from the numerous family photos on the walls seeming to follow him. The place pulsed with a warm, kinetic energy, mirroring the Thompsons themselves with their inviting, slightly chaotic charm.

As he removed his gloves and stuffed them into his helmet, he entered the living room. The crackle of the roaring fire was the first thing that greeted him, followed by the sight of Bronagh, and her husband Joe, who offered a tense nod. To his surprise,

Vanessa was there, too, her presence causing a momentary pause in Ru's step.

'Don't worry, Bronagh and I will be disappearing to the kitchen,' she said.

They both left the room, closing the door behind them.

Ru chose a spot near the fireplace, the heat seeping into his bones.

'Let me begin by confirming I am not AuthenticAegis, as you implied to my wife,' Joe said. His tone was calm, but Ru could detect the tension behind it. 'My technical knowledge is limited to what I need for my therapy sessions and the occasional PowerPoint for conferences. As for video editing, I wouldn't know where to begin. Not to mention the fact – as I just discovered when checking the dates of when these videos were uploaded – I was running a retreat upstate. A place off the grid, which means no Wi-Fi. I have proof. So if upload times are your evidence, I'm off the hook,' he said with an amiable smile.

'It wasn't just the upload times,' Ru said. 'Certain shots of the city skyline suggest they could have been recorded from upstairs,' he said, peering up at the ceiling.

Joe frowned. It was a brief moment but enough for Ru to bookmark. 'Park Slope is a large area,' Joe said. 'I'm sorry this isn't the breakthrough you hoped for. But, given the nature of the case, and having just spoken to my boss, there is another way I can help. I *can* talk to you about Cordelia.'

Ru settled deeper into his chair, the leather creaking under his weight as the fire crackled a comfortable soundtrack. 'I appreciate it, Joe,' he said. 'I know there are professional boundaries, but anything you can share within legal limits could be pivotal.'

Joe nodded. 'There certainly are boundaries. I don't even share who my clients are with Bronagh, not even when I learned she was involved with Cordelia's case. It's why these people come to us, we are discreet.' He sighed. 'But on this occasion, my boss has agreed we need some wiggle room. Cordelia was . . . struggling, significantly,' Joe conceded with a careful tone. 'There was an assault, about a year ago. She didn't give me details, just mentioned it in passing. It was clear, though, that it left its mark.'

Ru thought of the rumours about Maximilian Rossi assaulting girls.

'Add to that an ongoing battle with an eating disorder and the pressures of an industry that . . . well, it can be quite unforgiving,' Joe continued. 'There was a betrayal, too, a personal one. She found out she'd been cheated on. All of this led to her decision to step away from the digital world for a while – a detox of sorts.'

'I see. I suppose you won't be able to tell me this, but any names?'

'No. She never gave me specific names. She was such a *good* person, you know? Actually, genuinely, good. Too good for this industry.' Joe let out a heavy sigh, his eyes momentarily losing focus as if he were seeing Cordelia in the room with them. 'The industry my clients are involved in, it's gruelling. It can chew you up, spit you out. Let me reiterate, I am *not* AuthenticAegis. But I understand, to some extent, the rationale behind such videos. Cordelia being lumped in with those people makes me sad. She was genuine, just a girl pursuing her love of acting.'

Ru had to confess, it was something that continued to puzzle him, too. Cordelia seemed different from the other victims. Less . . . showy.

'So not the usual target of AuthenticAegis?' Ru asked.

He observed that same frown crease Joe's brow again.

Ru leaned forward. 'Joe, do you think you know who AuthenticAegis might be?'

Joe quickly shook his head. 'No idea. So, is this enough, Detective Hoshino? I really can't add much more unless you apply for a court order.'

Ru thought about it, examining Joe's face. He *seemed* to be telling the truth. But Ru, for once, couldn't be sure. He realised why. He was exhausted, his judgement impaired. It had been a long time since he'd worked at this level. It was taking its toll. In fact, maybe the fact he'd even considered Joe was AuthenticAegis was down to that impaired judgement. He closed his eyes, taking in a low, deep breath.

'This must be placing a burden on you,' Joe said softly, 'such a big case with few leads. It's important you look after yourself. Having the lead detective crash and burn wouldn't be good for Cordelia, for these other victims, either. Have you been eating well?'

'My mother fed me on Saturday night.'

'That was three nights ago. How about a warm Irish stew?'

Ru hesitated.

'Come on,' Joe said, standing up. 'It's all ready. It will take you just a few moments to eat, then you can get back to the case. I'll go get the kids. You go join Bronagh and Vanessa.'

As Joe ascended the stairs, Ru headed into the kitchen, finding Bronagh and Vanessa talking softly by the stove where a large pot simmered.

'Your husband is insisting I join you for dinner,' Ru said, breathing in the rich, hearty aromas wafting through the air.

'Yeah, you really look like you're being forced,' Vanessa said with a smile.

'You are more than welcome,' Bronagh said. 'As long as you're not about to expose my husband as AuthenticAegis?'

'I was convinced by his technical ineptitude,' Ru replied.

'It's been the bane of my life,' Bronagh replied. 'Sit, both of you.'

Ru took a seat at the table with Vanessa as Bronagh plated the stew up, chunks of tender meat and vegetables.

'Awful about the producer,' Bronagh said, 'seems never-ending.'

Ru sighed, raking his fingers through his dark hair. 'It does.'

'So you think AuthenticAegis has something to do with it all?' Vanessa asked.

'I don't know,' Ru admitted. 'It's all part of trying to find a connection between these victims. That's the key,' he said, jabbing his finger on the table, 'motive. Why target these particular people?'

Joe returned then, the thunder of footsteps announcing the presence of what looked like Bronagh's two youngest children.

'Simeon's got his nose buried in textbooks,' Joe explained, taking a seat. 'He'll join us if he can pry himself away.'

Talk of the case stopped and the dinner conversation was light. For a brief moment, the case receded into the background, allowing Ru a rare taste of normality in the midst of chaos. He took in the scene as he ate, the warmth and connection so foreign to his own existence. He noticed Vanessa watching, too, two lone wolves in the midst of this den-like experience. He supposed they were kindred spirits, bound by a dedication to the truth, no matter where it led. It was a life of sacrifice, but one they had chosen willingly.

'Hey, Bronagh,' Joe said, after they'd finished their plates, 'help me fetch the dessert from the garage freezer, will you?'

Bronagh's brows knitted together in a frown, but she rose from the table without protest. 'Of course,' she said, a hint of hesitation in her voice. They left the kitchen, leaving a temporary void at the table that was filled by the low murmur of whispering from the hallway, just audible enough to suggest a serious exchange but too quiet to discern any words.

'What was that all about?' Vanessa asked.

'No idea,' Ru replied, 'but I have a feeling dessert isn't the main reason for their departure. I have been making some enquiries about your mother, by the way, but as you can understand, it's been hectic.'

'No, it's fine. Dariel has offered to do some digging so that should take the pressure off.'

'Agent Valdez?' Vanessa nodded and Ru noticed her cheeks flush as she did.

'I was in Cortland, actually,' she said. 'Dariel invited me to learn a bit more about illegal insect trading.'

Ru tilted his head, watching her expression. It seemed she had a soft spot for Agent Valdez. Ru had encountered men like that most of his life. Confident, handsome, easily melding into society.

Joe and Bronagh returned then, this time with their eldest son in tow, his head hung low.

Bronagh gave a gentle but firm jab to Simeon's side. The teenage boy lifted his head, his eyes meeting Ru's.

'Detective Hoshino, I wanted to tell you . . . I'm AuthenticAegis. It's me.'

Vanessa's mouth dropped open. Ru didn't know how to react. He'd had so many surprises the past few days, he no longer had the ability to be shocked.

'I had a suspicion after what you'd told me, Ru,' Joe said with a sigh, 'and he admitted to it.'

'I didn't think it'd get so big,' Simeon said. 'It was just a sort of experiment to begin with. I swear, I have nothing to do with all these deaths, Detective Hoshino.' He looked like he was about to cry. Ru noticed Vanessa give Bronagh a sympathetic look.

'I'm not happy about this,' Bronagh said. 'Especially his most recent video about Cordelia's death, in particular. But Simeon's a good boy.'

Ru was quiet. 'I understand,' he said eventually. 'I was much the same as a teenager. Still am.'

'Simeon wants to tell you something else,' Joe said. 'About a private message he received via his AuthenticAegis account.'

'Yes?' Ru asked, paying close attention.

'It was on that recent video I did,' Simeon replied, 'after news about Cordelia Montgomery's and Maxmillian Rossi's deaths came out. Someone emailed from an anonymous account and said the *Chislington Post* was planning an exposé on Maximilian Rossi being a complete perv . . . and Cordelia was one of the people he perved on. But then the piece was pulled by the boss, Jerry Bowman.' His face went red. 'They also said Jerry Bowman was, you know, having *relations* with the journalist who was due to publish the article.'

'Did they give the name of this person?' Ru asked.

Simeon nodded. 'Kendra Grey.'

Ru raised an eyebrow. The journalist who'd received the wasp ring.

'Okay, Simeon,' Bronagh said, clearly clocking the name too. 'Go back upstairs, your dad and I will come up for a proper chat later.'

Simeon nodded and walked out.

'That name,' Bronagh said when he was out of earshot.

Ru nodded. 'Yes, she received a gift, too, and your son has confirmed a suspicion I had about Kendra and her boss.'

His phone rang then. It was Lieutenant Haworth. 'We have another target, and before you panic, he's alive,' she quickly said. 'I'll send the address, keep it discreet. And bring that bug lady with you. She's gonna love this one.'

Chapter 34

Vanessa followed Ru into the spacious apartment that belonged to the singer, Owen Harmon. His music wasn't her thing, but she'd heard of him – a former boy band member who'd become part of New York's trendy hipster set. She wasn't sure what to expect. Harris had been driving when he'd called Ru, so reception was patchy. All she knew is he'd recommended she be present.

She walked in, absorbing the loft's high ceilings and expansive windows, plus, rather predictably, Vanessa thought, a vintage guitar mounted on one wall. She was relieved when the singer himself came into view, sitting nearby on a leather sofa. He was in his twenties with deep auburn hair that fell in loose waves around the boyishly handsome face that made him so popular with his young fans. He was dressed in a long woollen jumper – or was it more a dress? – that reached his knees and frayed leggings, his feet bare.

'It's here,' Harris said, gesturing over to a secured area in the corner of the room, marked off by yellow caution tape. Within the boundary was a portable, transparent containment unit which hummed softly. Next to it were two forensics officers and a city health official, their faces set in grim lines as they guarded the potentially toxic artifact.

The brooch Owen had received as a gift looked tiny as it sat within the containment unit. But in reality, it was rather large, at least three inches in size. Vanessa leaned down to get a closer look. It was a masterwork of jewelled artistry, its border wrought with delicate gold and studded with diamonds. At its centre was a glass oval housing a living jewel – a peacock spider, its abdomen a kaleidoscope of shimmering blues and greens as it clung to the web it had made within its tiny home.

Despite the beauty of the display, there was something undeniably macabre about it. The spider, a creature of instinct and survival, reduced to an ornament, its natural habitat distilled into an artificial chamber. It was very still at first, but then it shifted slightly. Still alive, thank God.

'That's why the captain thought you should be here,' Harris said, 'to make sure the little guy survives.'

'Spiders can last a long time without sustenance,' Vanessa said. 'The back of the brooch must be aerated.'

'Is it another rare insect?' Harris asked.

Vanessa nodded. 'It's a peacock spider. They're incredibly rare, mostly found in Australia. They're particularly hardy as they've adapted to the Australian bush, where food can be scarce. They're able to regulate their metabolic rate.'

As she said that, the officials listened, their expressions a mix of wonder and concern.

Ru walked over to the singer. 'Mr Harmon,' Vanessa heard him say, 'when did you receive this gift?'

'Valentine's Day,' Owen replied, in his distinctive Australian accent. 'Didn't see it until this morning when I got back from my tour. My assistant left it here with all the other stuff I get.' He gestured to a large table full of post. 'Thank God I wasn't here when it arrived, eh? Wouldn't have known these things are fatal if it wasn't for your press conference.' He shook his head, his curls bouncing into his eyes. 'It's mad, especially after Cordelia . . .' His voice trailed off, and he shook his head. 'That was rough. I really liked that girl.'

'You knew Cordelia?' Ru asked.

'Yeah, we dated last year.'

Vanessa and Harris exchanged surprised glances.

'How long did you date?' Ru asked.

'Just a few weeks, but we were properly into each other.'

Ru frowned. 'Why did things end between you two, then?'

Owen shrugged. 'Just one of those things, you know?' He took in a ragged breath, hand brushing against his stubbled jaw. 'And now she's gone.'

Ru stood back up and joined Harris and Vanessa by the brooch.

'Hey, it's good we've tracked a piece of jewellery down before someone's hurt,' Harris said. 'Be good if we can find that moth necklace, too.'

'Moth necklace?' Vanessa said. 'I'm avoiding the news at the moment.'

Ru got his phone out and showed her a photo of the necklace Ali Perkins sold with a centrepiece made from a rare Atlas moth, the rich, coffee-coloured hues of its wings bleeding into a soft, cream border. What was most noticeable was its broken right wing, its jagged edges appearing to be sewn in gold.

Vanessa couldn't help but think about her mother. Vanessa had been fascinated by Atlas moths as a child, some of which spanned close to ten inches. Her mother would draw pictures of them for Vanessa. In fact, the broken wing of the dead moth attached to this necklace would be the kind of detail her mother would have added in her sculptures.

'It was sold at a craft fair in Williamsburg,' Ru explained.

'We're still trying to track the buyer down,' Harris added. 'Some broad in her sixties or seventies with long, greying black hair and olive skin.'

Vanessa paused. That sounded just like how her mother would look now.

The broken wing.

The Atlas moth.

The connection with the Thorsens' illegal insect trade.

'Do we have any photos yet of this person?' she asked carefully.

'Nothing, unless Adiche has managed to track down some CCTV,' Harris said.

'What's wrong?' Ru asked, perceptive enough to notice something was playing on Vanessa's mind.

'This sounds ridiculous,' she said. 'But that description sounds just like my mum.'

Ru stared off into the middle distance for a moment, clearly lost in his own thoughts. 'Not so ridiculous,' he said eventually, 'given her connection with the Thorsens. And don't her sculptures feature broken insects?'

A knot tightened in Vanessa's stomach. 'Exactly.'

'Do you have any recent photos of your mother?' Ru asked. 'We can share one with the actress who sold the item, see if she recognises her?'

'I'll send one to you now.' Vanessa got her phone out, finding a recent photo from the gallery website where her mother displayed her art. It was a side profile, of her standing outside, barefoot, in one of the long summer dresses she loved to wear, a flower in her long, greying black hair. Vanessa noted the lines around her eyes and the grey of her hair. So much time had passed since they'd seen each other last. She quickly shared it with Ru's phone over Bluetooth.

'You look like her,' he said as he studied it. 'I'll send it to Ali Perkins now.' He quickly composed a message and sent it.

'I'm sure it's not her,' Harris said, giving Vanessa a sympathetic look.

But Vanessa just chewed at her lip, hoping against hope he was right. The thought of her mother being in danger was a frightening one. But it was also confusing. She hadn't seen her in so long, it was hard to contemplate what it could mean for them.

Ru's phone buzzed and the three of them went very still. His eyes flickered up to Vanessa then down to his phone, opening the message. Vanessa watched him reading, her pulse drumming in her ears, her hands going clammy. She knew it before he even told her: 'I'm sorry, Vanessa,' he said. 'It looks like it was your mother who purchased the item. It's imperative we track her down.'

Chapter 35

Ru stood in front of the briefing room with Lieutenant Haworth. It felt even more personal now, a potential victim linked to one of their own. And Dr Marwood felt like one of their own now.

He scanned the faces of his colleagues, each one etched with the weariness that came from too little sleep and too many bad cups of precinct coffee.

'So,' Haworth began, 'we have our eighth and, we hope, final gift recipient. Dr Vanessa Marwood's mother was the one who purchased the necklace from Ali Perkins.'

A ripple of surprise passed through the officers who didn't know this news yet. Some exchanged glances, others just looked puzzled.

'That leaves us with one person to track down,' the lieutenant said. 'Ru, tell us more.'

Ru clicked a button on his remote and Vanessa's mother appeared on screen:

Name: Delilah de Souza
Job: Artist/Sculptor
Age: 65
Last contact: Sunday 19 February, 11 a.m., Craft fair in Williamsburg
Jewellery item: Necklace
Suspicious item: Unknown
Illegal insect: Atlas moth

'Let's start in Williamsburg,' Haworth said. She turned to Bouchier. 'Any luck with your canvassing there?'

'Hardly anything,' she replied. 'Some people recognised Ali from her stall and one remembered the necklace but nobody recalls seeing the person that bought it.'

'Maybe they will with a photo,' Ru said.

'Good point,' Haworth said. 'Get a printout and head back out there with uniforms, Bouchier. I'll get the photo circulated on the media, too.'

Bouchier nodded. 'I'll brief the media guys on the way out.'

'Any more general updates?' Haworth asked the room as Bouchier walked out.

One by one, the officers reported in. Leads had run dry; informants were silent. The frustration in the room grew palpable.

'Connections,' Ru said. 'Motives.'

He pressed some keys on his laptop and the faces of the eight targets came up.

Cordelia Montgomery
Maximilian Rossi
Jerry Bowman
Kendra Grey
Madeline Layton
Jimmy Tandy
Owen Harman
Ali Perkins

'Oh, Ramos left a note,' Adiche said. 'Sorry, I forgot. She reckons Cordelia and Ali worked on some film together, years back? When Cordelia started out. Ali was the lead.'

Ru frowned. It did keep coming back to Cordelia. He googled the film, and an insipid-looking romance came up: Ali's perky face smiling out, a younger Cordelia giving a wry smile behind her. He scrolled down, pausing when he got to an interview with a celebrity news item.

Ali Perkins Throws Shade at Former Co-Star Cordelia Montgomery: 'Some of Us Had to Work Our Way Up'

In a recent sit-down with *Celebrity Insight*, Ali Perkins didn't hold back when discussing her early career and the paths taken by her former co-stars. Reflecting on their shared project, *Love Beware*, the once sizzling romance film that introduced Cordelia Montgomery to the silver screen, Perkins remarked, 'It's interesting to see how some have skyrocketed to fame. I guess not everyone needs to grind it out in auditions and small roles. Some of us had to work our way up the hard way.' Perkins' comments have sparked speculation of a simmering jealousy towards Montgomery's rapid rise in Hollywood. This comes not long after speculation about the reasons for Cordelia's break-up with hottie Owen Harmon, involving a certain plump-lipped influencer, Madeline Layton.

'I have to ask,' Haworth said with a sigh, 'why haven't we noticed this before?'

'Cordelia had a few casual boyfriends,' Adiche said, 'and lots of snarky articles written about her. Ramos was following all the leads she could.'

Haworth nodded. 'Understood.'

'So,' Ru said, 'a snarky article from Ali about Cordelia. Rumours of her abuse at the hands of Maximilian Rossi. Her ex, Owen, cheating on her with Madeline, another target.'

'Oh!' Adiche said, 'another thing. There are rumours online that Jimmy Tandy made comments about Cordelia's weight after she turned down a role in one of his films.'

Ru thought about what Simeon had said about an article on Maximilian's abuse being pulled by Kendra . . . Kendra, whose boss was Jerry Bowman. He sat up straight. 'Most of these targets,' he said, 'if not *all*, have caused Cordelia Montgomery distress in some way.'

'Maybe whoever sent those gifts out on Valentine's Day did it for Cordelia?' Harris suggested.

'But why *kill* Cordelia, too?' Haworth asked, voicing the question Ru was turning over.

An officer popped their head in then. She'd been tasked with trawling sites like Etsy for any signs of the Japanese symbol Ru had noticed on the delivered gift boxes. 'We finally have a lead for the gift boxes,' she said, looking exhausted but happy. 'It's an Etsy page run by a packaging designer called Tillie Pearson.'

Tillie Pearson was just twenty-one, living in a small flat in Queens, and had, according to Adiche, who'd managed to gather some information on her, dropped out of Harvard Law. When Ru arrived at her flat with Harris, they were greeted by a young woman with brown owlish eyes and a smattering of freckles.

'I'm Detective Hoshino,' Ru said, flashing his badge. 'This is Detective Harris.'

She blinked. 'OK.'

'Is this one of your designs?' Harris asked, showing her a photo of the gift box.

Ru watched the woman closely, noticing a faint flicker of unease cross her face. 'Y-yes.'

'Can we come in?' Harris asked.

The woman opened the door wider and Ru walked in with Harris. She led them to a small living space with fake ivy hanging from the corners of the room, plus shelves of anime books and characters. Now Ru could understand the Japanese watermark on her packaging. They both took seats on the soft blue sofas across from Tillie. She looked like she was on the verge of tears.

'I saw the news conference on Sunday,' she said in a trembly voice, 'and I *swear*, I have *nothing* to do with those deaths.'

'We're not suggesting you did,' Harris said, voice gentle. He *could* be gentle when he needed to be. 'But you could really help. You want to help, right?'

She quickly nodded. 'Sure.'

'It would be useful if we could have the addresses of all those you've supplied these gift boxes to,' Ru asked.

'Most of them are through one client,' she continued. 'I don't sell many of these black boxes through my actual Etsy store.'

'What client?' Ru asked.

'I – I don't know who that client is. It's all done through my aunt. I design the packaging, that's *all*.'

'And your aunt is?' Ru asked.

Tillie suddenly burst into tears. 'I promised her I wouldn't tell anyone about all this!'

'Tillie, who is your aunt?' Harris pushed.

Tillie bit her lip. 'Heidi Stone,' she whispered. Harris's mouth actually dropped open and Ru took in a sharp breath. Tillie looked between them, a panicked expression on her face. 'Will she get in trouble?' she asked. 'She's a good woman, really, I swear! She didn't know the hair clip would be so dangerous.'

Ru frowned, confused. 'Heidi gave Cordelia the hair clip?'

'Yes. Heidi got it as a gift in the post, like all those victims,' Tillie said, wiping her tears. 'She – she showed it to me. It was so cute. She said she was going to give it to Cordelia.'

So Cordelia Montgomery hadn't been the target. It had been Heidi Stone.

Chapter 36

Williamsburg had transformed under the fierce grip of a winter blizzard. The snow, relentless in its assault, whirled around Vanessa as she braved the slippery sidewalks. Her breath formed clouds of mist in the freezing air, dissipating quickly but persistently replaced by the next frosty exhalation.

Vanessa's hands, despite her gloves, felt numb, clutching a now soggy photograph of her mother. She had ventured out into the storm, driven by desperation. She couldn't just sit at home and do nothing. The knowledge that Ru and the team were conducting their search did little to quell the storm of anxiety raging within her. She had seen the police cars – their lights a blur through the thick curtain of snow – and knew a recent photo of her mother was circulating in the media. But she needed to do something, too.

As she moved, Vanessa approached strangers, her voice barely audible over the howling wind as that frantic buzzing in her head grew to fever pitch. 'Have you seen this woman?' she asked, thrusting the dampened photograph towards them. But people only gave it a cursory glance then hurried by, heads bowed, their minds singularly focused on seeking shelter from the storm. The few who did stop squinted at the photo, shaking their heads apologetically before disappearing into the whiteout.

Frustration mounted with every unsuccessful attempt.

She'd have to head back soon. The roads would be impassable, even in her monster of a truck. She passed a man with dreadlocks who was sheltering under the awning of a closed coffee shop, seemingly at ease despite the chaos around him. Vanessa wrapped her coat tight around herself and walked over, holding the photo up at him.

'Have you seen this woman?'

The man took the photo from her, studying it closely under the streetlight above. 'Yeah, sure, I've seen her. That's Audrey Vee, right?'

Vanessa frowned.

Audrey, her grandmother's name. Vee . . . for Vanessa and Vincent?

'You related to her?' the man said. 'You look like her.'

Vanessa's heart ricocheted against her chest. 'When's the last time you saw her?'

'Actually, come to think of it, not for a couple of days. I usually spot her every day; she goes for a long walk most mornings right past my window, even in the snow.'

Panic clawed at Vanessa's insides. 'Where does she live?'

He pointed down the road, towards a block of apartments. 'Second floor.'

Without another word, Vanessa turned and ran, her feet slipping on the snow-covered pavement. When she got to the apartment block, she noticed graffiti on the wall outside depicting two laughing children and inside, through the glass doors of the entrance, one of her mother's sculptures, an intricate blend of metal and glass. Just as she reached the door, a young woman stepped out. Vanessa quickly moved to stop the door from closing, but the woman blocked her way. 'Not happening,' she said, voice firm. 'I don't recognise you.'

Vanessa didn't have time to be polite. She shoved the petite woman out of the way and raced up the stairs to the second floor. When she got there, she was horrified to see paramedics outside one of the apartments. Even more shocking, Dariel was there, too.

Vanessa regarded him with a frown. 'What are you doing here? I – I thought you were in Cortland.'

'Your mother's inside,' he said, without answering her question. 'She's not in a good way, Vanessa.'

Chapter 37

The townhouse where Heidi lived stood proudly in the upscale neighbourhood of the Upper East Side, its classic brownstone facade exuding the historical charm of old New York. Ru rang the doorbell, but there was no answer.

'You hear that?' Harris said as laughter rang out from around the back of the house. Ru walked over to the gate next to the house and tried it. It opened easily and the two officers walked in. As they drew closer, the laughter was replaced with moaning and they saw steam rising into the freezing late afternoon air.

'I feel like I'm in a porno,' Harris said as the moans grew louder. 'Is this the bit where the two hot detectives interrupt?'

They stepped into the garden to discover Anja Thorsen bare-chested in a jacuzzi, eyes closed as a muscular black man kissed her neck, Heidi Stone watching with a glass of champagne from nearby.

Heidi didn't know the Thorsens, according to the last time they'd spoken in her office. And yet here she now was, watching one of the Thorsen twins being pleasured by someone in her back garden.

The detectives exchanged a brief, bemused look, then Ru coughed. Anja's eyes snapped open and Heidi gasped. 'What in God's name are you doing here?' she hissed, wrapping her white fur coat tightly around her.

Anja tapped the man on the head. 'Sawyer, darling, we have company,' she said in her calm, Nordic accent.

Sawyer looked over his shoulder and let out a small, girlish scream.

Anja stepped from the steaming jacuzzi – seemingly unbothered that she was completely naked – and wrapped a towel around herself. 'If this is about Madeline,' she said, 'she's not a *real* friend, I barely know her.'

'We're actually here to speak to Ms Stone,' Ru said.

Anja quirked an eyebrow. 'Interesting. I'd better get out of your hair, then.'

She padded past Ru, narrowing her blue eyes at him as she did. Sawyer wrapped a towel around himself, too, and jogged in after her. When they were out of sight, Ru and Harris joined Heidi at her table.

'This is private property,' Heidi said. 'You can't just *barge* in like this.'

'The gate was open,' Harris said, 'and this is a multiple murder investigation.'

'I thought you didn't know the Thorsens?' Ru asked.

'I never said that,' Heidi snapped.

'You did,' Ru replied. 'I asked you "What about the Thorsens? Are you familiar with them?" to which you replied, "I know they own the hotel where Maximilian died. Otherwise, no."'

'He has a photographic memory,' Harris explained.

Heidi breathed in through her nostrils. 'Fine. I know them.'

'Why lie?' Ru asked. 'Especially to a detective?'

'*Because* you are a detective,' Heidi said. 'Wouldn't exactly go down well, would it? Me admitting I know a family rumoured to be involved with criminal activities?'

'Lying goes down a lot worse,' Harris said.

Ru held up his phone. 'Do you recognise this?' Ru showed Heidi a photo of the hair clip Cordelia had been wearing.

'No,' Heidi said after a brief pause.

'I'd strongly recommend you avoid lying again,' Ru advised.

Anja dipped her head out from the patio doors. 'Are you OK, Heidi?' she called out. 'Do you want me to call my lawyer?'

Ru noticed a flash of fear in Heidi's eyes as she looked at Anja. Then she quickly recovered herself, smiling. 'You don't have to worry about a *thing*, Anja, it's just a few questions about poor Cordelia and Maximilian. You can head off if you want – it's been a pleasure, as always. Tell Sawyer to make a start on dinner.'

Anja gave Ru another hard look, then nodded, closing the door and walking away.

Heidi sighed. 'I need a cigarette for this.' She picked a bag up from the floor, reaching a trembling hand into it. Ru noticed a bottle of pills in there. She pulled a packet of cigarettes out and lit one. 'OK.

I received the hair clip in the post on Valentine's Day, and assumed it was from the Thorsens as it was their packaging. I decided to give it to Cordelia, so had it couriered over the morning of fourteenth February, then called later to explain it was a gift for her.'

'Why leave this detail out when I saw you in your office last week?' Ru asked.

Heidi shrugged. 'I didn't think it was necessary. I have proof, I'll show you the box and label before you leave.' She shuddered. 'To think if I hadn't given this as a gift to dear Cordelia, I'd be dead.'

'But Cordelia would be alive,' Ru couldn't help himself saying. 'In the grand scheme of things, which option would be better?'

Harris gave him a sharp look.

'Do you recognise this?' Ru asked, showing Heidi a photo of the watermark.

She leaned forward. 'Something rings a bell. Why?'

'It's the watermark used by Tillie Pearson in her designs.'

'Your niece,' Harris added.

Heidi shifted uncomfortably in her chair.

'Interesting, isn't it?' Ru said, 'how the exact same watermark can be found on the gift boxes linked to multiple homicides, two of whom are your clients.'

'Yes, Tillie is my niece,' Heidi said. 'I introduced her beautiful work to Anja at a party last year, and as a consequence, they now commission Tillie to design their packaging. It's really as innocent as that. Honestly, there is nothing more I can say.'

'What about "sorry" for not coming to us sooner about this?' Harris said.

Heidi blinked. 'You don't understand. Jacqueline Thorsen is connected to some very powerful people.'

'So you were trying to protect the Thorsens by holding back this information?'

'More myself. As soon as I realised the connection between these deaths and the gifts – gifts featuring the same logo the Thorsens use for these special items – I knew it would be safer for me to keep my mouth shut. But why target me? I – I just don't understand.' She chewed at her lip as she peered into the distance. 'So, what happens now?'

'You let us take the gift box,' Ru said, 'then we talk to the captain about whether we need to bring you in for obstructing the course of justice.'

Ru's phone rang. It was Ramos.

'Excuse me,' he said as he walked down to the end of the garden, putting his phone to his ear. 'What's up?'

'Tillie Pearson's Etsy order list came through,' Ramos replied. 'In the past month, twenty-two orders had been made through the Etsy site, *eight* of which were delivered to a warehouse unit in Brooklyn Navy Yard.'

'Any names?' he asked.

'Sadly not,' Ramos replied. 'I spoke to the landlord. The units are rented out via an online platform and the person who rents this place, Unit 17B, has used a prepaid debit card which was purchased using cash. It's *completely* untraceable. But at least it's something.'

A surge of energy coursed through Ru's body – had they just found the site where their killer had been operating from?

Chapter 38

Vanessa shoved her way past Dariel and ran through her mother's apartment, her mind and heart racing. The space was small and cluttered, yet every inch spoke volumes about the woman who lived there. It was like stepping into a fragment of her childhood. The walls were adorned with paintings Vanessa recognised, their colours faded but still vibrant with emotion. In the corner, a small table held an unfinished sculpture.

But it was the framed photo on the mantelpiece of the bohemian open-plan living area that caught Vanessa's eye. It was a recent picture of Vanessa from the NovaScope website. Her mum really *had* kept up with her life, silently and from afar.

Vanessa turned her attention to the kitchen where two paramedics were working on someone who was lying on the floor. She darted over to see who they were tending to: a frail woman with greying hair spread around her head.

Yes, it was her mother. So different from the vital figure etched in Vanessa's memories, and yet so unmistakably her. The beauty spot on her cheek. The cluster of colourful rings adorning her fingers. A long, beautifully patterned dress.

Dariel approached her. She knew the time would come when she'd be asking Dariel why he was here before them. Even worse, why he hadn't called her to tell her he knew where her mother lived.

But now wasn't the time.

'We found her collapsed,' Dariel said gently.

Vanessa took in her mother's face, the slight swelling to her lips and around her mouth. The trace of dried blood at the corner of her lips. Her face was also very bruised, her arm, too, suggesting she must have fallen pretty hard when she collapsed.

'We think she's been here, alone, for a couple of days,' Dariel continued. 'We got here just in time.'

Alone. For a couple of *days*? Those words hammered Vanessa with – she realised in surprise – guilt. Rationally, she knew she couldn't have been here. Couldn't have known. Despite that, she felt some responsibility, like she did for her brother.

Dariel gestured towards a gift box being placed into an evidence bag nearby. 'It's the necklace,' he said. 'I think she was planning to give it to you, Vanessa. There was a note. She wouldn't have known about how unsafe it was if this happened a couple of days back, before it all hit the news.'

She'd bought the necklace . . . for her?

Tears welled up in Vanessa's eyes, but she blinked them back fiercely. She'd deal with the note later. Right now, all that mattered was the fragile figure on the floor. Vanessa knelt beside her. 'I'm here, Mum,' she whispered. 'It's Vanessa.'

She had fleeting images of her mum doing the same when she was a child. Rubbing her back when she was ill or upset, kissing her cheek. *I'm here, Vanessa. Mummy's here.*

But then she wasn't there, for so long. Why did she leave? Why stay away? Vanessa had to swallow the questions down, focusing instead on whispering words of comfort to her mother as the paramedics stabilised her.

'Is my mother going to be OK?' Vanessa asked.

'She's been unconscious for a significant period of time,' the older paramedic explained, 'so we're treating her for dehydration and respiratory issues.'

'What kind of damage could she have sustained?'

'If Agent Valdez's concerns are true,' the paramedic replied, 'and she's been exposed to a toxin, then it may have affected her organ function. We'll know more once she's at the hospital.'

The journey out of the apartment was a blur. In the back of the ambulance, Vanessa continued to hold her mother's hand, a turmoil of emotions churning within her, one sentence running over and over through her mind.

Live, damn it. Live.

Chapter 39

Unit 17B was located in a large warehouse-style building in the Brooklyn Navy Yard. After officers made a forced entry into the unit, Ru stepped in, musty, chemical-laden air greeting him. Inside, workbenches were cluttered with tools and materials. The walls, peeling with layers of old paint, were lined with shelves filled with jars and boxes. In one corner of the area a large magnifying lamp hung over a desk, illuminating an array of intricate jewellery parts and watch components. Tiny gears, springs and clasps lay scattered across the surface, alongside delicate tools tailored for minute work.

'Looks like we've found our place,' Harris said.

Ru nodded, walking around the room as officers began to search for evidence. Opposite the desk, another section was dedicated to entomology; various dead insects pinned and displayed under glass cases. There was also a makeshift laboratory. Vials of toxins, pipettes and beakers were arranged alongside protective gloves and masks.

'Hoshino, look.' It was Ramos, standing at the other end of the room and gesturing to a table. Ru walked over to it to find a dead ironclad beetle, half its back covered in the same colour jewels as those on Cordelia's hair clip. 'Looks like it died in the process,' she said. 'The one eventually used on the clip was probably a back-up.'

Ru nodded. 'We need this place thoroughly checked over by forensics. Photographs, fingerprints, everything and anything bagged up. The works. Collect any samples our colleagues at NovaScope Forensics can look at, too.'

Then his phone rang. It was the captain. 'We found Delilah de Souza,' he said. 'It doesn't look good.'

Ru leaned against the sterile wall of the hospital corridor, his eyes flicking from the clock to the emergency room doors and then to Bronagh, who was pacing up and down in front of him.

'She found her,' Bronagh said. 'Went out in the storm and found her.'

'Dr Marwood is a very determined woman.'

'That's one of the reasons why I took her on. Jesus, this is going to *mess* with her head. She hasn't seen her mother since she was a kid and now, all these years later, her first sight of her is collapsed on the floor?'

Ru nodded. 'It will be very difficult for her. But she is strong. She will cope.' He felt similarly about Madeline Layton, recuperating just one floor below, her condition steadily improving. Two lives had been snatched back from the brink of whatever malevolence was behind this. Yet, in his eyes, that was still two too many who had teetered dangerously close to death's edge.

A nurse popped her head out. 'Dr Marwood says you can come in.'

They both walked into the hospital room, the sterile white walls and the rhythmic beeping of the machines creating a surreal backdrop to Ru's turbulent thoughts. The breakthrough he'd made about the killer targeting people who had wronged Cordelia left him with some options. Options he would pursue as soon as he checked on Vanessa and her mother.

Vanessa sat quietly by her mother's bed, watching her as she slept, a figure so frail and distant from the vibrant artist in the mental image Vanessa had created of her. Her face was a painful sight with bruising around her mouth, and a hint of damaged teeth, a result of her collapse.

'I can't stop wondering,' Vanessa said quietly, 'whether she was in pain as she lay there, waiting and hoping for help?'

'She hopefully passed out straight away,' Bronagh said, taking the seat next to Vanessa and holding her hand.

'The doctors confirmed poisoning,' Vanessa said. 'They don't know how she survived.'

Bronagh nodded. 'Egbo and the team will work through the night on the toxicology tests. And Jamie's already checked the necklace. Whatever substance harmed your mother came from a tiny aerosol dispenser hidden in the necklace's pendant, triggered by a certain amount of handling. But thankfully,' she added with a sigh, 'it looked like the dispenser malfunctioned, delivering only a small dose. Enough to render her unconscious, but not enough to claim her life.'

'Thank God,' Vanessa said. 'And thank you – the whole team – for looking into it all so quickly.'

Bronagh squeezed Vanessa's hand. 'You're one of our own.'

Ru watched them. They clearly shared a bond.

He sensed movement behind him and turned to see Dariel standing at the entrance to the room. He'd heard Dariel had been at the scene a full half an hour before Vanessa arrived. And yet he hadn't called Ru, nor Vanessa, despite knowing they were urgently trying to find her mother. Why?

Then he thought of what Harris had said to him about Valdez being 'damn ambitious'. Maybe his priority had been getting a breakthrough on his illegal insect trading investigation, and he didn't want Vanessa and the NYPD ruining that.

'How did you know where my mum lived?' Vanessa asked, clearly struck by the same fact. 'You must have known what danger she was in. Why didn't you call me? And why were you back here, in the city?'

Dariel hesitated, his silence filling the room like a dense fog.

'You didn't care about her,' Vanessa said as it dawned on her. 'About *me*. All you care about is cracking your case.'

'Don't make it sound so fucking awful. I've been working on this case for years, Vanessa! And I'm finally getting close to putting some important people away,' Dariel said. 'But I genuinely like you, Vanessa. *Really* like you.'

'Fuck you,' Vanessa said, shaking her head and turning away.

'I'm serious.' Dariel reached out to place a hand on her shoulder, but Vanessa shoved him away.

'Seriously, don't even *try*,' she said in a calm voice. 'It's not worth it. Nothing was going to come of us anyway. So save your breath. Please leave.'

Dariel stayed where he was.

'Wasn't she clear enough?' Ru said, face impassive as he regarded Dariel. 'Please leave. Now.'

Dariel tensed his jaw then walked out. Vanessa's shoulders slumped.

'What an A-hole,' Bronagh said.

Vanessa let out a bitter laugh. 'Stupid thing is, I was lying when I said nothing was going to come of it. Deep down, I think I hoped something *would* come out of it.' She shook her head. 'God, I'm so bloody naïve, and I have the absolute *worst* taste in men.'

'Do not blame yourself for his bad decisions,' Bronagh said fiercely. 'You gave someone a chance – that's a *good* thing. It's not your fault he didn't deserve it.'

A doctor walked in then, nodding at them all. 'I'm Dr Jefferson,' he said, 'the hospital's oral and maxillofacial surgeon. I'll be looking at your mother's injuries. I believe you're a doctor too?' he asked Vanessa.

'Of forensic entomology,' Vanessa said.

'How *fascinating*.' The doctor leaned down and carefully studied Vanessa's mother's mouth. After a thorough examination, he straightened up and addressed Vanessa. 'So, it looks like I'll need to create a custom dental appliance to aid her recovery. It's quite a detailed piece of work,' he explained, a hint of pride in his voice. 'I believe your mother is an artist?'

Vanessa nodded. 'She is.'

'Well, I suppose we dentists are artists in our way. It takes dexterity and skill to create these intricate devices.'

Dexterity and skill to create these intricate devices.

His words ignited a spark in Ru's mind.

Cordelia's brother was a dentist . . . The craftsmanship and attention to detail required in dentistry could be very useful when creating intricate designs to turn jewellery into deadly weapons. Then another thought occurred to him: the user on the dark web forum, ByteCraft. He'd assumed it was a nod to computer hacking, but what if it was more literal, referring to a *craft* involving *biting*. Specifically . . . teeth?

Vanessa must have been thinking the same because her eyes widened. 'Levi,' they both said at the same time.

'Levi?' Bronagh said, looking between the two of them. 'You mean Cordelia's brother?'

'All the people attacked and targeted had in some way hurt his younger sister,' Ru reasoned. 'We've heard how protective and defensive he is, too.'

Ru slipped his phone from his pocket and googled Levi Montgomery. Among the results was a link to a video clip from a local news segment showcasing Levi's dental skills. He played it, Vanessa and Bronagh watching it too. In the video, Levi was demonstrating a dental procedure on a plastic model. His hands were deft, his movements precise. When the reporter commended him on his work, Levi replied, 'Well, delicate work often requires a strong and steady hand.'

'A strong and steady hand,' Vanessa murmured.

'And dentists could get their hands on medical supplies,' Bronagh said.

Ru was already walking out of the door. 'Keep me posted with your mother's progress,' he called over his shoulder. As he walked down the hospital corridors, he called Haworth, explaining their theory.

'You're not gonna believe this, Hoshino,' Haworth said. 'Adiche has been doing some digging around Owen and Cordelia's relationship. Turns out, Owen and Levi had words at an awards ceremony last year, and it got pretty heated when Levi confronted Owen about rumours he was cheating with Madeline. Jesus,' she said, 'what if Levi Montgomery *is* behind all this? It would make sense, if whoever's doing this all did it for Cordelia?'

'And he *killed* his sister by accident,' Ru said, 'if indeed she wasn't a target, as we suspect. What a tragic mistake. We need to bring him in.'

'Not yet,' Haworth warned. 'We *must* tread carefully before we rush in. Make sure we have as much evidence as we can get. He is the first victim's brother, after all. What do we know about him?'

'Thirty-two, married with two children,' Ru replied. 'The epitome of the perfect Jewish son – respected, successful orthodontist, pillar of the community.'

He heard footsteps behind him. It was Bronagh. 'I just had a call from one of my digital team. Detective Haworth, you asked me to do a deep dive of the PayPal account linked to the person who leased the unit – the one you suspect the killer used?'

'Yes?' Haworth asked.

'The user attempted to anonymise the payment,' Bronagh said, her voice holding an edge of excitement. 'But they didn't cover all their bases. They used a VPN, sure, but the email linked to the PayPal account was previously used to register a domain. That domain is now defunct, but I pulled the historical registration info from an internet archive service.'

'And?' Ru pushed.

'And it was registered to a private mailbox service. We cross-referenced the service with known associates of our suspects and found a match. The mailbox was rented out under a fake name, but the payment records for the rental tie back to a card used for – wait for it – Montgomery Medical Supplies.'

'Did you hear all that?' Ru asked Haworth.

'I did. I think we have the evidence we need. It's time you paid Levi Montgomery a visit.'

Chapter 40

Levi lived with his family in the suburban outskirts of New York City. As Ru pulled up outside the picturesque home, he took a moment to breathe in the neighbourhood against the setting sun, the epitome of family life with glimpses of a treehouse in the yard and tiny snow boots on the porch. The snowstorm had abated, leaving behind snow-clad trees and white paths.

The officers stepped out of their cars. As Ru and his team approached the door, Levi was already opening it. He was wearing a tux, his expression one of cordial surprise as he noticed Ru. Then it quickly shifted to confusion followed by concern as he saw the police cars parked outside.

'How can I help you, Officers?' he asked.

Ru didn't waste any time. 'Levi Montgomery, you are under arrest in connection with the manufacture of hazardous materials and assault.' He recited the Miranda warning with a practised ease, his eyes never leaving Levi's face.

'I – I don't understand. This is impossible!'

Harris stepped forward to handcuff Levi as the other officers flooded into the house.

'Call Lucy and my mother,' he called over his shoulder towards an older woman standing at the back of the hallway. The housekeeper? As Harris led Levi to the car, Ru walked into the house. He wanted to be there when the search team gathered evidence. This interview with Levi could be the most important of his career, and he intended to be thoroughly prepared.

'Question the housekeeper,' he said to Ramos. 'She may know something.'

'Will do.'

Ru strolled around Levi's house as the search team moved into action. As he surveyed the dining room, his eye landed on a collection of ribbons and an ornate gift bag lying on its side on the dining room table.

'What is this for?' he asked the housekeeper, gesturing to the gift bag.

'Mrs Montgomery runs a party supplies business,' the housekeeper answered. 'She has supplied gift bags for the winter gala event tonight in honour of Cordelia. Mr Montgomery was about to head there to meet Mrs Montgomery and the children. The rest of the gift bags are there now. This is a spare.'

Ru picked up one of the bags, carefully examining its contents. Chocolates from a boutique confectioner, miniature bottles of upscale champagne, small notepads and an empty aerosol perfume bottle. He thought of the aerosol mechanism in Vanessa's mother's necklace.

'What's in this?' he asked the housekeeper, pointing to the bottle.

'Some guests get a special perfume,' she replied. 'Just a small vial, but the aerosol on this one does not work, so it wasn't used.'

Ru's mind raced. Perfume. A vial. Could there be a connection?

'Were the gift bags labelled?' he asked.

The housekeeper nodded, gesturing to a printout. Ru scanned the list, noting that certain individuals were starred. One of them was the make-up artist from the funeral, Laife Ravenna.

Ru's mind raced. The vials in the gift bags might not be mere gifts; they could be potential weapons, akin to the aerosol in the necklace. This charity event could be a cover for a larger, more sinister plan. It might not be over.

'Where is this event taking place?' Ru pushed.

'The Damyanti Institute,' she replied. 'East 73rd Street.'

That was near the hospital he'd just come from.

Ru started running out of the room, calling Vanessa as he did.

'Did you get him?' she asked as soon as she answered.

'Yes, but I need your help,' Ru said, his voice tense. 'There's a charity event happening at a building a mere three-minute walk from you. I think the gift bags have been tampered with. We're sending officers, but the city's gridlocked because of the snow. It took us an hour to get here.'

'I'm looking out of the window now. I can see.' She paused. In that pause, Ru knew she was considering his unspoken question: would she go to the event and stop the gift bags being distributed? He imagined her standing at the window and watching the traffic lights trailing and unmoving below. Her instincts might be screaming at her to wait, to let the authorities handle it. But another part of her, a stronger part, would be thinking of how many more people might end up lying in a hospital bed like her mother, or worse, down below in the mortuary.

'I'll go,' Vanessa said.

Chapter 41

The dark streets were a blur as Vanessa ran towards the building where the winter gala was taking place. She rounded the corner and saw the venue up ahead, glittering with lights. Sirens sounded in the distance but no officers came running. It was rush hour, after all, in the heart of Manhattan on a snowy day. Only so many officers would be free.

Vanessa slowed her pace, moving more cautiously now. She needed to be calm enough to talk her way in. She peered down at what she was wearing. At least it was a dress, a pattern of vibrant red roses trailing down one side of the A-line skirt, her velvet blazer matching the colour of the roses.

The building where the event was taking place was an elegant piece of modern architecture with expansive glass facades that reflected the evening lights of the city. The entrance was marked by a red carpet, leading to a set of grand double doors that were flanked by tall plants. At the door, a woman was holding a clipboard. Vanessa approached, her heart rate quickening. She knew she wasn't on that list, and she couldn't declare she was an officer of the law without a badge.

'Your name?' the woman asked with a smile.

'I'm sorry, I'm not on the list, but Felicity – Cordelia's mother – knows me. She'll vouch for my presence.'

The woman at the door looked sceptical, her eyes scanning Vanessa's gothabilly attire with a hint of doubt. 'Do you have any way to contact her? I can't just let you in without confirmation.'

She didn't have Felicity's number, but she pulled out her phone anyway, relieved to see there was no reception. She grimaced and showed the woman her screen. 'Reception isn't great here.'

'I'm sorry, I can't let you in. Reception is better at the back – you can go down that alleyway and try there. Maybe then get her to come out and speak to me?' She shrugged. 'Sorry.'

As she said that, Vanessa noticed a blonde woman striding over. She remembered her from the funeral. It was Levi's wife, Lucy, and judging from the smile on her face, she had no idea yet that her husband had been arrested. Vanessa waved at her. 'Lucy!'

Lucy looked over, frowning as she took Vanessa in.

'Do you know this woman, Lucy?' the woman at the door asked.

'I suppose I do,' she said hesitantly.

'Felicity invited me,' Vanessa lied, hating herself for it. 'She must have forgotten to put me on the list.'

'Typical Felicity,' Lucy snapped. 'Please, come in.'

Vanessa stepped in. 'The gift bags. Where are they?'

Lucy frowned, perhaps thinking Vanessa was just there for the swag. 'They won't be given out until the end.'

'I need to know where they are. They may have been tampered with.'

Lucy's eyes widened. 'Th-that's impossible. I did them myself.'

'Alone?'

'Well, no, Levi was there and—' Vanessa gave her a pointed look and Lucy quickly shook her head. 'Absolutely not.'

'I'm afraid he's been arrested, Lucy. I'm so sorry.'

'No, that's impossible.'

'Please, Lucy,' Vanessa said, grabbing her hands. 'I need to make sure nobody's near the gift bags.'

Lucy gulped, tears flooding her eyes. Then she gestured for Vanessa to follow her. Together, they walked into the main area of the gala. As Vanessa and Lucy made their way to the back of the room, Vanessa's phone buzzed with a flurry of messages. Finally, some reception. She glanced at the screen to see one of the messages was from Ru, informing her that two officers were a five-minute walk away.

'The gift bags are in there,' Lucy said, gesturing to a door.

'You stay here.'

Lucy nodded, already checking her own phone for reception and putting it to her ear.

Gift bags in back room, she quickly typed back to Ru. **Heading there now.**

Vanessa opened the door and slipped into a small back room, away from the buzz of the gala. Lined up on a table at the back were carefully arranged rows of gift bags, each adorned with delicate gold accents and a subtle floral pattern. As Vanessa's eyes scanned the neat rows, she imagined the deadly perfumed weapons that might be hidden within them.

'Oh. Dr Marwood!' a voice announced.

Vanessa turned to see Felicity appear through a door at the back of the room, a gift bag clutched in both hands. Her expression was troubled, her usual poise replaced by a pallor of distress. Had she heard the news about her son? The ashen look on her face suggested she may have done.

'I didn't realise you were attending,' she said.

'Felicity, I need you to put those gift bags down. They could be dangerous.'

Felicity looked confused as she peered down at the bags. 'I don't understand.'

'We believe there may be tampered items within some of them.'

'T-tampered? What on earth do you mean?'

'The small bottles of perfume,' Vanessa said. 'Please, put the bags down, then I can explain. I don't want to risk you getting hurt.'

Felicity blinked, tears flooding her sad eyes, the bags still hanging from her hands.

Why wasn't she putting them down?

And then something occurred to Vanessa.

'Felicity, what work did you do before you retired?'

'I don't understand the relevance.'

'What job did you do?'

'I helped run my husband's medical supply business. Before that, I was a biomedical engineer.' She frowned. 'Dr Marwood, I really don't understand—'

A horrible realisation settled. Vanessa looked down at the gift bags. 'A biomedical engineer. So you know something about designing intricate items to place in bodies, like tiny aerosol dispensers and pressure pads?' she asked.

Felicity's face suddenly dropped. 'Oh.'

It was one simple word but it spoke volumes. Felicity Montgomery was the killer behind all these deaths.

Chapter 42

'Police officers will be arriving imminently,' Vanessa said, putting her back against the door so Felicity couldn't leave through it. She just needed to hope the other door didn't lead outside. 'It would look better if you gave yourself up.'

Felicity nodded, placing the gift bags down and smoothing her silver hair from her eyes. 'Of course. I suppose it's a relief in many ways.'

'Your own daughter . . .'

Felicity flinched, squeezing her eyes shut. 'Cordelia was *never* meant to come into contact with *any* of those items. Why would that awful agent of hers *gift* her such a thing? And why would Cordelia *wear* it? I did all this *for* my girl. It was never meant to happen like this.'

'So you purposefully targeted a list of people with gifts, pretending they were from the company that supplied insect jewellery?' Vanessa asked, trying to wrap her head around how the woman standing before her could be capable of something like that.

'It started as a fantasy,' Felicity said, placing her hand on one of the gift bags. 'I was angry at them all, starting with that bastard, Maximilian Rossi. You know he *raped* my daughter?'

Vanessa squeezed her eyes shut. 'My God,' she whispered.

'I *pleaded* with her to report it, but she refused. Said it was her fault because she'd agreed to stay behind after a photo shoot.' Felicity let out an angry sob. 'I even went to Heidi, that terrible woman, but she fobbed me off. So I took it to a newspaper journalist I know.'

'Kendra Grey.'

'That's right. She said she'd look into it but then she just started avoiding my calls. Guess what? Turned out she was seeing her boss, Jerry Bowman. And he was friends with Maximilian Rossi! He must have convinced his little mistress to pull the article . . . *All* so incestuous and so rotten.'

Vanessa sighed. She could see the frustration etched on this mother's face and she could understand it, too. 'Then at the Golden Globes last year,' Felicity continued, 'I overheard Heidi discussing some dark web insect jewellery venture. I asked her about it, and she had a brochure sent to me.'

She caressed the top of the gift bag with her thumb, closer and closer to that perfume. 'The items were as sickening as I imagined,' Felicity continued. 'Even worse, I began noticing more and more celebrities wearing them when I accompanied Cordelia to events.' Her expression faltered. 'That was around the time I noticed Cordelia's mental health unravelling. This industry was picking her to pieces, bit by bit. What had happened to my mother, was happening to my daughter.'

'Your mother?'

Felicity's glassy eyes met Vanessa's. 'She was an actress, too. Not as successful as Cordelia. She got pregnant with me before she really had a chance to make it.' She closed her eyes, black mascara tears squeezing from her lashes. 'She took her life when I was fifteen, after she tried to return to the industry. This unforgiving celebrity world drove her to it. Cordelia knew that and yet still, she insisted it was what she wanted to do.' Felicity opened her eyes and shook her head. 'I couldn't have her taking her life like my mother had. I started fantasising about ways to remove the threat factors in her life. It was the insect jewellery that pushed me to it. I saw so many of the people in her world – the ones who hurt her – wearing those awful things. It sickened me, these shallow, dreadful people using living creatures as accessories, even more so when I learned she was falling for Nils Thorsen, the very man whose family was behind such horrendous items.' Felicity tilted her head, examining Vanessa's face. 'You probably think I'm a hypocrite, seeing as I've used living creatures for revenge.'

Vanessa didn't say anything, so aware of how easily Felicity could grab a bottle of that perfume and spray it at her.

'Do you have children, Dr Marwood?'

Vanessa shook her head.

'Well, you won't understand, then, the things you will do for your children, even if those things go against *everything* you believe in.' She began to open the gift bag. Vanessa tried to listen for the sound of running feet, but there was nothing, just the revelry of the ball, and it was just her, alone, with a woman who'd killed five people already.

'I began imagining targeting those who had wronged Cordelia,' Felicity said. 'I imagined injectors with poison and release pads with toxins.' She tapped her head. 'It was all up here to begin with, that's all. Just something to tame my anger.'

'What turned the fantasy into reality?' Vanessa dared to ask.

'When Cordelia got worse, I got angrier. Did you know she tried to take her life six months ago?'

'No,' Vanessa said. 'I'm so sorry.'

Felicity let out a bitter laugh. 'No, no, of course you wouldn't know. Heidi was very good at keeping it quiet. Couldn't have her most lucrative client being *tainted*. But yes, that's when my fantasies turned to reality.'

She smiled slightly, as though she'd enjoyed the process. Maybe it was because, in a helpless situation, she had felt she was doing something, even if that something was horrific . . .

'I researched the dark web and how I might be able to source insects like the ones I saw in the brochure,' Felicity continued. 'Finding similar jewellery pieces was easy enough from places like Etsy and thrift stores. I even went so far as to order an item from the Thorsens' brochure and track down where they had their gift boxes made. I could kill two birds with one stone and implicate Nils Thorsen in it all. I suppose,' she said, brow creased, 'that when I started designing the little mechanisms in my notepad, it became more serious. I have to admit, I enjoyed it. It took me back to my engineering days, sourcing equipment from old contacts.' She was lost in thought for a moment, then straightened her back. 'When I signed up for a lease on the warehouse, I knew the fantasy was becoming reality. Eight people, I told myself. Eight people to remove from my darling girl's life and she'd be all better. Or I suppose it would be nine, if Nils Thorsen and his family's sickening enterprise was tangled up in it all. Some of their addresses were easy to get hold of. An indiscreet celebrity photographer, or simply following them to see where they went. Eight *stupid*, shallow people. In the end, it would be up to them. If they were indeed stupid and shallow enough to wear such an item, then they would deserve to die.'

Vanessa couldn't help herself. 'But one of them wasn't your intended target. Cordelia, your own daughter.'

Felicity's face collapsed slightly. 'I never dreamed of such a horrific outcome. You know, Dr Marwood,' she said, taking the gift bag and hugging it to her chest as she took a step towards Vanessa, 'I very nearly took my life the evening Cordelia was found. Luckily, my son found me, insisted on staying with me. Then I saw Maximilian had died. It made me realise I had a new purpose. I *had* to make her death worth it.'

'Worth it? With *more* death?' Vanessa asked, gesturing to the gift bags. 'What have the guests here done to you? There are *scores* of them out there.'

'I won't hurt all of them, just some. They're labelled, see,' she said, gesturing to the bag in her hand to show a name written on the side: Ottilli Holmes, the feather-hatted woman from the funeral. 'Thing is, Dr Marwood, more of these leeches came out of the woodwork after Cordelia died. People claiming to be her friends, like that awful Laife creature. I had to continue, for Cordelia.'

'And take more children from their mothers?' Vanessa said.

Felicity shook her head. 'No, you're looking at it the wrong way. If I *don't* do this, more mothers will suffer grief. More children, too, as their parents take their lives.' Her eyes flickered with memories, no doubt thinking of her own mother. 'If I want to ensure Cordelia's death wasn't for nothing, I *have* to see this through.' She straightened her shoulders. 'And I'm sorry, Dr Marwood. As much as I admire you, I can't let you get in my way.'

She quickly reached into the gift bag she was holding and pulled out a tiny green perfume bottle with insect patterns etched all over it. She held it up to Vanessa, her finger on the pump. 'If you leave now,' Felicity said calmly, 'I won't have to hurt you.'

Vanessa stared at the perfume bottle, imagining what the contents would do to her. *Not now*, she thought. *Not now I've found my mother again.* For a moment, she considered doing as Felicity ordered and just leaving. But then she thought of all those people Felicity had killed. Had hurt.

Vanessa shook her head. 'I can't let you hurt more people like you hurt my mother.'

Felicity frowned. 'Mother?'

'Yes. The actress you targeted, Ali Perkins? She sold her piece of jewellery to my mother.'

'Your *mother*?'

Vanessa nodded. 'She's in hospital right now. She's around your age, in fact.'

'I – I had no idea.'

'I'd like to say she was as devoted a mother as you are,' Vanessa continued. 'She was, at first . . . But then she left us. It did things to my brother and me, her leaving, *here*,' she said, pressing her fist to her heart. 'How do you think your mother would feel, to know what her death did to you? The number of subsequent deaths it caused? What it's also doing now, to your remaining son. To your grandchildren?'

Felicity faltered, lowering the hand that was clutching her next weapon.

As she did, officers suddenly burst in through the door at the back. Felicity turned and, for a moment, Vanessa thought she might spray them with the substance. But instead, she just crumpled, falling to the ground and screaming her daughter's name. All this time, she'd been holding her grief at bay, and redirecting it into her twisted plan.

But now, finally, it was all tumbling out.

Chapter 43

Vanessa sat in the hospital room, her mother a frail figure beneath her white sheet. She'd been slowly regaining consciousness, and seemed confused as she did, not recognising Vanessa and quickly going back to sleep.

But now, as her eyes fluttered open, a croaky whisper escaped her lips. 'Vanessa.'

'Mum, you're going to be OK,' Vanessa said softly.

'How did you find me?'

'Perseverance.'

A faint smile. 'Yes, always one for perseverance, our Nessy.'

Vanessa flinched slightly, to hear the same nickname her brother used for her come from her mother's lips.

'You have grown into such a beautiful woman,' her mother said as she explored Vanessa's face. 'So strong. So successful. I've watched you from afar, you know.'

Vanessa clenched her fists, trying to hold in the emotion. She knew it wasn't the time to get into the past and the recriminations.

Stick to the now, Vanessa told herself. *To the facts.*

'They caught who did it,' Vanessa said. 'It was Cordelia Montgomery's mother.'

Her mother looked shocked. 'My God, she killed her own daughter?'

'She didn't mean to.' Vanessa shared what she'd learned.

Her mother tried to sit up, reaching for her drink which Vanessa passed to her, helping her to take a sip. Her mother smiled, stroking Vanessa's face. 'Maybe I understand a little,' she said, 'the lengths we go to for our children.'

Vanessa stiffened. No, she couldn't keep it in. '*Do* you understand, though? You left us.'

'I had no choice, Vanessa. All I thought about was protecting you both.'

'Protecting us? From *what*?'

'I – I did something stupid. I disposed of an important item. A *very* important item.'

'You mean something you were supposed to smuggle?' Her mother nodded. 'So it all started as far back as that?' Vanessa asked.

'Sadly, yes. I was so horrified when I came across the piece that I had to destroy it. I had no idea where it would lead . . . When they found out what I'd done, they threatened to have you and Vincent harmed. Your father, too. The *only* way to keep you safe was to leave and do what they asked.'

Vanessa absorbed her mother's words, her anger tinged with a dawning understanding. Her mother had made terrible choices, but maybe they were born out of desperation and fear.

'So what, you've been working for this criminal gang all this time, smuggling their stuff?' Vanessa asked. Her mother nodded.

'It was the only way.'

'When did you come to New York?'

'Two years ago. Jacqueline, my old friend, tracked me down. Said if I helped her, she might be able to convince the people running the operation to drop the debt they believed I needed to pay, and let me see you.'

'A debt that spanned over thirty years? For one item?'

'You don't understand these people. You wrong them in any way, and that's a lifetime of regret.'

'Why didn't you just go to the police?'

'Oh, Vanessa,' her mother said, pity in her brown eyes, 'you don't know how deep-rooted this is. It goes back so long, so deep . . . and so high up, too. The police can't touch it.'

'What do you mean, high up? Are the Thorsens *really* that powerful?'

Her mother pursed her lips, looking away. 'They're just a small part of it, like the Oberlins were.'

'Part of what?'

'I can't tell you that. I can't risk your safety, Vanessa. That's what this has all been about.'

'I can handle myself.'

She smiled. 'You still think you're bulletproof, my darling. I suppose, in many ways, you are, proving my decision to walk away for your own good was right. Look how far you've come,' she said, squeezing Vanessa's hand.

Vanessa yanked her hand away from her mother. 'Do you know what it took for me to be where I am today? Every choice I made was a fight against the void you left. And what about Vincent? It didn't work out for him, Mum, did it?'

Delilah sighed. 'I would never have dreamed he was capable of what he did.' She squeezed her eyes shut. 'Oh, Vincent . . .' Her voice trailed off.

'Yes, Mum,' Vanessa said, voice trembling. '*What he did*, killing all those people. Have you ever asked yourself why?'

'Of course, Vanessa!' her mother said, voice desperate. 'Every single day since I turned on the news and saw his face six months ago. Why? Why would he do that?'

'Brain plasticity,' Vanessa said, recalling the conversation she had with Vincent.

'I don't understand. He had a brain injury?'

'Of sorts, if you consider the way abandonment impacts the neural pathways in our brains.'

Her mother sighed. 'I see where you're going with this. But what else could I do? I couldn't have lived with myself if your brother and you had been the ones to suffer because of something *I* did. Can you imagine how much it hurt me to leave you, my darling? Both of you? It broke me apart. I just had to focus on the fact that you had your father . . . And *you* are safe, at least.'

'Safe from *what* exactly? Why are you being so bloody cryptic?'

She clutched Vanessa's hand. 'You'd understand if you knew.'

A bitter laugh escaped Vanessa's lips. 'You think I won't try to figure it out for myself?'

Fear shot through Delilah's eyes. 'You absolutely can't.'

'You lost the right to tell me what to do when you walked out on me, Mum. I was *seven*.'

Then she got up and walked out of the room, unable to take any more.

Halfway down the corridor she noticed Ru and Harris talking to Ramos, who was standing in her dressing gown, her baby in her arms.

Her mind swirling, Vanessa walked over, pleased for some distraction as she looked down at the tiny bundle of black hair and soft skin. 'Gorgeous,' she said. 'Congratulations.'

'Thanks, Doc. Kicked her little way out five weeks early, so I think she's gonna be a handful.' Ramos examined her face. 'Hey, you OK? Your mom doing OK?'

'Of course Bug Lady isn't OK!' Harris said. 'She nearly got poisoned last night and her mom, who she hasn't seen since she was a child and happens to be an illegal insect smuggler, is lying in a hospital bed.'

'You summed it up pretty well,' Vanessa said. 'Speaking of poison, did you find anything at Felicity's apartment?'

'Yes, we found evidence of Felicity's work on the aerosol dispensers for the perfume bottles,' Ru said. 'With her usual unit not being available to her, she had to use her own house.'

'It means we have enough evidence to charge Felicity even before the forensics come back from the unit,' Harris said.

'I still can't wrap my head around it,' Ramos said. 'Cordelia's own mom. Damn, that must have been another level of grief to discover she'd killed her own daughter with the plan that was supposed to save her . . . And yet she kept going.'

'To punish those who harmed her daughter,' Ru pointed out. 'As she said to Vanessa, she needed to make it worth it . . .' He shrugged. 'Maybe there is some logic to that. I might not be a parent myself, but I imagine parents do some pretty strange things for their children.' He looked at Vanessa meaningfully. Was he trying to say her mother had done the same for her?

'We sure do,' Harris said. 'Right, better get on with it.'

'You're going to question my mum?'

Ru nodded. 'We'll call you in when we're done.' He went to walk off with Harris, then paused, surprising Vanessa by putting a cool hand on her arm. 'You can attend if you wish? Your mother may need you.'

'Yeah, well, I needed her for a long time but she wasn't there,' Vanessa found herself saying.

'There's a saying in Japan,' Ru said. '*Sugita koto wa mizu ni nagas.*

It means let past things flow away like water. It's up to you.' Then he walked away.

'He's a wise man,' Ramos said as she smiled down at her daughter. She squeezed Vanessa's arm. 'Take care, yeah?' Then she strolled off, cooing down at her baby.

Vanessa watched her, thinking that once, nearly forty-one years ago, her mother had done the same with her in her arms. She dug her phone out of her pocket, finding the email Dariel had sent that morning with her mother's gift note attached. She ignored his pleas to answer his calls – not in a million years – then took in a deep breath and clicked.

My darling Vanessa,

One day, I hope you'll understand the choices I had to make and why I have kept my distance for so long. Or maybe you won't, I can't be sure of that. But there is one thing I am and always will be sure of: that I love you with every ounce of my being. I love that little girl who would run around the garden, spotting butterflies. I love that teenager, strong and fierce enough to refuse to speak to the mother who she thought – still thinks, no doubt – abandoned her. And now the adult, a world-leading forensic entomologist, proof I made the right decision. I am always watching, Vanessa, and everything I sacrificed is for YOU. You are everything now.

Please forgive me.

Mum

Vanessa squeezed her eyes shut, feeling warm tears build up behind her eyelids. She realised then that the buzzing in her head had stopped. In fact, she hadn't felt it since she found her mother lying on that floor. Is that what it had been about? Finding her mother?

She started walking back towards her mother's hospital room with a renewed determination, as the tears slid down her cheeks. It wasn't just the note. She still wasn't convinced about this 'I abandoned you for your own good' narrative. But what she did know for certain now, what she had finally learned, was that she wasn't like her mother. She didn't abandon those she loved. So she would walk into that hospital room. She would hold her mother's hand while she was questioned by Ru and Harris. She would tell her she loved her, and that she would always be there for her.

But she would also resolve to find out what her mother had got herself tangled up with all those years ago. Something that went deeper than the Oberlins. Even deeper than one of the most powerful families in New York: the Thorsens.

If her mother was right and it went straight to the top, then Vanessa knew what the next few months would hold: climbing to the top *and* toppling it all down.

A Note from the Author

Hello!

It's a thrill to welcome you to the end of this latest journey with Dr Vanessa Marwood. As I write this, I'm also putting the finishing touches to the next book in the series, *Moth to the Flames*, spurred on by the brilliant early reviews for *Venom in the Blood*. Your enthusiasm and support have been nothing short of inspirational.

If you've enjoyed your time in Vanessa's shadowy world and aren't quite ready to leave it behind, you can subscribe to my *Words & Dark Wings* newsletter on Substack. It's not just a newsletter; it's an entry ticket to a world of exclusives and freebies crafted just for you. From sneak peeks and early chapters to behind-the-scenes content and personal insights, it's all there, and it's all free. Subscribe today at Substack to ensure you don't miss out by heading on over to wordsanddarkwings.substack.com

Want to keep the conversation going? I'm always eager to hear your thoughts – what captivated you, what sent shivers down your spine, or even what you're looking forward to in our next dark adventure. Find me here:

- www.facebook.com/TracyBuchananAuthor
- www.facebook.com/groups/thereadingsnug
- www.instagram.com/TracyBuchananAuthor
- www.tiktok.com/@tracybuchananauthor

Thank you for journeying with me and Dr Marwood once more. Keep reading, keep exploring, and remember – the shadows aren't as empty as they seem, and sometimes, they watch back.

See you soon in the pages of *Moth to the Flames*!

Tracy

Acknowledgements

This book is dedicated to my agent, Caroline, a constant presence amid the ever-shifting sands of the publishing world. And boy, do they shift! Throughout the years, she's always been there to calm me down during my most exuberant moments, offering sage advice that I sometimes initially resist – but then I soon learn she was right. But more importantly, she's a constant, so important for an author.

A heartfelt thank you to the Embla team, whose enthusiasm for this series never wanes. Special mention must go to Jane Snelgrove, my editor, who has worked tirelessly and brilliantly to sculpt this manuscript into shape. To Martina Arzu, for her overseeing eye, Katie Williams, a marketing maven whose zeal for this project mirrors my own and Jon Appleton, my eagle-eyed copy editor – all the Embla team's dedication does not go unnoticed.

To my daughter, Scarlett, who is blossoming into an incredible writer with a knack for crafting characters and plots as dark and evocative as any I could hope to conjure. Whatever path you choose, Scarlett, I know it will be creatively spectacular, and if it leads you to storytelling, the world is in for a treat.

My husband, ever the cheerleader, feeder (honestly, the man just loves encouraging my chocolate consumption!) and constant oak tree of support.

Also a big thanks to former NYPD detective Patrick Lanigan, who provided invaluable insights into the workings of the NYPD Homicide Squad and the unique rhythms of New York City itself – a city that is as much a character in these pages as any.

To my friends and family, whose support is as unwavering as it is cherished – particularly my dad, who champions my work to anyone who'll listen (AKA, forces people to buy my books!).

And finally, to you, my readers. Your enthusiasm and support fuel my passion for storytelling. Without you, these pages would remain only whispers in the wind. Thank you all for being part of this journey.

About the Author

Tracy is a bestselling author whose books have been published around the world, including chart-toppers *Wall of Silence, My Sister's Secret* and *No Turning Back*. She lives in the UK with her husband, their daughter and a very spoilt Cavalier King Charles Spaniel called Bronte.

About Embla Books

Embla Books is a digital-first publisher of standout commercial adult fiction. Passionate about storytelling, the team at Embla publish books that will make you 'laugh, love, look over your shoulder and lose sleep'. Launched by Bonnier Books UK in 2021, the imprint is named after the first woman from the creation myth in Norse mythology, who was carved by the gods from a tree trunk found on the seashore – an image of the kind of creative work and crafting that writers do, and a symbol of how stories shape our lives.

Find out about some of our other books and stay in touch:

X, Facebook, Instagram: @emblabooks
Newsletter: https://bit.ly/emblanewsletter

Made in the USA
Middletown, DE
05 December 2024

66185440R00163